THE ROCKY ROAD YEAR

by Marion H. Youngquist

FIRST EDITION

©opyright 2009 by Marion H. Youngquist

ISBN-10: 0-9770533-8-5
ISBN-13: 978-0-9770533-8-4

DrurysPublishing.com

Kentucky

Produced in The United States of America.

Contents

PREFACE

Years ago, my friend Sara Hill in Glen Ellyn, Illinois said, "Marion, you live in the midst of drama". She made this remark because I was a minister's wife and often, I observed human dilemmas. Although my husband never betrayed any confidences, I became aware of some situations. At times, women would come to me and pour out their concerns. I was not a counselor and felt very inadequate. I could only listen and console. Sadly, I wondered what their future held. I never forgot them. I always wanted to write their story. Now that they are no longer alive, I feel permitted to include their poignant experiences.

Often, cultural changes brought heartbreak. For some, marriage and family life were sacrificed for a career. Now, monogamous marriage is threatened by other forces which encourage just living together, or an introductory "first" in serial marriages. Education, sports and technology have become new idols while the media shapes national morals. Our economy depends on more and more consumption which impacts marriage and family life. Judeo-Christian values are shaken and tested.

In our own family, we were part of the mobile society, too, as we moved across the country and met friends again from earlier decades. Tara's experience of twelve moves in eighteen years actually happened to a friend. This novel honors those women who accept mobility in church or corporate life. Some things aren't addressed—primarily, the financial difficulties when a woman is left with children and the husband's income is gone. That would be a different story. Neither are the many problems of people in Third World countries. My story is localized about a very small tribe.

When my husband and I celebrated our sixtieth wedding anniversary, our grandson Jeffrey Karalis said, "You're the only couple I'll ever see married that long. My friends are already divorced." That is a very sad statement.

This is the background for this contemporary novel about Tara, a wife suddenly abandoned. I expected her to always be bitter and her husband Cal was going to be a difficult man. There was no mission trip on the horizon. However, as Tara and the others began to "speak" to me, my original story changed to one of hope and redemption.

I want the readers to enjoy and reflect on Tara's story.

People ask where my stories come from. I wish I knew. The characters present themselves and reveal their own personalities. Imagination is just that—imagination. Maybe it is like the ability to solve equations. It can be cultivated, but it helps if you have an innate talent.

I was thrilled that my first novel *Procula* (about Pontius Pilate's wife) was so well received. Many people tell me they enjoy rereading it. It is the same with *Maple Tree Tales* (inter-related short stories) and *Christmas Presence* (poems). That I've given pleasure to others is very rewarding. So I hope the reader finds joy in Tara's story, too.

A "Thank-You" goes to many people at Calvary Lutheran Church, Brookfield, WI. who contributed to the first draft and gave helpful information about their Guatemala mission trip. These were: Marty Almin, Cindy Busche, Pat Corcoran, Sue Gaskell, Bill Jordan, John and Mary Lau, Mario Lopez, Jim and Nancy Marsho, Carolyn Mijokovic, Pastor Phil Nybroten, Tom Schramek, Barbara Swanson Snyder, Jane and Leslie Taufner, Lee and Kari Tyne, Wayne and Carol Wegner, and Terry Wussow. Among other friends who gave valuable support and critiques were Grace and Gordy Gunnlaugsson, Martha Zipsie, Dorothea Winek, Ruby Hauch, Sue Jacobson, Susan Klopfer, Jim and Ruth Brostowitz, Bill and Sue Romo. Special thanks to Adra Klopfer who provided Spanish translations.

Two other couples have our heartfelt "Thanks" for the use of northern Wisconsin cabins, so we could work on our writing projects without distractions. They are Joanne and Don Krause as well as Eleanor "Ellie" and John Ellison.

A special acknowledgement is for Ted, my husband. We have shared so many blessed years—sixty-three—and special times together, including a trip to the Mayan ruins in the Yucatan and several cruises through the Panama Canal with a stop in Guatemala. A true test of our devotion is sharing a computer. Our own story is private.

As always, my appreciation goes to Gary Drury, publisher for faith in my effort.

Marion H. Youngquist
Wauwatosa, Wisconsin

Dedicated to all who love, have loved,
or hope to love
Que Dias te acompane
The Lord be with you.

Truly, to tell lies is not honourable,
But when the truth entrails tremendous ruin,
To speak dishonourably is pardonable.

Sophocles,
Causa Fragment 323

…and if I have all faith, so as to
remove mountains,
But have not love, I am nothing.

St. Paul
1 Corinthians 13:2

Suffering produces endurance, and
endurance produces character,
and character produces hope, and
hope does not disappoint us.

St. Paul
Romans 5:3-5

A new commandment I give to you,
that you love one another,
Even as I have loved you,
that you also love one another.

Jesus
John 13:34

SHOCK,

N. A SUDDEN AND STARTLING EFFECT ON THE MIND OR EMOTIONS; PATHOL., A SUDDEN DE-BILITATING EFFECT ON THE BODILY FUNCTIONS DUE TO SOME VIOLENT IMPRESSION ON THE NERVOUS SYSTEM, AS FROM A SEVERE INJURY, A VIOLENT EMOTIONAL DISTURBANCE OR THE LIKE; THE RESULTING CONDITION OF NERVOUS DEPRESSION OR PROSTRATION.—OR TO STRIKE WITH INTENSE AND PAINFUL SURPRISE; TO SUB-JECT TO BODILY OR NERVOUS SHOCK; TO STAR-TLE BY OUTRAGING THE SENSE OF PROPRIETY OR DECENCY.

It's already past ten o'clock. I'm alone—driving through darkened streets on this wet January night after choir practice. I rush into Klopfer's before closing for a quart of hand-packed rocky road ice cream, so I can celebrate my excitement with Cal. Brad, the choir director, signaled me tonight to sing the alto solo in Sunday's anthem. I'm feeling really good. On a dark night like this, bad things happen to good people, but good things do, too—even to me, an alto in the third row of Trinity's choir.

It grew warmer today and the streets are slick from sleet. I slide too widely into Knollwood Drive, so I slow down. Often, Cal teases me about my reluctance to take a chance. He says I miss half the fun in life—being so careful, so proper. I say life is a gift from God, so I take care of mine, just as I take care of him and our daughter, Anne.

When I pull into the garage, I realize that Cal's golf clubs are missing from the far wall. Did he leave them at the Country Club? No, it's winter and he hasn't played for two months. I'm anxious to tell Cal about my solo—well, only two lines—in Sunday's anthem. Maybe that will get him into church. No, he'll miss it because he leaves early tomorrow for Atlanta. So odd for Mirron/Molten to have weekend meetings. He'll be back on Tuesday which is strange timing, but I don't ask questions. I'm the good wife, full of trust and acceptance of his erratic schedule.

I call, "Cal?" Silence. There's a note on the kitchen table. "Tara, I'm turning in early. I feel I'm taking a cold. I'll take a couple of aspirin. Maybe you should sleep in the guest room. See you in the morning."

The usual XXX isn't there with his hurried scrawl. I stash the ice cream in the freezer and rush upstairs to see if Cal has enough blankets, but the door is closed. I push it ajar, but the room is dark—his figure covered in blankets, his face turned away from me. His suitcase is packed for his departure tomorrow, but I worry about him. Maybe, he's caught a bad case of flu.

14

Before I went to sleep last night, Cal tossed and turned a lot. I awoke (the digital dial said *three-twelve*) and saw him standing at the window. He had pulled back the drapes and in the dim moonlight he looked tall and strong like a Michelangelo statue.

"What's the matter?" I asked, rubbing my half-closed eyes.

"I thought I heard a noise. Go back to sleep."

"Come back to bed."

"All right," he sighed. He crawled in beside me and turned away. I rubbed his back awhile, easing the tenseness in his shoulders.

I'm sure he's worried about his business trip to Atlanta this weekend. I remember the card that I bought today. It's a black and white photo of an owl high in a tree. Inside, it reads, "Come up and See Me Sometime!" I signed it *Your ever-loving Tara* and slipped it inside his attaché case on the hall table. He'll find it in the middle of a report when he's on the plane tomorrow and grin that cocky grin, thinking of me. Often, I leave pink love notes in his suit pocket or a chocolate bar tied with a pink ribbon in his tennis bag. It's a silly habit, but I want to remind Cal that I'm always thinking of him.

I assume he wants me to drive him to the station so I set an early alarm and bed down in the guest room. My last prayer is about Sunday's anthem. *Dear God, keep me calm so my voice will be true and steady on Sunday.* I fall into a gentle sleep as in childhood when I was held and rocked by my mother.

I wake up and hear Cal in the shower. He runs the water a long time so I pull on my navy sweat suit, ready to work out later with Arletta who is my best friend now. Back in our McNaughton college days, we lived on the same floor in Hopkins Hall. Although we were never close friends, we

15

connected again after almost three decades when Cal and I moved here. We found each other over produce at the supermarket. Immediately, I knew her, still funny and blonde and full of suggestions—*Try this new Bibb lettuce.* She filled a plastic bag and dropped it in my cart.

Automatically, I pour orange juice, make coffee and put bread in the toaster. I slice bananas for our morning cereal and scan the morning Herald as the minutes tick by. If Cal wants to catch the seven-twelve, we'll have to hurry. I'm nervous, but I don't know why.

"Cal—," I call upstairs. I pour fresh water in the vase of yellow roses. He sent them last Monday. Dear precious thoughtful Cal. I carried yellow roses at our June wedding twenty-seven years ago. When we celebrate our thirtieth, I want to see the Taj Mahal in the moonlight. Last week I gave him a travel brochure, but he ignored it. Too busy.

Cal comes downstairs with his suitcase. "I'll throw this in the car before I leave." His face is grim and his jaw, hard as stone. His blue eyes are as cold as icicles. I know Cal. He's troubled about something.

Obviously, he intends to drive into the city which is very strange if he flies to Atlanta today. I hear him slam the trunk. I pour his coffee and wait for him. The garage door grinds open. I hear the motor running. Will he skip breakfast? Something's wrong. The muscles in my neck and shoulders tighten. Cal stands in the doorway, tall with his clipped executive manner. He's still trim and handsome. I'm so proud of him—proud to be his wife. That's my job. I'm good at it. I rise to kiss him goodbye.

"Don't move!" he orders, his voice taut and hard. "I have something to say." He takes a deep breath. "I'm leaving!"

"I know that. You said it was Atlanta. You'll be back on Tuesday."

"Listen carefully." Cal's in a hurry. He talks fast. "I'll be in Atlanta on the weekend. I'll return to the office on Tues-

16

day, but I won't come back here. I'm leaving—leaving here for good. I've sublet an apartment. I can't take this—our life—anymore."

I stare at him, trying to grasp his statement. Surely, I didn't hear him correctly.

Cal holds up his hand. "Please—no hysterics! I'm out of here now. Later we can straighten out the details. Call Anne and tell her that I left. I'll talk to her when I get back."

He heels around and slams the door behind him. I stand frozen, immobile. I hear his Infiniti purr as he backs out. I race to the door to see his fleeing car turn into the street and speed away, lurching slightly on the slick pavement. I run down the drive, onto the sidewalk as he speeds out of sight. I wave my arms. I yell, "Come back! Come back!' in the still damp air. I run down the street, crying all the way. I stumble, and fling out my hands to steady myself. It's too late. I fall, scraping my hands and my face on the hard cement. I lie there with a pounding heart. I don't want to get up. I want to die.

A passing motorist stops and asks, "What happened?"

I lie, "I was jogging. I slipped."

Warily, she looks at the abrasion on my right cheek. "Did you bump your head? I'll drive you home." She pulls into our garage so I won't slip again.

I thank her and walk into the kitchen, now chilly as air seeps through the open doors. My cold coffee waits on the blue place mat. The juice glasses remain untouched. I stand there shaking, numb from shock. I ignore everything. I collapse on the living room sofa, my body trembling from an impossible new reality.

I listen as the walnut grandfather clock strikes eight. My parents gave us that—*to be an heirloom for you that will mark your happy years together.* The chimes ring every quarter hour. One hour. Two hours. Time passes. Is that thunder? Does an ambulance speed down Central Avenue several blocks away? Sound mean nothing—not the clock, or the phone, or a siren. I sit there shaking, my mind numb.

Presently, Arletta walks in through the kitchen because she seldom knocks and always ignores the doorbell. She stares at me.

"You weren't at yoga this morning. I saw your car in the garage," Arletta frowns. "Oh—your face! What happened to you?"

"I'm numb," I whisper. "Cal's left me. He says he's not coming back. How can he leave? This is his home. He picked out this house because he wanted to live in this old Windsor neighborhood."

The Windsor homes are meant to look like British places, each with a marker. Ours says, "Wellington—1928" in old English script. The outside has lots of brick and stucco with diagonal wood strips on the second story, and ivy climbing toward them. Inside there's warm mahogany woodwork and a stairway with a carved newel post. Even the leaded windows have small stained glass inserts with Tudor roses, and innocuous shields and fleur-de-lis. There are Austrian crystal chandeliers in both the dining room and front hall. I admit they sparkle, especially after I clean the prisms twice a year. I won't let a cleaning lady do them.

The rooms are overpowering, because Ursula, the interior designer ("I'm not a decorator!"—said like it's a naughty word!) ordered lots of chintz furniture—Victorian peonies and muted stripes, damask draperies and roses in our master bedroom. Anne rebelled and insisted on plain walls in her room, so she could hang posters of pop stars. She's smarter than I and got her way with Cal and the designer. I didn't.

Arletta frowns, "Cal? I can't believe it!" Arletta puts her arms around me. "—Poor baby."

I begin to cry. "I don't know why—."

Arletta, who is usually too talkative, turns quiet and holds me, gently rocking in rhythm to my sobs. "There—there," she comforts, "When the time is right, you'll find out."

I lift my head and wonder if she knows something that I don't. "It isn't fair! We've been married almost thirty years."

"Life isn't fair, but your life isn't over." She sounds like a counselor. I don't want a counselor, I want Cal.

"You're wrong. My life is over. I can't get along without Cal. He's the center of my life. I knew Anne would go off to college—have a career—get married. I thought Cal would always be here." I keep sobbing. "I've tried to be a good wife. I tuck love notes in his pockets. I put an expensive three dollar card in his attaché case this morning." I pause, worn out from all my tears. "That makes me mad. Why didn't I settle for a fifty cent card from the outlet!"

Arletta laughs at me. "See, the old Tara isn't destroyed."

"I am! What did I do wrong?" I'm shaking from shock.

"Nothing," Arletta assures me.

I realize that's the reason. I've done nothing. I'm dull. While Cal built his career, I managed our many moves without complaint. How many? Twelve, so far. A miscarriage in Houston. A tiny grave left in Greenville. Anne's rebellion when we left Chatham for Denver. Twice we lived in Hartford. I handled everything—even that stormy summer when Anne had a crush on a Yale junior—too old for her. Too often, I was alone while Cal worked as a Mirron/Molten Corporation executive. Good old Cal. Got a problem? Send for Cal. He can pick up the pieces. He's a great salvage man.

Cal is colorblind. He always looks sharp because I coordinate his shirts and ties. How can HE get along without ME? I was a perfect hostess for those occasional dinners, when old F.A. Mirron thought it was necessary to celebrate something. As Cal moved up the company ladder, I've been the capable wife, always aware that I'm watched and judged to see if I'm really equal to Cal's position. I could have easily lost my values. It didn't matter where Cal was sent, because I always found a church to keep me grounded in "plain living and high thinking", as my parents taught me. Now, I wonder if my effort really mattered?

"What can I do?" Arletta asks.

I muffle my sobs long enough to stammer, "Call the choir director. Tell him that I have a terrible cold and I can't sing on Sunday." One lie after another. "How can I go to church and face people?"

"They'll understand—."

"How can they? I don't understand." That's wrong. I do understand one thing. "I'm a failure."

"You can't say that! Maybe Cal needs a breather."

"—From me?"

Arletta ignores my question. "Cal's has been in his office these last six months so maybe he needs this trip to Atlanta. He'll be back." Arletta doesn't sound convinced.

"There's a few changes at Mirron/Molten. I thought he'd be glad to get rid of airports and hotel rooms. Evidently not," I sniffle. "I don't wish this on anyone. Tell Sharlene to think twice about getting married in August. I don't want her to ever hurt like I do."

Arletta smiles faintly about her daughter's wedding. "Sharlene and Jared planned their ceremony at Happily Ever-After Farm with a huge barn for the dinner and dance. Farmer Ahab has a license to perform the ceremony, so they ignored our own minister. Now, they want to cancel the farm site and sail to China on a freighter!"

"—But Jared hates water. He doesn't even swim!" I dab at my eyes, "How can they do that when the date is set and you've contracted for the farm and catering service?"

"It doesn't bother them. It's our money." Arletta sighs, "I'm ready to send them to Las Vegas for a drive-by quickie. Oh, let them elope!" She adds wistfully, "I wanted a church wedding—at least, start them off the right way."

Cal told me to tell Anne. I don't want her driving after she hears what happened, so I phone her Saturday morning to alert her that I'm coming that afternoon. Maybe I'll be hit by a semi and I won't have to reveal that her Dad has walked out.

"Gee, Mom, that's awfully inconvenient. Five of us will head for Old Town tonight for pizza and a blue-grass concert."

"I'll come anyway." I can't put off Cal's awful message any longer.

She doesn't answer right away. Maybe she hears my anxiety. "Well, if you insist, but we leave about four-thirty."

"Fine." I warn, "Don't plan too much for Sunday. You'll need your rest."

She'll need more than that, but I'll be here when the shock waves hit her.

Anne is a junior at Northwestern University. She lives on one of Evanston's tree-lined streets in an old home. Her apartment is on the second floor. Slowly, I climb the steps with leaden feet. The oak banister feels solid beneath my trembling hand. I rap on her door. Why didn't I bring a pot of early spring tulips to soften my awful news?

Anne stands there in a terry cloth robe, a towel wrapped around her hair. She's barefoot. Somehow, I'm reminded of a child dressed in a fleecy white polar bear costume. "Come in!" she says with a quick hug.

I look around to see if she's crowded more stuff into her space. She's added a twig-and-yarn wall hanging over a bookcase. Students today are too well equipped with their microwaves, toasters, laptops, TVs and CD players. And don't forget the cell-phones and I-Pods. Invent something new and they get it. Technology they have—hopefully, with brains to manage it, too. They're wired to their wireless.

Anne studies me a moment, and sees that my eyes are red and puffy. I cried until the clock struck three early this morning. She asks, "What's wrong?"

I brace myself. It won't be easier ten minutes from now. I blurt out, "Your Dad has left."

"I know. He went to Atlanta this weekend."

"I mean. He's left us for good. Out the door yesterday morning. Not coming back—ever!"

Silence.

Anne's eyes widen in shock. "I don't believe you. This is a sick, sick, sick joke that some stupid yoga friend suggested."

I take a deep breath. "I wish it were. Unfortunately, he spit out his sick joke and walked out. He sped away as fast as he could." I pat my face—still sore from stumbling on the sidewalk. I'm worn out from just recalling those awful minutes.

"Get Dad on the phone. Tell him to come home."

"I can't reach him. Try your own cell phone."

More silence.

Anne walks to her window. "Something's not right. This isn't like Dad. Maybe, he's sick."

"He probably is." I don't add that he's probably sick of me, maybe of Anne—although they're alike in many ways. Maybe Cal's sick of the corporation and has a middle-aged fantasy, although that is highly unlikely since Cal's goal has always been to sit on the Executive Committee someday.

There's a knock on the door. Maye, an Asian coed, peeks in. "We're leaving early for Old Town. We want to shop, too. Can you be ready in twenty minutes?"

"Sure." Anne's blue eyes have turned as hard as cold marble. She turns back to me. "I'll think about what you said. The whole thing isn't right. You've misunderstood. I'll talk to Dad."

"Do that. I tried Atlanta this morning and he hasn't registered as yet." I hug Anne and we cling to each other for an extra minute until she pushes me away. She's confused and so am I. The shock hasn't hit her yet. All her anger will be unleashed later.

I drive home on state roads. I can't take a fast freeway when I can't concentrate on driving. I keep seeing Cal in the kitchen and his abrupt departure. Also, I see the shock and disbelief in Anne's eyes. A wave of anger hits me—the one that Cal expected when he announced his decision. A car swerves around me and surprised, I brake slightly. I must think clearly and arrive home safely for Anne's sake. She doesn't need to lose two parents.

Once inside, the clock chimes. Cold emptiness fills the house. I want to call out "Cal!" and hear his rich voice answer, "I thought you'd never get here. Come upstairs!"

Instead, there is complete silence. I dissolve into tears.

I don't keep track of time. One week slides into two. I can't face anyone. My nights are sleepless. Lena, my cleaning lady, comes on Tuesdays. She's Polish, I think, and in the States to improve her English. Usually, I have everything clean and in order so she can vacuum and polish without difficulty. Cal always teased me about cleaning before a cleaning lady came. I don't do that now. Lena knows something is wrong when she sees too many daily papers (still in their blue plastic sleeves) on Cal's brown recliner.

"I'm ill," I always stammer in a hoarse voice. "Just clean downstairs and leave when you're done." I hand her an envelope. "Here's your money."

I stumble upstairs and crawl into bed. I pull the covers over my face. The vacuum cleaner drones away and mercifully, I'm lulled to sleep on Tuesdays.

Anne drives home for an overnight. She waits as I go over again Cal's abrupt departure. She frowns, "It doesn't sound like Dad. Are you sure that you didn't say the wrong thing to him? I know he doesn't like an argument." She half-smiles, remembering the times she tangled with him over her high-school allowance. She leaves her slice of pepperoni pizza half-eaten.

I ask her if she wants a dish of rocky road ice cream.

"No, it won't taste the same, if Dad isn't here."

The silence hangs between us. We half-watch some inane TV sit-com and then say "Good-night". Before she goes upstairs, we hug each other for a long time.

"Dad will come back," Anne whispers and repeats, "He just has to come back."

The phone rings. I wait before I pick it up. I hope for Cal. The answering machine clicks on. Instead, it's our insurance agent. He's always ready with another deal.

"Hello," I say cautiously.

"Cal wanted a quote on some new coverage."

Is the policy on me? My heart's already dead. I ask, "What kind of coverage?"

"Automobile—on the new BMW he's looking at."

A new car sounds like Cal. He sent me yellow roses for New Year's Day and then took Anne and me to Gustav's for Sunday dinner. On Friday, he walked out. He has great style. I have nothing.

The agent asks, "When will Cal be home?"

"I don't know—if ever!" That's the truth. I slam down the phone and I cry some more.

I traipse down to the basement so the neighbors can't hear me rage at Cal, at God, and the world. Why don't I end my misery with a rope and a plumbing pipe, except I can't fix a noose. I wasn't a Girl Scout. Instead, I scream, "Bring Cal back! Dear God—if you're there—bring Cal back!"

I listen to the silence of God.

I cancel my hair appointments. The third week Elena, who owns Elena's Elegante Hairem calls, "What's with you?"

I burst into tears. "Cal's left me. I can't do anything."

She orders, "You get here at eleven-thirty and I'll make you over—a whole new you."

I pull myself off the sofa where I've slept all night. I manage to shower and grab some dark slacks and a very old cerise velour top that I intended to throw away. I start the car and realize I could leave the motor running and end my misery, except Anne would never understand. Arletta would never forgive me that I didn't ask for her advice so I don't dare use a gun or ram a passing train. That's me—no talent for living or dying.

In her salon, Elena hands me a glossy magazine with numerous hairstyles. "Pick something out—nothing proper and staid this time."

I thumb through the pages, cover-to-cover. Sloe-eyed young people stare at me with pouty lips and hair—frizzled, spiked, flipped, clipped, curled, or swirled in whatever way it can be plastered.

Elena asks, "What have you found?"

I shrug, "I don't care. You can try anything new."

She runs her hand over my scalp. "—A younger style—away with those few gray hairs!"

For the next two hours, I'm washed, cut and colored. She holds each wisp gently, then brushes and wraps it in foil. Monet in a salon. I sit there like an alien moppet with spiky silver coils. She's not an illusionist or magician. The old me doesn't disappear. I'm still Tara with a broken heart, but my hair has changed. A cover-girl style—whatever that is. It's streaked in three shades. I'm an ash-blonde raccoon.

Elena leans down beside me, her hands on both my shoulders. "How do you like it?" she beams.

I turn my head from side-to-side. "It is—ah—unique," I murmur and close my eyes. I like her to touch my shoulders. I miss being touched. I want to be hugged. I want to feel Cal's warmth at night.

I leave a generous tip and get out of there.

While I'm gone, Cal returns and empties his closet of his lighter clothing. He's rushed the season. He leaves a note that I should store his winter suits. Maybe I'll send them all to Good Will. Did he arrange his timing with Elena to keep me at the salon? My trust is gone.

It's time to change the security locks. I don't trust anyone.

It's difficult whenever Anne comes home for a strained weekend. I brace for angry remarks about her Dad's desertion. She wears a purple tee shirt and frayed jeans. Her tan remains from last July's seminar in Cuernavaca. No doubt she perfected her Spanish at the Institute's pool. Now she wants to leave for Salamanca this June to study more Spanish. It's not her major, but she thinks it might come in handy someday.

Anne looks a lot like Cal with her thin nose, high cheekbones and laughing blue eyes. Her long blonde hair is slightly tousled, falling in waves around her smiling face. She drops her duffle bag.

Anne studies me. "Your hair looks awful."

I choke back tears and whisper in a hesitant voice, "I can't take living here. Your Dad is gone and you're away at school."

Silence. She struggles to spit out what she's been holding back. "Why do you do this to me? Other parents get divorced. You can't!"

"Ask your Dad. It's not my idea. Nothing's been decided. We don't talk. I hope that he'll come back. He doesn't call."

"You don't understand Dad." She clenches her teeth, "I'll talk to him again."

"Do that whenever you can get past the secretaries—or his administrative assistants. He doesn't care if we get sick or—."

Anne drums her fingers in staccato time. "I tell my friends he's on a business trip."

Wearily, I reply, "You should tell them the truth. You don't know what happened— nor do I." She's been through shock and she wants an answer when there is none.

Anne's anger bubbles up. "It's your fault! You always run everything around here. You never did anything important with your life except make our lives miserable. The house was so-o-o important. You were always after us to pick up everything. Me—clothes. Dad—newspapers. Oh yes—put our towels in the hamper! I wanted to run away when I was in high school! Now he leaves and you don't beg him to stay!" She starts to cry and runs upstairs and closes her door.

I'm speechless. Is Anne right? In high school, I let her have pajama parties and a big New Year's bash. How much chili did I cook for that? Many late nights I washed her favorite jeans so she'd have them the next morning. I took her to summer camps—the one in Maine was a long tiring drive. We visited various colleges, so she'd find the right one. I was ready to let her go and spread her wings. Cal never had much time for her. First, the Mirron Company and then the Mirron/Molten Corporation dictated his life.

Is she right about me? I thought that making a home for her and Cal was important, although at McNaughton I sat in

27

Dr. Burke's Economics class and heard her promote a wealthier United States if women worked with men in offices and factories. She spoke enthusiastically about children being raised by workers in day care centers and schools. A new world was ahead if women as in Russia were freed from being household slaves.

I was one of the few coeds who didn't believe her. I thought homemaking was an important career. A family separated all day might sleep in the same house, but would it be a home if they had no time for each other?

Would Anne be happier now if I'd climbed the corporate ladder, too? I could have left her in private boarding schools. Would Cal still be with me if I had a career? If I sat on an Executive Committee? I explore every possibility and I know nothing.

I am defeated. I am numb.

This morning Anne leaves for Evanston with a small apology. "I know I shouldn't be mad at you. Everything's so confused. Perhaps I can persuade Dad to come home."

"Call me when you get there." I force a small smile. We hug, but something's been lost in her outburst yesterday. I feel guilty that in a way Cal's left her, too, and I didn't prevent him from wounding her. It's a relief to see her leave.

She backs out and spins her tires. She, also, can't wait to get away. Like father. Like daughter. Now a junior, she's full of self-assurance with her red sports car and an unlimited credit card. I wanted her to have everything I missed when I was young. She hasn't worked her way through college as I did. But Cal and I did her a disservice. She has no pride in earning her own way. She doesn't think about others. Often, her tongue is used thoughtlessly and becomes a sharp weapon. If she loses friends or a flunks a class, I can't be her protector or cheerleader any longer. Perhaps she will grow to think of others or else she will suffer more than any hurt she imposes.

Has my tie with my daughter been damaged? I put my head down on the kitchen table and let the tears flow. Already, Arletta hints that I will remarry someday. I might find another husband, but how could I replace a daughter? Losing her would be too great a casualty to bear.

Arletta stops by on her Monday call—just to make sure that I'm still breathing. I tell her about Anne.

"She's still in shock, but she doesn't mean what she says." Arletta eyes me critically. "You must keep busy." Arletta likes to keep busy. I don't.

"Busy-ness doesn't help the hurt go away." My thoughts scatter and fall like dried petals in an October wind. "I can't concentrate on anything."

"—But busy-ness will help time pass. What household chore do you dislike the most?"

"—Cleaning our bedroom. I shut the door when Cal left. I haven't gone in since—only to move my clothing to the guest bedroom."

"Then we'll clean it up right now!"

I follow Arletta upstairs. She opens the chintz drapes, patterned with full-blown roses on a trellis. A matching border runs around the ceiling. The bed is still unmade. Cal's drawers are open as he left them. One pair of his Allen Edmunds remain partially hidden under the bed skirt. Did he forget those in his haste? I'll put them in a Good Will box along with his green tropical shirt and an old fishing cap with the Mirron logo, but I push his clothes to one end of the closet instead of the thrift shop box. I think I'm being nice.

Arletta insists that we change the sheets on the rumpled bed. We slip on white satin stripes—so bridal looking.

I explain. "Cal always wants white sheets—never colored or printed ones."

29

Arletta plumps the pillows and tosses on the quilted chintz spread that's celadon green with pink and cream roses. Ursula insisted that it wasn't too feminine for "such a terrific executive like your husband."

I hated the spread, but Ursula was right because Cal said, "This spread reminds me of your wedding bouquet." How could he say that when I carried yellow roses?

The bedspread stayed, but Cal left. He's still gone.

Arletta breaks into my reverie. "I've got to go. Be sure and eat the pasta salad I left in the refrigerator."

Weeping, I fall on the bed, reaching out for Cal's warm hand. It's not there. My own hands are icy cold.

After Arletta leaves, I sit on the celadon slipper chair. The beautiful room is in order again. I could sleep here nightly, but it wouldn't be the same without Cal. I shut the door and cross to the welcoming guest room. Now, this is my space. I'll buy a bowl of yellow daisies. How can I get on with my life, as Arletta advises? The daisies will wither and die, too.

I'm filled with a huge mountain of despair for my heart has turned to stone. I'll never survive. My life is over.

Anne calls from Evanston. "I had a long talk with Dad. I told him that I'd never speak to him again if he didn't come home. He said that I would understand someday and that he will always love me." She sniffles and draws a deep breath. "I don't understand why he doesn't care what I think or say."

I'm at a crossroads. Do I really destroy her relationship with Cal, or do I try to keep his damage to a minimum? I know I have no right to interfere. I, too, take a deep breath. "I'm sure that your Dad cares very deeply for you and for your feelings. Just keep in touch with him and tell him that you love him."

I hang up and feel stronger that I've done the right thing. Anne will have to work things out with Cal in her own way. Someday, I must deal with him, too.

The monthly bank statement arrives and I slit the envelope. I frown at the balance in our checking account. Half is missing. Something is terribly wrong. I haven't shopped or even entered a supermarket since Cal left. Arletta sees that I eat a little something each day even if I toss out a half portion. Where is our money?

I call the bank and I can't get information on the phone. I must come in person. So I'm forced to shower and dress decently just to go there.

The customer service representative sits behind her desk with a computer at her fingertips. I want to argue about the laxness of their system that misplaces a lot of our money. She's efficient and taps out some numbers and frowns a little at the screen. "It seems that your husband withdrew half the checking account on the third of the month." She purses her lips. "You have this much left." She scribbles some numbers on a pad and hands it to me.

I don't look at the paper. I know the amount. It makes me angry that Cal did this without telling me. Only a big excuse will save my dignity.

I take a deep breath and give her a crooked smile. "Oh, my birthday's in two weeks. No doubt he's buying me the mink stole that I've always wanted!" I arch my eyebrows and force a smile even more widely. "He's such a dear man!"

She knows better, but I walk out, my head held high. I'm really angry that he doesn't trust me with money. I drive five blocks to the Jefferson National Bank and open a new checking account in my own name with the remaining funds. Now, Cal can't touch MY money. I'll never share a dime with him again.

Cal's new financial arrangement has snapped me out of my numbness. If he can make secret plans, so can I. I feel a rising spitefulness. He should be wary. I want to skewer him and hold him over a big bonfire until he's charred from live coals. What will I do with this rising anger? Neither he—nor I—know. I dump his untouched quart of rocky road ice cream down the disposal and listen to it grind away. It is a moment of grim pleasure.

Is it possibly a turning point.?

ANGER,

L. *ANGERE,* N. A VIOLENT, REVENGEFUL PAS-
SION OR EMOTION, EXCITED BY A REAL OR
SUPPOSED INJURY TO ONESELF OR OTHERS;
PASSION; IRE; CHOLER; RAGE; WRATH. ANGER IS
MORE GENERAL AND EXPRESSES A LESS STRONG
FEELING THAN WRATH OR RAGE, BOTH OF
WHICH IMPLY A CERTAIN OUTWARD MANIFESTA-
TION AND THE LATTER, VIOLENCE AND WANT OF
SELF-COMMAND.

Alone at night, I bargain with God. "Dear God—bring Cal back! I'll do anything —pray on my knees every morning—feed the poor—chaperone the teens ski trip— ANYTHING! Just send Cal back to me." God doesn't listen to me, nor does Cal call or return. Although Brad, the choir director, contacts me, I won't go back to choir and I won't see anyone because I don't want to admit that Cal left me.

I'm as mad at God as I am at Cal. I deserve better than this. One night I yell out to God, "Is this the way YOU treat a faithful worshipper? Where's the plan for my life? I trusted YOU. I even prayed that YOUR will be done. And what do YOU do? YOU let Cal walk out without even a parting Thanks for the memories. Where are YOU when I need YOU?"

I skip worship for several weeks. Then the Pastor phones, and invites me to the church office. I want to turn him down, but I can't because he is my Pastor and I know he's genuinely concerned about me. Soon Ash Wednesday will be observed. I should be at worship.

I climb the steps of the Church of the Holy Trinity, sometimes called "Holy Trinity", but usually shortened to "Trinity". When it was built, the church was in a cornfield. The town grew, so now the church stands on a busy thoroughfare with a pizza palace and a gas station on opposite corners and a branch library across the side street. I really don't have to meet the Pastor. I could go to Arletta's huge church and be lost in a crowd.

When I met Arletta, she invited me to attend Glen Springs Community Church, which is a big sprawling complex—a mega-church with theater seating for lectures, concerts and programs. The double TV screens seem alien to any humility or awe—for me, the marks of religious experience. Arletta's daughter Sharlene belongs to a liturgical dance group that choreographs psalms with circles and leaps, raising arms and hands like flying angels. A combo, complete with two guitars, drums, keyboard and tambourines rap out one-line songs thrown on the large screens.

It was hard to pray while watching the screens, theatrics and applause at the opening service. Then Brother Ollie, Jr., with his large screen head and broader smile called on the Lord for "riches to flow like the Jordan River". It didn't feel like worship, but a spiritual pep rally. Arletta says the upbeat service makes her and Boyce feel alive.

After several Sundays, I told Arletta I needed liturgical worship and a greater tie with the historic church. When Anne and I came to Trinity. Anne liked a smaller group of friendly young people. To me, the nave seemed filled with "holy space". We found that the giant hammered bronze cross, marble altar, candles, stained glass windows and dark wood was a place for quiet silence, prayer and reflection. The building was erected when architects still used the Gothic arch over the doorways and the nave with its interior walls of natural wood and stone.

Arletta teases me that I'm too traditional. "Tara, you don't think you've really prayed until you kneel."

I say nothing in response, but she's right. I kneel and bow my head because that's what worship means—the acknowledgment that I'm a selfish creature and come before my creator—the Eternal God—for forgiveness and strength to live another day.

I'm not surprised that the Pastor calls to find out why I'm not attending services. No doubt Brad told him that I've dropped out of choir. I don't fill out a communion card each Sunday because I'm absent. The Pastor knows something is wrong.

The Pastor's door stays open which is *politically correct* according to the guidelines from some church official. Once there was absolute trust in the clergy, but who can be trusted anymore? Not husbands either.

"I'm mad at God!" I snap. "What have I done to deserve Cal's rejection? I've prayed every night since he left and all day, too. Not a-a—(I want to swear)—nothing at all has happened." My shoulders slump as I struggle to hold back tears.

The Pastor studies me. "Maybe God and Cal don't talk. Are you sure they're on daily speaking terms? How can God order Cal to go home if Cal doesn't listen to Him?"

"You're right! Cal doesn't listen to me either." I remember our big quarrel a year ago when I wanted a screen porch, but Cal insisted on a wooden deck. The deck was built and he never sat there. Too many bugs. Sometimes, I reminded him that I was really right. I still think that the porch would have been a better choice..

Cal seldom comes to church—maybe Christmas and sometimes, Easter. He always says he believes in God, but he can talk to Him on the golf course on Sunday mornings. I needle him. Does he pray for a hole-in-one? I don't tell the Pastor about these little differences that I have with Cal.

I weep. "I'm destroyed—utterly destroyed. What have I done to deserve this?"

"Nothing—that I know of—."

"—I'm dependent on Cal. I can't take living alone."

"You're not alone," the Pastor says. "We believe that God hears our cries—the moans and groans from the depths of our soul, as the prophet Isaiah reminds us. Like any good parent, He knows our needs and desires. All we can do is wait—and trust that God will bless us in some way."

"Then HE CAN SEND CAL BACK TO ME!"

The Pastor gives me a rueful smile. "God is neither a magician nor does he manipulate us like puppets. We have free will—free to make our own decisions and mistakes." He pauses and says softly,. "Are you sure you want Cal back or is your pride hurt?"

"Cal has no right to do this to me. Life's not fair!"

"I agree on both counts. Cal broke his commitment. Life isn't fair for many of us."

I ignore for many of us. What does he know about what is fair? "I feel so deserted, so alone."

"That's why we pray. We're not alone because prayer assures us of the presence of God. When we're helpless, we experience the grace of God and the help of others."

"I have prayed, but it doesn't work for me anymore."

"Then come back to church where others will pray with you and for you. Not even Jesus carried his cross alone. A bystander helped him. You'll be surrounded by friends who will help you." He looks at me with kindness. "Let us grieve with you."

"My life is over. I can't live without Cal."

"You can and you will. You're still young—in the prime of life. You see your life as a failure, but you can find other people to love. I'm not talking about marriage. I know you can create a new life—a full life—perhaps with even a few surprises. The Easter story is a triumph over tragedy, but no one expected that on Good Friday."

"I don't want surprises. I want my old life back. It's gone."

"Are you sure? Do you think that everything would be wonderful if Cal came back? That's an illusion. You can't repeat the past—even if it was a great one. Yesterday is always gone. Tomorrow may never come. You're given today—this moment." He pauses. "Perhaps God has something even better in mind for you."

"That's no comfort! I wish I were dead!"

"Really?" He narrows his eyes. "Come with me to Sarah's home. She's in hospice care now. Tell her that you wish you were dead. Complain to her two small children. Rave to her worried husband." He repeats, "Tell them angrily that you wish you were dead."

"Life's not fair!" I repeat, spitting it out just like I snapped at Arletta.

"You're right! Life's not fair! Uncertainty—along with our mortal bodies—is also a part of life." Quietly, he adds, "Remember—we worship the Eternal God who creates life and preserves it. When you learn to be thankful for your life and health, and ask only for strength to live another day—when you learn to truly forgive—you may find joy will return and your life's worth living. You don't want to miss that." He added, "Remember, you're not half a couple. You, Tara, are a whole person."

I turn away bitterly, "You sound like a preacher."

He sighs, "That's all I am."

I look at him—older, graying, shoulders beginning to droop. How many burdens does he help others carry? I know he is right. Other church members will help—like smartly dressed Francesca with her jangly bracelets, and middle-aged Lillian who will never share her mother's brownie recipe but brings five dozen for the Sunday coffee hour. I miss Hank who lost a hand in Vietnam and always asks about Cal's health. Others, too, are ready with hugs and support. If I can't sing anymore, I can sit among them and feel the closeness of a church family. But how can I confess my sins of anger and resentment against my errant husband? That will be most difficult of all.

"I'll try to pray again," I say with some hesitation, "but it won't do any good. There aren't any good days ahead for me. The memory of Cal is too bitter. I'll never forgive him."

"Then you'll continue to have a hard time with prayer. You blame Cal and consider that you are the righteous one. You must change and instead, remember Christ's death. He died for both of you—Cal's failure as well as your own mistakes. The love of God is there for both of you."

I shrug. "I don't feel very loved. I can't pray because I want Cal back." I don't add that if I ever see Cal, I'll hurt him as deeply as he's hurt me.

"You kneel at the Communion rail as a sinner, and another person kneels beside you who is a person whom God also loves. I pray that one day Cal may kneel there with you and you can both leave your bitter memories at the altar."

"It will take a miracle to get Cal to kneel at any altar—."

"I believe in miracles." He states this quietly and with confidence.

"—Cal worships the almighty dollar and serves as a Mirron/Molten corporate priest." I add angrily, "Everything is his fault! It's hopeless to pray for him."

The Pastor studies me until I look away. "Then you pray for others, and I will pray for you and Cal." Slowly, he says. "Remember, prayer is about your relationship with God. Be careful. You may find He answers your prayer." He adds, "You can start to build a better life, or you can become a bitter woman."

That is parting advice from my well-meaning Pastor. He doesn't understand my heartache—at least, I don't think he does. I repeat to myself, If I get the chance, I'll hurt Cal, as he hurt me. I wish he were dead.

A perceptive look crosses the Pastor's face. He knows what I'm thinking. I leave.

Every day I phone my younger sister Jill in California who tires of my calls. Abruptly she says one night, "You're better off without Cal. He's one big bore. Always slaps his knee when he thinks he's funny. He sounds so pompous when he clears his throat before he gives his latest financial advice. I'm surprised his company didn't dump him years ago. Get rid of him and get on with your life." She doesn't understand because her fiancé died in Vietnam and she never married. Her film career and her cat Micah are her life.

"Cal is my life. His promotions prove how smart he is," I sob, "You don't understand. Other people don't understand. I can't live without him."

Jill's voice takes a hard edge. "You had twenty-seven years with Cal. I never even had a wedding night. Don't complain! Get over him!"

Jill works for a talent agency in Los Angeles. She asks me to stay with Micah while she goes to Nome to screen natives for an Alaskan documentary. I fly out to Burbank and lounge beside her small pool, surrounded by a high fence. I hide from the world, just as I wanted to do when Cal left. Except it's boring. I stroke Micah and wonder if he will run under Jill's bed—which is his sign of a sudden earthquake. Let Jill's walls tumble down on me and put me be out of my misery. Micah purrs and I get a sunburned nose. Sunny California—land of granola and gurus. I eat granola and wish for a guru. Young—not a handsome Latino that Anne would flash her eyes at and flirt with. In fact, I want a guru who doesn't talk. Cal talked too much and told me nothing. Just left.

Two Mexicans paint the upstairs bedrooms—moss green in one and pale peach, the other. When they go to lunch, I give them ten dollars to bring me a sandwich. I am surprised when they come back with a lukewarm Reuben. I wanted a burrito. My luck's run out. I'll never get what I want. I want Cal.

It's Easter Sunday and it seems strange not to be in church. Micah and I watch a TV broadcast from some cathedral. Easter signifies hope after the tragedy of Good Friday. Once, I hunted daily for one little ray of hope after Cal walked away. I never found one. I reheat soup for myself. Even Micah's cat food looks better than my watery meal.

The phone rings. I stroke Micah and pick it up. It's Anne calling from Destin on her spring break which means she wants money. Why don't students really stay on a campus anymore? I hear excited voices in the background. Last summer, she went to Europe with a great purpose. She planned "to interview farmers about soil erosion on Spain's southern plains and save the planet." Instead, she went to Norway. Now she has a perfect excuse to go to Salamanca this summer—for environmental studies. In Spanish? Of course.

"Mom, I'm having a blast," she says.

I hear noise and I needle her. "Have you interviewed any Floridian on beach erosion?"

"—Better than any interview. I'm attending a Latino dance festival tonight."

I'm silent. Has she moved beyond Cal's abandonment? Maybe she's in denial.

She rushes on, "—I've lost three pounds because we walk everywhere. I feel wonderful."

"Good. Maybe you should give up your car when you come back—just to prevent more pollution."

"I can't do that! How can I attend the rallies to clean up the environment?"

I stifle a laugh. Long ago I marched on McNaughton's campus to extend late hours at the library. No one listened, but we were militant students, impressed with our fruitless efforts and we talked about it for weeks. Anne's that way about greening the earth again.

"Anne, you can ride your bike, or a bus—."

"—I don't understand."

"When you get back to Evanston, convince your friends to get rid of their personal TVs, refrigerators, and micro-waves. Roommates can share a computer. There are many significant ways for the students to cut down on wasted energy—."

"Mom—you don't understand—."

She irritates me with her carefree trip when I'm falling apart. "Library hours can be cut back at night. The Student Union should close at ten o'clock."

"Mom—you can't be serious!"

"Speaking of that—cut down the lovely trees on the campus and erect those energy windmills. Make NU a major first example to other institutions across the country."

"Mom—I think you've lost it!"

"While you're at it, contact the head electrician. He might install low-wattage lights in the hallways."

"Stop it! You're too sarcastic. I thought you'd take me seriously. I'm very dedicated to a clean environment and understanding other cultures."

"Great! Give up your car and ride a bike."

Anne pauses. "Well, actually, I am thinking of giving up my car. It's a real gas guzzler."

I'm taken aback. She lives in that car. "That's wonderful. Biking and walking are are so healthy."

"Oh—I don't mean that. I mean—I'll buy a hybrid instead." She yells "Wait!" to someone in the background and gives me a quick "'Bye."

I smile. Mirron/Molten and the other corporations don't need to worry about student rallies. America's relentless consumption is in young hands.

I close my eyes, pet Micah, and remember when I was still married to Cal. A year ago Jill asked me to fly west for the Academy Awards. She had worked on a documentary that was nominated for an Oscar. I called Cal nightly. One night I gave up after the late night news. I told myself he didn't hear the phone.

However, the next night Cal confessed, "After work, I went grazing with some younger staff. They go to different places and sample appetizers."

"That's grazing?" I needed to respond quickly, so I add, "How—ah—unusual."

"Diedre invited me. I expected only a sociable meal and then I'd catch a later train."

Diedre? She is a tall rangy brunette with full lips and stiletto boots—a smart and very ambitious aide. I know her kind—another office piranha, ready to eat anyone to reach the top. She knows what she wants. At the last annual holiday buffet for Cal's department, I stopped to greet the CEO's wife. Over her shoulder, I saw Diedre standing close to Cal and wearing a short dress of clingy white fabric, perfectly showing off her long legs. The neckline draped down toward her cleavage in a sophisticated flowing design. Small diamond earrings matched her diamond pendant. She looked very chic with her long dark hair artfully arranged in a coronet with a few curls dangling at her temple. Every man in the room wanted to run his hand through her lustrous hair. Every woman over forty felt plain and dull beside her. She looked like Snow-White while I was a gray-haired Witch in my long black skirt and black-and-silver top.

She and Cal seemed perfectly matched because they were both tall—she, a brunette, and Cal, with silver temples and lighter hair. He stood there with his face and genial grin bent toward her in the confident manner of a successful executive. He was a big man in every way, looking handsome in his black tux with a red cummerbund. (I barely reach his broad shoulders which means I always look up to him).

Diedre's head almost rested on his shoulder. They were a handsome couple standing so close together. When she saw me coming toward them, she moved toward the buffet table.

I looked at Cal's margarita with surprise. "Well, that is something new."

Cal reddened because he has a personal rule to hold only one glass of merlot during an evening. He's seen too many careers ruined by too many drinks.

"Diedre suggested I try this instead. It's what young people prefer."

"How interesting," I murmured coolly. I knew why I was wary of Diedre and her ambition. She had Cal's attention every day in the office. Was that enough for her?

Cal's voice interrupted my memory. I listened to his comment about grazing. "The younger ones don't eat real dinners. Instead, we hit some crowded bistros and sushi bars." Silence. "Well, you were gone." My fault? "I knew it didn't matter when I got home."

"It must have been very late."

"Actually, I took a limo home."

"—Oh. You must have been very tired."

"I—I didn't notice." Silence. Cal continued, "Really, it was great fun to be with the younger staff. They sound a lot like Anne with their ideas about green space and clean air." Another pause. "We exchanged ideas—opinions. I felt that I fit right in." He gave a little self-conscious laugh. "I almost felt young again."

Mixing socially with the younger staff has always been a no-no with Mirron senior executives. Those kids were smart. They fawned over Cal to cultivate his approval —and would stab him in the back to get ahead. Did he really want to repeat being twenty-five again?

Instead I said, "Jill wants me to stay through next week. She has a private screening of her latest project.".

"—Stay as long as you like. I'm getting along fine here."

That's not what I wanted to hear. I was irked at Cal's stupidity and slung a sandal down the patio. Micah jumped aside, carefully paced toward me and leaped into my lap. I rubbed my cheek along his back and whispered, "Oh, Micah, it's time to go home."

When Jill returns from Alaska, I complain about my empty life without Cal. No sympathy from her. Instead, she's snappish. "Cal's such a dull stuffed shirt. Be glad you're rid of the jerk! I mean—he had only three jokes. We heard them so often he sounded like a broken record."

I argue. "Cal is charming. People love his humor, his smile, the way he joins in laughter when he finishes his funny dialog about the lawyers and St. Peter—or the clergy-man out on a limb—or three guys in a fishing boat." I defend him some more. "They love the way his eyes crinkle in the corners and his great smile. He enjoys entertaining people."

"No one else ever sees him that way. We're tired of his old stories. People don't walk away because they don't want to embarrass you."

I defend Cal. "He's very good-looking—proud of Anne—."

Jill adds, "—Proud of each new car! He recites all the upgrades. And he always parks in the middle of two spaces, so no one gets near his precious car! Don't get revenge—get money! Besides, who stays married any more? Men are dependent. The guys always have someone waiting in the wings." She waits for me to respond. "Stay here in the California sun. Date a movie star. Get on with your life! Get with it!"

I'm confused by Jill's attitude. I didn't know that she disliked Cal. Surely, he wouldn't cheat on me. Not Cal who got an "A" in Business Ethics years ago. Now, I'm unsure.

"I can't stay." I hunt for an excuse. "I have so many things to do—." I really want to be home in case Cal calls and says he wants to come home. Then I remember when he left in January. I called Atlanta to confront Cal directly. I meant to wake him up at two a.m. and ruin his golf game the next day.

When I reached the hotel, a young desk clerk with a Latino accent said that no person by Cal's name was registered there. Where was he? Scottsdale? Greenbriar? Overseas at St. Andrews? Cal had lied to me.

Jill hugs me when I leave. She's relieved not to listen to me any more. I promise myself that I'll only call her once a week. I must find someone else or find something to do— like smash everyone of Ursula's Austrian crystal prisms..

When I return home, I take off my wedding band and drop it in my jewelry box next to a rhinestone lily pin. Both sparkle with the same glitzy luster. I put a cheap turquoise and silver band from the Woodstock era on my middle finger and wear my engagement ring on my right hand. I should sell it, except I should pass it on to Anne. Without my wedding ring, I feel like a more independent woman. Am I'm really with over shock? Do I want Cal to come back? I wonder.

Aunt Cleda, Mom's sister, calls weekly from Naples. "It's a male menopause thing, Tara," she advises. "All men get anxious when they hit forty-five. Cal can't face fifty plus. Women are relieved to be past all that monthly business. We never did like wiping noses and dealing with moody teenagers. Men are only bystanders. Be patient, Cal will be back."

I want to believe her. "I don't hear from him."

"He can't get along without you. You're his rock—."

"Aunt Cleda, I'm more like a pebble that he's kicked aside."

"—Come down here," she continues. "It's quiet without the snowbirds. Soon there will be summer concerts. We'll go out to dinner every night. I meet my friends at the pool around ten and we plan where we'll eat at night. I'll send you back with a fabulous tan and great bikini!"

Aunt Cleda makes Florida sound like one long party. I don't feel like a party. I'd be at my own wake. And I won't be any better with a tanned body or a drinky-poo every morning at ten.

Besides, the state leaves me cold. A plane accident in Florida killed Mom and Dad. It was their first real vacation—after they sold our old Iowa farm and its big white square clapboard house with a wooden swing on a wide front porch. It was a special place because my great-grandparents homesteaded the land. Mom and Dad headed for Disney World. On their return trip, the plane went down in a swamp.

I will always remember our farm where Jill and I planted and picked melons. We managed the farm stand by the road while Dad cultivated the corn fields, the rows as even as the worry lines on his forehead. People came from miles around for our great produce and we carefully counted our profit every night. Jill and I went to McNaughton College. I wanted to teach English. Jill appeared in every play and dreamed she would be the next Audrey Hepburn. We both worked for our room and board.

When a freeway raped the land, my Dad sold the farm to developers. Originally, a motel was planned, but the new partnership saw the potential for an Indian Springs Shopping Mall. A nearby tribe objected to the name which was then changed to "Pioneer". A statue of a rugged westerner on a horse was placed at the entrance, except he faced eastward toward Chicago instead of looking westward. A feminist alliance objected that women weren't represented, so a pioneer woman was added, complete with sunbonnet and billowing skirt. She carried a baby (sex unknown) and held the hand of a young girl. The mall was in business.

That awful March when the plane went down, Jill and I met in Chicago and drove to Muscatine. Cal was in Hong Kong and couldn't get back in time for the funeral. Proudly, I wore a maternity dress, although I was only in my third month of our first child.

I glanced toward Pioneer Mall and realized it sold discount linens and tableware where my mother once set her Sunday dinner table with a white damask cloth and Grandma's treasured china. I looked away, feeling a terrible heaviness in my heart.

The funeral service was at St. Paul, our white frame country church set on a slight rise. It held a special memory because Cal and I were married there in a sweet and simple ceremony. Mom made my white satin gown. Cal brought me yellow roses and Jill, my only attendant, was in yellow taffeta. Like Jesus feeding the five thousand, the church women provided a huge buffet. Looking back, life seemed simple and pure.

My parents funeral was large. Many people came, both to pay their respects and see us again. We were almost strangers, examples of local girls who "made good"— successful in a world of big cities and urban life. I was an executive's wife. By now, Jill's acting career had been replaced by her knack for casting actors in favorable roles.

We were both numb with grief. Death robbed our parents of retirement years when at last they could afford to enjoy life. I felt a terrible bitterness and my stomach was queasy. I went outside for the clear clean spring air of the rural landscape. I stood beside the two fresh earthen mounds and began to weep. Their deaths were too soon, too unfair.

A breeze rustled through the nearby evergreens. I believed I heard a voice distinctly say, "Do not grieve. They have come home to me." I looked up, turned around. Only an eagle circled high above in the cloudless blue sky. The breeze continued to gently sway the spruce branches. It was a Holy moment.

I stood there, transfixed, until Jill came up behind me. Her arm encircled me, and I nestled my face on her shoulder.

"You okay?" she asked.

I nodded. "I'm all right. I'm ready to leave."

We drove back to Chicago and I flew back to Houston alone. Three days later, a neighbor rushed me to the hospital. I had a miscarriage. Cal was on a flight from Hong Kong to Houston.

He came in late that night. When we hugged each other, Cal softly asked, "Are you okay?"

I nodded in tears, "I guess so. Everything was going so well, and then there was that awful crash, and the quick flight to Chicago, and the funeral—." My voice trailed off as I cried harder, "I tried to hold on. I really did."

Cal's voice was gentle, "I know you did."

"It was a little boy. They could tell already that it was a little boy." I sobbed, "I don't know what happened—what happened to him."

"The important thing is that you're okay. Give yourself time to recover. We'll have another child. I promise." His voice changed. "I do have some news. Mirron wants us to move to Greenville. That's a big step for me—for us. You'll be very busy packing for that move."

Did Cal ever grieve? I don't know. He was too full of plans while I wrestled with large cardboard boxes.

My heart was heavy with anguish.

When Cal deserted me, I waited two weeks for Cal's mother to phone me. Cal always called his mother *Anne* until our daughter was born. Instead of *Grandmama*, his mother became *Nana*. Somehow, she's always been a puzzle to me. She divorced Cal's father when Cal was small. Then, she married her boss who died and left her a tidy sum. Soon, she married Kip, a younger man who expected her to support him—and divorced him. Now, she's married to Wendell, a retired lawyer. They winter in Mexico, at the American colony near Lake Chapala and travel. Maybe Cal wants serial marriages like Nana. That's the way some people live.

Nana's back from a long cruise to Australia, so I phone her. I want her sympathy, some reassurance that she still approves of me. I'm sure that Nana likes me. At our wedding, she beamed, "Cal is lucky to have you. You're so sensible."

Instead, she says, "Tara, you're very sweet, but you've never really sparkled. Men want something more than a housekeeper. You could have helped Cal more. I know that he'll be on the Executive Committee someday, and well—." Her voice trails off. She's really thinking, *Cal needs a trophy wife—young, suntanned and smart.*

"I tried to be everything. I really did."

"—Of course, you're very capable," Nana says. Why doesn't she add dumb. too?

"I'm so capable that I put Cal through grad school!" I slam down the phone and try to absorb Nana's criticism. How could I sparkle? Did Cal expect me to wear a purple thong and sequin pasties?

Doesn't anyone support a forever marriage anymore?

Arletta drops by. She checks on me almost daily by phone or in person. She always has an excuse—"in the neighborhood" or "on the way to the dentist", or "had to run out to the drug store". She doesn't fool me. She knows that I know, but the charade is easier than the truth. She knows I'm desperate and she doesn't want me to do anything foolish.

Arletta stands in the kitchen with a plastic container.. "I made too much gazpacho for Boyce." She opens the refrigerator. "My-my. This is almost empty. It's time we went out to lunch. Today. No excuse."

"I don't feel like eating. I talked to Nana last night. She's destroyed me, too."

"Nonsense!" Arletta says and leaves the soup on the first shelf. "She can't destroy anyone. She's too busy remodeling her body. What's it this time—new ear lobes or liposuction? She had so many tucks, she's pleated."

"I don't sparkle," I sniffle as tears roll down my cheeks. I reach for a chocolate kiss.

Arletta frowns at the almost empty dish. "You can't live on chocolate kisses."

"They're the only kisses I get. Besides, they beg to be eaten." I sniff some more and ignore her comment. "What should I do? Dance veiled—draped in plastic wrap? Add some dangly earrings? Nana's right. I'm dull and stupid, too. I need more chocolate." I pop another piece. "Dark chocolate is healthy. I read that it mends a broken heart."

"Stop that! Nana's wrong and you know it."

"Then what am I?" I sob.

"You're Tara, who's bright, warm, and funny with your off-beat humor. Everyone loves to be near you. It doesn't make any difference—rich or poor—you're always glad to see them. That's a gift."

"There's nothing—ah—special—about being nice to people. I like being nice."

"Listen, we've lived here twenty-five years while Boyce built his business. Yet, there are women who barely speak to me because Boyce doesn't put on a sharp suit and catch the seven-twelve to the city. When we met, I said that my husband mowed lawns. I always say that just to judge a stranger's reaction. I wondered if you would ever speak to me again. You never batted an eye. Instead, you invited me over to trade McNaughton memories."

"Well, I was so glad to find one friendly face in the supermarket. You're the best friend that I have here." I reach for another tissue and blow my nose.

"Likewise. I want to you stay healthy and get past this bump in the road."

"It's more than a bump. Some days I wish I were dead. If I had a gun, I'd shoot myself," I shrug my shoulders, "—except I'd fail at that, too."

"Yes, and you'd miss and shatter your Austrian chandelier. Don't ever consider that!"

I never wanted that glittering glass—or this Tudor mansion or the chintz draperies. I say, "It means nothing. How did I end up with all this stuff? That's what it is—stuff."

"I've wondered that, too. This house is not you."

"We're back to Nana's remark. I don't sparkle. What am I?"

"You're Tara—the best friend I have. If you get rid of stuff, I'll give you mine, too. But don't rush it. The answer will come. In the meantime, let's eat Chinese for lunch and read our fortune cookies."

At the Bamboo Hut, we order plate lunches. She chooses sweet-sour pork and I take almond-ding chicken. I'm a ding-bat so it fits.

We pour more tea and crack open our cookies. Arletta grins, "I will receive a gift in the mail. I can't wait!"

"Mine says, You will take a long trip." I make a face. "I don't want to go anywhere. I prefer to be here and miserable with a good friend who listens to my complaints."

"That's what friends are for." She picks up her purse. "Let's stop at The Coffee Place for a latte. If you want, you can have hot chocolate."

I get through another day because Arletta helped me.

Two days later, Arletta calls. "Guess what? Like the fortune cookie said, I received a gift in the mail! It's a sample of a new rice cereal that looks like spiders and bugs."

"Forget my fortune cookie. I won't take any long trip." Instead, I go to the mall and buy Anne a summer outfit. Will she wear it in Salamanca? Probably not. She prefers jeans and tee-shirts. My shopping fills one afternoon. Every day is too long, but summer is bound to arrive sometime. Maybe things will get better. That's a hopeless wish.

Two things signify Cal and I are still married—our daughter Anne and taxes. Our Accountant sends a courier with some statements to sign. I refuse.

"Cal must ask me in person," I tell our accountant through gritted teeth. "And I want a copy of everything for my own file."

Cal comes on Saturday morning. He wears jeans and a new golf shirt. It's a pasty oatmeal color and hangs on him. He's lost weight and looks different. His sparse hair is fuller, blown dry, and now a sandy blonde color. He doesn't look so handsome anymore. He stares at me.

"You've done something with your hair."

I pat my striped raccoon mop. "Oh—so have you,"

Silence. A stilted conversation between two people, sitting across the living room, as far apart as possible. Two ice cubes at the North Pole. Remember, Cal—when we first married—no one could pull us apart? We devoured each other.

"Well, I must keep up with the younger ones," he says. He doesn't grin. "It's a young peoples' world. Do you realize that they don't look at you, anymore? They don't make eye contact. They only stare straight ahead, like they're at computers."

I look at Cal sharply. There is something wistful in his tone—without the confidence he usually has. His jovial informality is missing.

"How's work?"

"Fine. Fine." He pauses, "There's a few changes. Rumors, mainly. A lot of buyouts now." He glances away, "Who knows what will happen?" He stops again. "How about some lunch?"

"I've quit cooking."

"No, I meant that I'll take you someplace."

"I've already made plans." It's not true, but I can't hold back tears much longer.

Silence.

"Oh, I hope we can still be friends."

"I doubt it. When something is over, it's over." I look away. Where will I be in September? Christmas? Next Valentine's Day?

"I never said that our marriage is over. I need time to think."

"You've been gone long enough. You've had time!" I glance at the clock and back at him with a cold hard flat look.. "Let me sign the papers. You can leave!"

Cal reaches in his attaché case and hands over the pages. I take them to the dining room table, so he won't see my shaking hand.

"I hope these numbers are wrong. Then I'll be sent to a federal prison. I hear every prisoner gets his own TV and gourmet meals. Where are the duplicates?" I ask.

"I forgot," he says. "I'll bring them next Saturday. Then we can lunch together."

"Mail them. I'm spending the week-end in St. Louis." Another excuse.

Cal looks at me sharply, "Who are you going with?"

"A tour group. Through the local woman's club." I know how to hide the truth. By now, I'm really good at lies. He believes me.

"Oh—well, I'll send copies Monday." He hesitates and steps forward as if to kiss my cheek, but I step away. "There is one other thing—." Will he say *Divorce*? "—Could I have my big lounge chair and the small table beside it?"

Slowly, I reply, "Sure—I never sit there." I've always hated that bulky brown recliner, so I'm glad to be rid of it.

"I'll send the movers on Saturday."

"—Do that. Is there anything else?"

Cal moves to the hall and looks at the Murano glass vase, reflected in the tall baroque mirror. We bought it in Italy and I awkwardly lugged it home while Cal directed the porters with our luggage. It glistens with its variegated colors of royal blue, purple and olive green. It's shaped like a lily bulb with a long neck and a flaring fluted lip. Often,I add an orchid spray, and enjoy the reflected image.

Cal asks, "How about the vase? I persuaded you to bring it home."

"Of course," I say smoothly, so very smoothly. I pick it up. "Let me carry it out to the car for you."

Cal holds the door while I walk into the fresh air. He climbs into his sports car and reaches out for his vase. I lean forward with it and the vase slips, crashes. Smash! The glass splinters into a dozen fragments on the hard driveway. Cal leaps out and avoids the jagged pieces. He yells, angrily.

"Why did you do that?"

I lift my hands like an innocent bystander. "—It slipped."

"You'll regret this!" he threatens, coming toward me, shaking his fist. "You need a shrink!"

"Get one yourself! Leave!" I run into the house and slam the door. I lean against it, breathing hard.

I hear the tires squeal as Cal speeds away. This time I don't run after him.

I assume that Arletta found out that Cal's been here, because she stops by. I brace myself for a dozen questions, but she doesn't ask anything. Instead, she wants to talk about Sharlene's wedding.

"Guess what?" Arletta sounds weary. "Sharlene's changed her mind again. She wants to be married beside the pond at McKinley Park with a cook-out—brats and chicken—and a tent with a dance floor and a blue-grass band."

"When did she change her mind?"

"She says she wants her wedding to be a lot of fun. She and her friends got together and hashed around ideas, as to what would be FUN! That's what they came up with."

"Has she thought about the mosquitoes? Or if there's a sudden thunderstorm?"

"That's the problem with young people. They don't think. Their heads aren't screwed on right."

I think of Cal. "I know a few middle-aged men who aren't too bright either."

Arletta ignores my remark. "Tara—you've got to help me through this wedding. I'm counting on you."

She shouldn't depend on me. Right now, I'm against weddings at any age. My own was a mistake, except for Anne. I want to forget weddings, so I change the subject.

"Arletta, Cal's birthday is next week. Two years ago when I went to Florida to visit Aunt Cleda, Cal joined me. I arranged a deep-sea fishing trip to celebrate his fiftieth birthday. Maybe, I'll send him a bouquet of wilted yellow roses this year."

"Tara, you're wonderful! You won't do it, but it's very funny." Arletta shakes her head. "Send a clever card. You're good at finding one."

I continue a trail of angry words. "He'll get nothing from me—now or ever! Do I mean it? Yes! And I wish he were dead and I don't regret saying it! I don't feel guilty about feeling that way! No way!" I grit my teeth and snarl, "Let him roast in he—!" I stop. I won't waste my breath. I'm too mad to swear.

Arletta gives me a long probing look. "Tara, be very careful. In your anger, don't destroy yourself."

In our childhood Mama said the same thing when Jill made me angry, like times when she read my diary or borrowed my favorite pleated skirt. What do people expect? That I will always be nice—always calm, always self-controlled? But I know Arletta is right.

At McNaughton, I once read a French philosopher who said that without good friends to correct our bad behavior, we would go mad.

Arletta is such a friend.

SADNESS,

N. L. *SATUR.* FULL, *SATIS*, ENOUGH. N. SOR-
ROWFUL, MOURNFUL, AFFECTED WITH GRIEF, IN
A STATE OF MELANCHOLY, WEARY, SICK;
GLOOMY, CAUSING SORROW, EXPRESSING SOR-
ROW.

When I let the Italian vase slip from my hands and saw Cal's anger erupt, I felt a victorious moment because Cal takes pride in his self-control. However, I didn't expect to miss the vase, but I do. The hall table seems empty—like an old friend who's gone away. I buy a low colorful Mexican pitcher and fill it with trailing ivy. Somehow, it doesn't look right—like a heavy coffee mug in place of a delicate china teacup.

I'm filled with melancholy over all the things that I've lost in our moves—the china doll that Aunt Cleda gave me on my eighth birthday, the fine pillow slips with Mama's crocheted lace, the book of poems that Cal gave me on our first Valentine's Day. What happened to these things? Other precious items were lost in our moves—a box of Christmas ornaments, Cal's boyhood electric train. I tell myself they were only "things", but they were part of our lives—just as Cal is gone now from mine.

I regret my angry effort. I didn't hurt Cal as much as I hurt myself when the vase shattered. My tears flow.

Arletta reports that maybe Sharlene and Jared will choose a church wedding with a big reception after all. They've dropped two ideas—a large tent in a city park or a destination wedding. Arletta's so relieved and happy that she even has another solution for me. I should join a WOMEN ALONE—GIRLS TOGETHER group at her church.

"It's networking with others who have problems," she says.

I don't have problems. I only have one HEADACHE—Cal is gone. I'm filled with a terrible melancholy. I feel like I've fallen into a ravine and no one hears me. Although people are nearby, I can't move. I'm too paralyzed with fear and indecision. I sob too often.

Arletta keeps nagging until I agree to go on Tuesday night. I have another excuse. "I'll go alone, but I'll leave early. Anne promised to call. I can only stay a little while." I pull on my new royal blue slacks and a patriotic red, white and blue tee-shirt. I don't intend to look like I'm pale and listless from Cal's abandonment, although I've lost weight. I still can't eat very much.

I clump down the basement stairs of Glen Springs Community church. All church basements seem the same— sickly hospital-green walls (or beige), with asphalt tile floors scratched by spindly chrome-legged chairs. There's that flat stale air, too. At least Glen Springs basement has one improvement—new rose plastic chairs with curved seats that fit like a cup, sliding the listener forward. Maybe an audience seems more interested that way.

There's a metal coffee maker marked *Decaf* on a table and a stack of white plastic foam cups with red stir sticks. Plates of chips and assorted cookies are nearby. Women drift in and form clumps of three or four and glance my way. A younger woman holds out her hand. "I'm Betsy. Do join us." There's Rosita and Darla and Isobel and Aisha and Corrine—until I can't remember who's who. We blend together like rag dolls. When they sit down, I grab a back row seat so I can get out of there.

I'm introduced. I shrink from their eyes that look expectantly at me. I don't want to admit that Cal left me and that I'm slowly shriveling up from loneliness.

There's a lady lawyer who speaks on the problems of child support and the court system. She looks sharp in her smart beige suit and low heel pumps. She's young, savvy, and will gain a couple of clients, because she loves to hear their personal problems. She snaps out answers in staccato time and hands out cards with a smile and "Call me."

"My husband lost his job, and he's left the state."

"My ex has hidden bank accounts, but I don't know how to find them."

"The louse that I married gambles his paycheck before he pays any bills."

"The bank is ready to foreclose, and I need to find a place for me and the kids."

"Whenever my husband misplaces anything, he yells and asks me where I put it. I'm tired of being blamed for everything. Can I get any settlement for emotional abuse?"

"The hospital bills me for two nights after he beat me. I think he should pay."

"He and his girl friend flew to Las Vegas for a long weekend. Can I make him pay for a week at a spa for me?"

"My ex waits until the end of the month before he coughs up child support. I get penalized for a late rent payment."

"My in-laws have removed my name from any inheritance and the kids' money will be handled by my ex's brother—who is a real jerk."

"My husband got his girl friend pregnant. He thinks the three of us should buy a house together."

Betsy leans over and says, "Don't be shy. Speak up. Ask her whatever. We're very understanding."

I panic. Cal isn't like any of those other husbands. "Mine is a very personal problem."

I stammer, "My—my dog Fido doesn't sleep well—paces all night. We're both dying of loneliness."

Betsy frowns as if I'm on another planet. "Oh my! Oh, you poor dear."

"I gotta go," I whisper. "It's time for my poodle—uh, Fido—and me to have our heart-to-heart together before we go to bed."

I dash up the stairs into the night. I must be crazy. I don't have a dog. I don't even like dogs. Deep down, I know why I had to get away. I don't want to admit even to strangers that Cal left me. If I believe that he'll come back soon, that's a huge mistake. Like Jill says, *Get over it*. How can I make new life for myself? I weep and settle into the den, pulling a fuzzy plaid coverlet over me. I punch the remote.

I watch Garbo sit in a Paris opera box, beautifully gowned, curious as she surveys the crowd below. I rouse, whimpering, and feel my wet cheeks. I have been crying in my sleep because now Gable is on the TV screen, standing at the Saratoga race track with his confident and debonair grin. A small pain creeps through my chest. I lie quietly and breath carefully until it passes. If I were in bed with Cal, he would hold me close until I went back to sleep. But he isn't here and he never will be. Finally, I doze off again.

I awake to sunshine and find my vision blurs. Arletta calls the eye clinic for me. I can't get an appointment for a month. She describes my condition and persuades the stern guardian of appointments that I must see a doctor As a good friend, she takes me out to lunch, orders chicken salad for both of us and then drives me to the eye clinic. I'm scared. What if I can't ever read again?

In the ophthalmologist's office I try to decipher his charts, but I can read only the top, halting before each large letter—T,Z,O—or is it Q?—R, V. The nurse puts stinging drops in my eyes. I stare at various bright lights in a darkened room while a technician takes pictures from different cameras. Later, the doctor looks at the images and studies my eyes closely. He pulls down the lids and clears his throat.

"You must stop crying or your tear ducts will be damaged forever," he says gravely."That's an order."

Arletta drives me to the drugstore for medicine. "Spring is already gone and you've never cleaned out your closets," she hints. "It's time to begin. Get rid of things." Her closets are always clean and in order.

Slowly, I take action after a few tears. I start in on the basement and work all morning. It feels good to be active, to get rid of extra curtain rods, Cal's old golf clubs, faded Christmas wreaths (two for the front door), a box of vases (including the one with the dozen roses from Cal before he walked out). I'm surprised how much has accumulated since the last time we moved. Why do we hang on to stuff? That's what possession are—stuff. The word keeps going around in my mind.

I go into Cal's closet.. In my hardened heart, I mean for Cal to move everything out. Why should I lift a finger to help? He always left things scattered across our dresser, drawers pulled out. Now dust covers everything. I sneeze, but I don't cry. That's progress.

I settle into our guest room permanently. No more late night movies in the den, or stretching out on a chair and ottoman. I like the order, the simplicity of our guest room. Arletta helps me buy a quilted yellow bedspread and hang an abstract print above the bed. I put a pot of daisies at the window and open the drapes to bright sunshine. Soon it will be summer and perhaps my long spring shower of tears will—no, must—be over.

After the divorce, I'll move away. I don't want to live here anymore since Cal left. With Anne away at school, I have no use for this house. I never liked the room arrangement. When we moved here, Cal insisted that we get a decorator. Did Ursula, who must be sister of Attila, the Hun, think that chintz reflected my personality?

I won't look back anymore. I'll get a nice condo or apartment and fill it with purple furniture. Or an Oriental screen with an Eames chair. Start a whole new life.

Arletta approves of my new guest room decor. "You're back in the real world."

I make a mistake when I mention that I'm ready to move forward—start a new life.

She says, "If Cal's gone, do as you please. Get rid of the living room drapes. You've always hated them. Change the wallpaper." She wants me to keep busy. She's full of projects. "I'll rent a steamer for you."

"Too much work. I'll plant a garden." It seems an easier alternative.

Arletta goes to the dining room window. It overlooks the deck which overlooks the backyard. "You have a perfect yard to develop. It's private with that yew hedge and that great oak tree."

"I'll cut down the oak and plant wheat. Grind my own flour. Be self-sufficient."

She hears my bitter tone. "Nonsense. Think positively. You could have a lovely fountain—something slightly Victorian—to go with your house."

"I don't like Victorian. I hate these stripes and peonies."

"Change them later. You'll have more fun working in the yard. Boyce knows a great young landscape designer."

I don't argue. Maybe Arletta is right. Maybe I need to work outside—away from the house, waiting for something to happen. For Cal to phone. For Cal.

I buy two landscape books and let Boyce send Berkley with design plans. I expect a handsome woodsy guy and instead, get an experienced capable young woman. She spends an hour with me, tch-tching about winter damage to the grass. She shakes her head negatively about the hedge.

"We'll pull it out and in this corner, a rock garden—."

"I'm only interested in a fountain over here—."

"Impossible. It might upset the oak tree."

I look at the oak, at least seventy years old. "Does our—my—oak have feelings?"

Berkley stares at me as if I were an ignorant six-year old. "—But it does! It will die if the roots are disturbed."

I see this is turning into a much bigger project than a mere fountain. "I just want a fountain here by the deck," I say firmly. "I'm not sure how long I'll stay here. I want something that has good resale value." Something that will help to sell the house quickly so my pain will end.

Berkley shrugs and walks back toward the deck. "Maybe a small square with a brick inlay pattern and a fountain in the center." She squints her eyes and adds, "A low brick planter around it can be filled with seasonal flowers—spring bulbs and summer impatiens. Very simple. Very attractive. A real eye-catcher."

"Draw up the plans and send me estimates."

By the time, everything is finished—prodded by Arletta—June is gone. I plant scarlet impatiens and have a sore back for a week. The fountain gurgles and the squirrels run around the edge. The robins leave their droppings on the bricks, so daily, I spray off their calling cards. Simple? Yes. An eye-catcher? Maybe. At least, the flowers bloom.

But Arletta is right. Now, I have something to do. I hose down bird splats.

Cal leaves messages on my machine. I don't return his calls. Anne phones from Salamanca and begs me to answer Cal's calls.

"Dad says he's lost weight," she says. "You're terrible—not to talk to him."

"You're right!" I reply. "I hope you're never in my situation." I want to say What goes around, comes around. I'm almost single now, like you, Anne. Only, I'm a has-been. The extra woman. What do they do with me in a couples' world? The invitations to dinners have stopped. No engraved card came for the concert fund-raiser this spring. I fit in at a bridge benefit. They can always use an extra there.

I've taken the veil—our home is my own isolated convent.

Arletta says I'm still angry, that I need a worthwhile project to get rid of my rage. At Glen Springs church a women's group, the Knit-Wits, knit prayer shawls for the shut-ins. She thinks I should join them. Who? The knitters or the shut-ins? Either way, the name fits. I'm a real live nit-wit.

"Look," I protest, "When I was fourteen, Aunt Cleda came to visit. She was bored to death on the farm. Her summer project was teaching Jill and me to knit. Neither of us became adept with those pointed needles. I dropped stitches like a bowling ball."

Arletta doesn't hear me. "You never forget a skill." She rattles on. "We meet for coffee and a devotion and then we just click away until eleven." She's very confident. "Afterward, we'll go shopping."

I know her aim—to get me up in the morning, keep me busy, and get me fed, because we'll lunch together, too. She kills three birds with one yarn ball. She's so earnest, so concerned that, reluctantly, I agree. We're off to a yarn shop and I choose a variegated yarn of lavender, blue and turquoise. Then I buy huge needles that would be perfect for stabbing Cal in the back. Several times.

She picks me up on Tuesday morning and I join the Knit-Wits. I know Josie from the Garden Club, so I sit next to her and wait while Arletta directs the prayer time. Silently, I pray for Anne, but not Cal. I'm done with him. I take out my needles and Arletta nods for me to cast on my stitches. The needles are slippery and awkward. I look around while the others click-clack away because they know what they're doing. I don't.

Arletta reaches over and takes my supplies. "Casting on is the worst part. I'll get you started." With nimble fingers, she winds the yarn around those long metal needles and produces a row of stitches. "I'll do the first row, because that's harder." Quickly, she knits three more rows, too. She pushes the strip toward me. "Now, you just knit away!"

Slowly, I try to recall what Aunt Cleda taught me. I push one needle between two stitches and wind the yarn around the second needle. The yarn slips off and falls into my lap. I try again. This time, my first needle jabs at the strip and I separate threads instead of finding the right space for the next stitch. The morning is spent with dropped stitches and extra looped ones. I'm as miserable as the morning Cal left.

Arletta looks over, "You're doing fine. It will get easier." Meanwhile, she's finished a long section of her own prayer shawl.

The knitters leave at eleven. I drop to the floor to retrieve my yarn which has rolled under Josie's chair. I'd like to sprawl on the floor and go to sleep. I'm exhausted from the past two hours. I managed just one inch. I jab the needles into the yarn. At the rate that I knit, I'll be ready for a prayer shawl myself when it's finished.

Arletta will not be defeated and I promise to work at night. But in a couple of weeks, I'll find a different reason to give up.

"Arletta," I will say, "The yarn makes me sniffle at night. I don't think that knitting a prayer shawl is for me— especially in warm weather."

Arletta will know it's an excuse, but she'll take the yarn and finish my shawl. All's well that ends well. And she will tell me to move on. A wave of melancholy hits me. Move on to what? Where do I belong? I'm nothing.

A new show opens at the Art Museum. I go with Arletta and the Garden Club. I wander away from the group into the mid-European gallery. I linger at a painting that I've never really studied. I stand there a long time. A guard walks on to another room. I stop longer than the usual two minutes, so I'm still there when he returns later. Maybe he's glad that someone spends time in his gallery.

The painting is of a weary sad-eyed peasant girl, at the edge of a forest, her arms full of firewood. An old man, stooped and wrinkled, is nearby—perhaps following her. Has he piled the branches on her thin arms? The painting speaks to me of some sorrow that I can't identify, but I feel the child's heavy burden as never before. Is he her grandfather? Does she wish to build a fire to keep him warm. Has he ordered her to help him? Do men at any age feel that women—even a young girl—must take care of them?

I'm sad, too, but I also realize that Cal will never return. I need to accept that fact. I need closure.

Can I find a release in art? How?

Cal wants to meet me, but I say I'll be gone which is true because wonderful Arletta provides me with an excuse. She's excited for me to replace her at a Women's Weekend with Clotilde, a professional retreat leader. "I can't go because Sharlene's wedding is in twenty-two days," she says. "This is the trip your fortune cookie predicted! You'll love the weekend! Everyone gains so much. You'll really be inspired to start a new life in the fall. Clotilde will set your feet on solid ground and send you on your way!"

Clotilde should send me to Reno for a quickie divorce. Where can I go when I don't have any direction? I just fill time. I depend on Arletta. Too often she conveniently asks me to replace her at a bridge benefit or garden walk or an art show. I can argue, but she'll dismiss my excuse. It's hopeless, but I try. I don't like to see other people.

"I'll be a stranger. The other women will know each other."

"Josie from the garden club and Knit-Wits will be your roommate. She'll drive, too." Arletta rattles on while I make a decision. "Last year, Clotilde used a LAY theme—."

"—Meaning?"

"LOVE and ACCEPT YOURSELF. This year Clotilde has a LAM theme—LOVE and AFFIRM MYSELF. She's terrific. You'll come back really focused." Arletta is excited. "Wait until you hear Darya. She's back this year as the inspirational speaker." Perhaps I look doubtful because she quickly adds, "This isn't a church retreat. You don't have to say prayers or stuff like that. This is to find the real you!"

I admit I'm lost since Cal left. "Do I want to find me?"

Arletta adds a last clincher. "It'll be like camp when you were a kid!"

That gets me. Will I really feel that young and that free again? "Okay. Count me in. I'll be ready Friday morning."

I don't want to disappoint Arletta. She tries so hard to take care of me. I pack a bag with my old tennis shoes and jeans for roughing it. Will Clotilde hold the pole as we erect our tent? I doubt it. I'm skeptical about people like her and Cal who run things.

It's a two-hour trip. Away from my Tudor prison, I relax and enjoy the ride. Then Josie pulls into a long wide drive, lined with scarlet geraniums. On the velvet green lawn there's a large oval of tall red cannas and yellow marigolds, edged with chartreuse and wine coleus. Against the tall evergreens, it's especially colorful in the warm bright sunshine. The main lodge is a huge stone and brick edifice with golf courses spreading in all directions and small lakes scattered over the terrain. Condos and cottages stretch out along the winding roads. No tent will blow down on me tonight so I'll have an easy time. Even if the group doesn't say a prayer, I'll thank God that I'm away from the phone. Cal can't reach me here.

At the entrance, a handsome young man opens my door with a flourish. "I'm Mark. Welcome to Shining Waters Lodge!" He must be a college student on a summer job.

Josie pops up the trunk, while Mark puts our luggage on a brass rack. Another young man drives her car off toward a parking lot as a red Porsche pulls up and two bronzy golfers get out—the kind of guys who invite a lingering smile. I wish I'd brought my classy white slacks and a black and white tee shirt. Then I look away. I tell myself that I don't like men. They can't be trusted.

Inside, Josie and I are given plastic room keycards and pointed toward the Northwood lounge, designated for AFFIRM's activities. Women stand around with cold drinks. I'm introduced to Wisteria (I look twice at her name tag),

Phyllis, Pat, Joyce, Enid, and Annabelle, until I retreat behind a smile and a nod to others. Enthusiastically, they greet each other with hugs and a noisy "Hi, there!" It's a reunion of a sisterhood I'll never join.

Finally, I whisper to Josie. "I want to unpack and explore the gardens."

In our third floor room which overlooks a golf course, I stretch out on a queen size bed with huge pillows that almost force me into a sitting position. A corner tub with jets could substitute for a small swimming pool. I look around at Josie's bed, the large TV screen hidden behind a mahogany armoire, and the refrigerator hidden behind more carved doors. The luxury amuses me. This sure isn't like Camp Wittenberg.

The summer when I was ten, Jill and I had our one and only camp experience. The Sunday School superintendent and his wife drove their twin daughters, Jill, and me to Camp Wittenberg while they toured St. Louis for a week. I was excited because I was oldest, leggy, and wouldn't be staying near my squirmy eight-year-old sister and the twins.

I was put in St. Matthew cabin with other fifth grade girls while Jill was across the clearing and became a St. Luke girl. Each cabin took turns ringing a huge bell that called us to meals in the weathered frame Augsburg dining hall. Another clearing held Luther Chapel, an outdoor space with plain wood benches that faced an altar of logs with a brass cross, the only thing that represented a civilized world beyond our rustic camp. Down by the lake there was a fire pit for nightly devotions and toasting s'mores.

I don't remember the other seven cabin mates, but I can clearly recall our counselor, Rosalee—hired because her uncle was pastor of a large church in Des Moines. Rosalee had dark limpid eyes and a busty figure. She left her loose shirts unbuttoned to her cleavage until the Camp Director told her to "button up" because she must set a Christian example for the little Christians around her. At nightly prayers in our cabin, she defiantly left her shirt unbuttoned and we saw her white lacy bra.

Rosalee was always last to reach morning chapel, or the dining hall. And she faded into the dark at campfire time, which seemed strange. One night, I was curious and whispered to a cabin mate that I had to go to the bathroom, a cement block building that smelled awful and we avoided as long as possible.

It was scary to quietly tiptoe back alone on the winding path to our cabin. I was sure that the very name St. Matthew provided protection. One light shone above the door. The cabin was empty, but through the window screen I saw Rosalee leaning against a tree, smoking! She realized that I saw her, so she ground out her cigarette and came inside.

"Tara, I got tired of s'mores and doing the same thing every night. Would you like to have some fun?"

Right away, I knew I was in danger because FUN wasn't listed on the daily schedule. My mother didn't smoke and Dad said it was a "dirty filthy habit", but I didn't want Rosalee to think I was another dumb little farm girl like Jill and the twins. "Fun? Like what?"

"Tonight, when the others are asleep, let's go skinny-dipping in the lake."

"Gee—I don't know—."

"No one will hear us. We're closest to the path. If anyone stops us, we can say that we want to pray by the lake in the full moon." She waited for my response. "You'll have a secret, just like I have secrets."

"I'm afraid we'll get in trouble."

"No one will find out. You'll never have any fun, unless you take a chance."

I felt very small and scared, but I said, "Okay."

"When it gets late enough, I'll wake you up."

Rosalee didn't need to worry, because my heart pounded with anticipation and fright. I was wide awake when she jiggled my sleeping bag and held her fingers to her lips. We crept away, quiet as garter snakes on a mossy bank. Down by the lake, we dropped our thin summer nighties and slipped into the cold dark and foreboding water. Scared, I treaded water by the long pier, the sandy silt squishing up between my toes. Rosalee went farther out. What if she cried *Help! Help!* How could I save her?

It seemed an eternity before Rosalee swam back and said it was time to go. We shook ourselves and put on our gowns which clung to our wet skin. I crawled into my sleeping bag and promptly fell asleep.

Next morning, I was exhausted from our escapade and could barely wake up for the breakfast bell. I saw the Director speak to Rosalee. Soon, she left camp and the Director's wife took Rosalee's place at our table.. I knew I faced punishment when the Camp Director called me to his office. Ole, the night watchman, had seen us sneak back to our cabin.

"Tara, tell me everything about last night."

Tearfully, I confessed to breaking the rules, and blamed it on Rosalee.

"—But you knew it was wrong. And yet, you went along with it. That's a lesson. You must develop an inner strength to turn away from wrong even if it sounds like fun."

"I didn't want to sin—I really didn't." *Sin* was the right word to say and I rolled it around on my tongue like a sweet-sour lemon drop. Adults sinned, so somehow my one mistake was a glimpse into an exciting world ahead where I must make choices between good and bad things.

"I believe you, but there has to be punishment. What do you think that should be?"

"No ice cream at snack time?"

"—Nor dessert in the dining hall either."

I didn't care because those ice cream cups always had a cardboard flavor and camp desserts, like gummy tapioca or chocolate glop, were dull, dull, dull. I knew my mother would bake us a fresh cherry pie when Jill and I got home—or would I get any pie after my sin? That was a real worry.

The Director paused, "It wasn't only that you broke the rules, but you were in great danger of being out there without a life preserver or a lifeguard. If you had drowned, we would all be very sad. We would miss you very much."

I heard the concern in his voice and that made me really regret my foolishness.

When we drove into the farm yard, Mom and Dad enveloped us in their arms. Jill, like a mean little sister, began her chant, "Tara got in trouble! Tara got in trouble!"

I stuck out my tongue at her, but Mom said, "We'll talk about this privately."

In the kitchen, I tearfully recited the whole skinny-dipping episode over again. Mama just held me close. "You've learned a lesson. Throughout your life you must to choose to do the right thing, but all that matters is that you're safe at home with us again." In my mother's arms I felt the love that was and always would be there.

That night we had cherry pie for dessert—with ice cream, too.

After dinner, Clotilde quickly reviews the LAM weekend. "This is your time—your place! You must expect the unexpected—of endless possibilities for YOU!" Her tone reminded me of a television evangelist. "So—find YOURSELF!"

We tramp down a path for the evening's moonlight yoga session. A great bonfire illuminates the night and creates interesting shadows among the trees. We take plastic mats from a colorful cart and fling them down on the glazed brick patio. There's no roughing it here.

Clotilde is a tall broad-shouldered woman with a commanding voice. She's dressed in white slacks and a gauzy top. Her long blonde hair is wound into a top-knot. She stands there like a sculptured goddess in a shadowy niche. She turns to a young woman from the sports center, who's dressed in a trainer's black and white knit outfit.

"This is Toni who will lead yoga tonight. So relax, look at that gorgeous full moon, and breathe deeply." Clotilde vanishes into the dark and Toni begins with the standard stretching exercises. Soon we're doing cat-and-cow moves, along with wobbly tree poses and warrior lunge movements. "Breathe deeply! Breathe deeply!" We inhale the fresh clear night air. We finish with "Ha, Ha, Ha!"—ten minutes of laughing yoga.

When we're through with guffaws and lion roars, Toni disappears and Clotilde returns and claps her hands for attention. "Aren't we having fun? It's time to tap into the CHILD in us—which is the first step to AFFIRM our true self. Throw up your hands—your arms. Reach higher! Reach higher!"

Awkwardly, our arms are thrown out at all angles. Some people yell "Ouch!" when an unexpected fist hits them in the ribs.

"Stand tall! Stand tall!" she repeats. "Circle the fire! Sway like a tree."

I peer at the rigid evergreens. They've gone to sleep for the night. It's been a long day. I want to do the same.

"Dance!" Clotilde orders. "Be free as a child! Say I can! I can I can!"

We repeat like a Greek chorus, "I can! I can! I can!" swaying and circling the bonfire. Someone slaps a mosquito—or maybe a sand fly. I want flop down on my puffy pillow haven.

"Be free!" Clotilde urges again. She likes to repeat herself. "O Great Mother of Fire, who lights our way, inflame our lives! Inflame our hearts! Lead us to leap into the future with the gayety of children! Come! Mother of Fire—Come!" she chants and lightly skips forward.

I wish she wouldn't have us jumping around. If we get any closer, we could be her first martyrs—burned at the bonfire. Others take up her litany. A red-hot log splits apart so some pieces shift, sending sparks skyward. A few fire-worshipers pull back and shriek, as Clotilde dances ahead, toward the Lodge and the brightly lit boutiques. We follow our guru, past the beautifully manicured flower beds, to another large stone patio and the lodge doorway.

Josie taps me on the shoulder. "The Lodge boutiques are open until ten. I want to see what's available. I'll be up shortly." Others head for the stores, too, because shopping is a big part of feeling good at the LAM weekend.

Not for me. I wave her on. "Take your time. It's been a long day. I'm going to bed."

The child in me falls asleep.

After breakfast, Clotilde directs us to cross our arms and hug ourselves. Then we hug each other. Someone murmurs in my ear, "You're terrific!", but I watch as Darya quietly enters the room. She's a slim tiny person of far-eastern ancestry, perhaps from Kashmir or Madras. Her black hair is pulled back in a severe chignon and she wears gold earrings and several gold chains. It is her sari that is so beautiful—navy blue shot with gold threads in a fine intricate design. She speaks in a low warm tone, so we are almost lulled into a trance.

"You can't live in isolation, but you must live in relation-ships," she intones. I watch others jot down her words as if they're directly from some ancient god. I half-listen as she gives us her RECIPE FOR LIVING—Release old hurts, Respond to new relationships and Relish each day which includes healthy eating—further explained in her new diet book.

Darya steps closer with her final wisdom. "We face a future reality with a new and vibrant clarity. Each of us transmits light if we are open and transparent enough to let our light shine through and be a beacon to those around us, so they can experience light like the trans-illumination from a chandelier of fine crystal," Darya concludes, hands uplifted in an ethereal way.

We sit hushed until Enid jumps up to lead rousing applause. Others follow, smiling and nodding in agreement. With her psycho-babble, Darya said whatever she meant and said it very well—and in such a musical voice.

When Darya mentioned a crystal chandelier, I almost double-up with laughter. I've lived with trans-illumination for several years, thanks to Ursula, and didn't know it. Open? Transparent? Did Cal see through me and give up? Maybe I don't shine enough and that's what Nana meant. I'm dull like a clouded lamp chimney. Her remark still stings.

Release old hurts? I think about Cal and myself. Often, I knew we were drifting away from each other. Finally, we seemed to be worlds apart—he with the corporation and me with suburban life. But when we collided, I always felt we melded again, and belonged together.. Does he have a love affair with someone other than Mirron/Molten? I wonder. If Darya's right, where do I find new relationships? When will I relish each day?

While we take a coffee break, Darya moves to a table to sign her new book, *A New You for a New Day*. Afterward, I join a buzz group for ways to LOVE and AFFIRM MYSELF. I think hard as I listen to the others. Enid collects winter jackets for inner city kids and Phyllis campaigns to save oak trees from a land developer. Astrid hosts college exchange students and Violet collects hospital supplies for Aids patients in Ghana. They look at me expectantly.

Once I wanted to pursue a master's degree in children's literature. Instead, I put Cal through grad school. I gulp, "I'm good at moving. I mean—I've moved twelve—or is it thirteen?—times." I stammer, "Some wedding presents are still in their original boxes—." I stop. "I've done nothing with my life. I do nothing."

Silence.

Finally, Phyllis says softly, "It's not too late. If you have an empty life, find a place to use your talents."

Violet takes my hand, "That's why you're here. You matter. You can make your life so fulfilling." They smile at me expectantly.

"I'll think about it."

In the afternoon Josie goes off to shop again with the others. I decide to read beside the blue-green pool with its striped umbrellas and cushiony lounges. As I lay here, I review our years of marriage and that January morning, trying to find a new clue. Why did Cal leave? Nothing is clear. I mull over Phyllis' remark. Maybe it isn't too late for me—with my empty nest and single state—to start a worthwhile life. Other women have been abandoned. I'm not alone.

We gather in an open area when the first star shines at twilight. Bright scarves in various colors form a large spiral, leading to a silky red one in the center. It is a labyrinth without stones and Clotilde stands there while Annabelle, in a flowing Egyptian robe, sits on a bench with a bongo drum between her knees. Clotilde's hair shines like a silver halo in the dim light. She's a reincarnation of an exotic blonde gypsy dressed in a long paisley skirt and peasant blouse.

"Tonight, we're to feel our oneness with the universe. Line up—two together—and walk with the scarf line between you.. Line up!" She claps her hands again to hurry us along, like a first-grade teacher on a field trip. "First, you must clear your head of old negative thoughts and find your Zen-zone and your Zen-tone" She closes her eyes, lifts her head, puts a hand on each temple and hums a deep "Om-m-m". She must have great lungs. "Now, the first couple will move two steps ahead and repeat their mantras. The rest of you follow. Come, come! Soon we will be in the heart of the labyrinth, chanting together! A great chorus of women, like our Greek sisters in ancient Athens."

Josie and I are the third couple in line. I sound an "Ahm" and half close my eyes. The automatic sprinklers sprayed the lawn this afternoon, so I feel damp grass underfoot. I stifle a sneeze and wonder if it means a summer cold. Finally, we're bunched together in the center, droning away like bees in a rose garden as Annabelle beats the drum ever more loudly. It reminds me of a tolling death bell.

Clotilde, has one more order. "Now slowly unwind, reach down, and take a scarf. "We'll do a moon dance in a circle. Think of the Blue Danube—as we waltz and sing, *O Mother Moon, Bless me! Bless me!* Dance and twirl ! Dance and twirl!" Annabelle responds with a bongo waltz beat—Da Da Da Da Dahhhh, Da Dahhhh, Da Dahhhhh while we sing the moon chant to the Strauss tune.

Clotilde leaps around, waving her scarf, "When you're radiant with joy, you SMILE at Everyone!—SMILE at Life!—SMILE with Joy!—SMILE for You!—SMILE!" She urges us on. "Play! Sing! Dance away the night! Life is Wonderful! " Her voice rises, "You WILL sleep peacefully tonight for you are a CHILD of the UNIVERSE!" I believe her. She's in command.

I grab a scarf as a bug runs over my hand—or is it a vole? This time, I softly sneeze. Violet whispers, "Bless you." Awkwardly, we circle around chanting and waving our scarves at the moon. I circle twice and only feel cold wet feet, so I dance away. I take a hot shower and an aspirin before Josie enters our room. She is radiant from the moon dance and I'm cozy warm, snuggled down in the pillows. I agree with Arletta's promise that there's something for everyone at a Clotilde retreat. I'll take a luxury bed over damp feet anytime.

On our return, Josie drives with her left hand while her right gestures about the fantastic week-end. "What do you think?"

I struggle to be polite. "It was most—most unique." *Unique* saves me every time.

"You're so right!" She's remains enthusiastic about Clotilde. "Inspiring—that's what I tell my friends. I mean—Clotilde has it all together," Josie says, her hazel eyes darting right and left like sparks from the campfire. "And I love the purse I bought. It made the retreat worthwhile. And these earrings, too!" She waves her head left and right.

I wish she'd keep both hands on the wheel. "Well, Clotilde commands attention."

"That's what I mean," Josie repeats. "She makes us feel so at one with the universe. Everything is so full of meaning. Everything. We can't take one moment for granted."

I nod, unable to feel at one with anything because Josie's driving makes me nervous. She keeps waving her right hand and looks at me, not the road.

Josie continues, "Things that we overlook just fit together. Like the labyrinth. Last summer I picked up an orange scarf. Guess what? This year in the dark, I picked up another orange scarf. What do you think it means?"

I try for a light touch. "—That you're a CHILD of the SUNSETS?"

Josie's eyes widen and her voice is serious. "You're right! That's what it means! I should use sunsets for meditation, for feeling oneness with the universe." She turns to me as a car swerves in front of us. "Oh, Tara, you have such insight! This LAM retreat has really deepened our relationship. Let's meet every week—."

"Well, I might be involved—." I struggle and quickly remember, "—I—I—I may go to Florida to care for my aunt."

Josie doesn't hear me. "We'll be great friends. What color was your scarf?"

"Lavender."

Josie is silent, now both hands on the wheel. "It may mean that your ancestors were royalty—wore the royal purple."

"I doubt it. My great-grandparents came through Ellis Island, after their ship was lost for six weeks due to a drunken captain. They were Norwegian peasants—that's for sure."

Josie giggles a little. "Some peasants had royal blood. Sometimes, the princes went a little wild." She winks and waves her hand, as another car slows in front of her. She brakes just in time to avoid a rear-end collision.

I yawn extra long and extra wide. "Excuse me, but I'm really tired—."

Josie is sympathetic. "Oh, I know how you feel. Clotilde runs a really INTENSE weekend."

"I have to catch up on my sleep."

"That's okay," Josie says. "I bought two tapes from Clotilde, so I'll listen while you nap."

While Clotilde drones on about Positive Affirmation through Love Relationships, I lay back and close my eyes. I recall riding with Cal when I took him home the first time to meet Mom and Dad.

I sat near Cal. He lifted his right arm and pulled me closer to him. There wasn't much traffic, but I slid out from under his arm and put his hand back on the wheel. "Keep your hands on the wheel, because one-hand drivers make me very nervous!"

Cal gave a throaty laugh. "Why? What's wrong? Are you afraid your parents won't approve of me?"

"Oh, they'll like you. I'm just afraid—afraid of the future."

"We've got a great future." Cal stopped the car. "Now, Tara, tell me the truth. What do you really fear?"

"I intended to go to grad school, and then you come along and change everything—."

Cal put his arms around me. "You're the one. You came along and changed my life. When I transferred to McNaughton, I didn't intend to meet a girl who makes it almost impossible to study or eat or sleep without thinking about her."

I look away through the right window to the cornfields. "This is wonderful now, but how do we know we'll still be in love next year, or the year after that, or ten years from now?" I bury my head in Cal's shoulder and start to cry.

Cal gently wipes my eyes. "Tara, we'll make it last. I promise our love will last."

"Don't ever leave me."

"Never."

How many times have I recalled that conversation on state road 34? When Cal took the Mirron job, he began to travel. Because of business, he left me many times, but he always came back and I welcomed him with open arms. I'm not allowed tears anymore, but when I think of that afternoon I want to cry. What ever happened to our promises? To us?

I unlock my front door and notice that filmy dust still covers the hall table. I miss Lena who has returned to Poland or wherever. Cal isn't here to drop his golf card or leave his keys on a freshly polished surface. Can I continue to blame him for my listless life? Here in isolation, it would be so simple to end everything—or would it? My Phi Beta Kappa pin from McNaughton College didn't guarantee me any smarts. I've hung on to my tattered marriage because I lied to myself that Cal would come back. Anne will soon return for her senior year at NU and I'll be alone next winter in this large Victorian house, decorated by Ursula, the designer who knew what I wanted and I didn't argue.

I stand still. A Bible verse flashes through my mind, *Be still, and know that I am God.* God is my problem, too—maybe worse than a husband who walks away without notice. I've cried. I've yelled. I've bargained, but God doesn't answer my prayers. Yet, I want to believe that He watches and loves me, because God is a God of life—not death. Perhaps He will still give me an answer. I live in hope.

I know the Pastor, Arletta, Phyllis, Violet and the others are right. I have my health—even with poor eyesight—time, and a car. It's not too late to rejoin the human race.

I call the Senior Center and offer to volunteer. An automated voice instructs me to leave my name and number. A return call from the Director says there's a new Partner-to-Patient program. Volunteers will visit nursing home residents who have no friend or relative nearby.

"It's really very simple," the Director continues. "Hopefully, you will visit twice a month and remember a birthday with a card or flowers."

I hesitate. I don't want anyone to depend on me for anything. I don't want to get emotionally involved with people anymore—certainly not a stranger. I hunt for a quick excuse. "My husband and I travel a great deal so MY time is so limited—."

"Oh, the residents love to get postcards. If you send your new friend a picture from wherever you go, it will be shown to other patents with a certain pride. In many ways, you become a surrogate relative."

I know I haven't a good excuse. I'm not sure that I can help anyone, but my effort will fill an afternoon, so I say "Yes" and make an appointment for Thursday.

Christ the Shepherd Manor is a rambling complex of old and new brick buildings. I park close to the stone-arch reception entrance as an ambulance races down a side drive. It is a constant reminder that sickness and death are always nearby. What if I am living here someday and need someone to visit me?

I push through the heavy plate glass doors and register at the reception desk. Soon,I face the director who appraises me with an experienced eye. I hope she doesn't see my hesitation, but I can't fool her. She knows the difference between real volunteers and those with good intentions. She asks me some basic questions and then pushes a paper across her desk.

"Here's a form to fill out. We'll have an orientation next week. If you decide to join the program, bring it with you."

I find myself back in the parking lot with a grim determination to come back and befriend someone. I'll prove to the Director that I'll follow through on my commitment.

I don't tell Arletta about my new activity, because she's wrapped up in Sharlene's wedding plans. But the Pastor will know because I list his name as a character reference. I sit in the orientation and listen to the needs of elderly patients. I'm assigned to Irma who is seventy-eight years old and has no relatives nearby. Already, I feel a tie. Although my errant husband is in town, I don't see him. My daughter's in Spain, my sister is in California and my aunt is in Florida. I'm sympathetic to Irma who is alone.

She's in the fifth room down a long hall in an aged building. Each old door has four white rectangles—covered by many layers of paint, chipped from years of wear. Irma's door is open and she sits motionless in front of a small television. An old "I Love Lucy" rerun plays with Lucy stuffing chocolates into her mouth. Irma doesn't laugh. The aide lightly taps Irma on her shoulder.

"Here's someone to visit you," the aide says. "Her name is Tara." She walks out —her duty done.

I take Irma's hand—small, limp and frail with raised blue veins. She looks at me without interest. I explain, "I'm Tara. I want to visit with you today."

Irma says, "Who are you?"

"I'm Tara—," I repeat, "—I—I—I want to be your—your friend."

"My friend? I have no friends." Irma fumbles with a crumpled tissue in her left hand. "My friends are all gone." She dabs at her eyes.

"Well, then," I say too brightly, "I'll be a new friend." I think of Arletta and the choir and the Garden Club members.

82

I can't complain because I know a dozen women I can call if I'm lonely. I should never be sad. "Tell me about yourself."

Irma frowns, "There's nothing to tell. I'm here."

"Where were you born?"

"Kansas."

Silence.

"I've never met anyone from Kansas," It's not the truth. When Cal and I were in college, I met at least a half-dozen students from Kansas—Wichita, Shawnee Village, Glasco, Kansas City, Olathe, Topeka. "What did your father do?"

Suddenly, Irma shakes her head back and forth. "He left me. My mother died when I was born. So did my twin sister. My father gave me to my mother's sister. He left. He never wrote. Once he came to see me when I was eight. He had another family. He never cared about me. Why didn't he send me a birthday card?" she asks with trembling lips.

I try to soothe her. "Maybe it got lost in the mail."

Irma doesn't believe me. "No one ever really cared about me. I married my husband when he came back from overseas. Oh, he worked in a factory and I kept house for him. He really liked to go to Legion meetings and play cards on Friday nights with his friends. I don't know if he really loved me."

"I'm sure he did. Husbands don't always remember to tell us." Cal was thoughtful. He always sent me yellow roses on my birthday, no matter how far away—Seattle or Boston, Guadalajara or Buenos Aires.

"Did I tell you that I had a twin sister who died at birth? I love her. All my life, I've missed her. We would have taken care of each other." Irma faces me with troubled eyes. "Will I see her in heaven?"

I want to comfort her so I put my arms around her, "Of course! And it will all be quite wonderful." I see that it is an effort for her to speak. "I must be going, but I'll see you next week," I promise.

I know I'll come back—next time with a bouquet from the garden. I count my many blessings as I drive away—for Anne, for Jill and our phone calls, for Aunt Cleda, for Arletta, for all the church friends—yes, and for Cal, too, and the good memories of our years together even if he's a jerk! Thank you, God, for them all.

Arletta is too busy with Sharlene's wedding to worry about me. The wedding will be at the farm after all. Sharlene and Jared have decided that all the pre-payments to Farmer Ahab should be used. Besides, Jared might get a migraine in a church because he has claustrophobia even in a sports arena. That's why he likes to be outside mowing lawns for Boyce's company.

I return the response card which looks strange without Cal's name. I choose salmon with champagne sauce—which means cream sauce, light on the champagne. I'll wear a long black dress with my mother's rhinestone pin.

I drive to Happily-Ever-After Farm which has a large heart-shaped entrance made of weathered branches, as in an old western movie. The huge parking area is at the end of a rutted lane. The lumpy ground is covered by dry grass so people half-stumble toward the farmyard. It's a hot August afternoon and the distinct smell of swine from another farm wafts across the road. The guests mill around in a former feed lot. Arletta has banked the bridal portico with palms and large urns of lilies and delphinium. Pink balloons and multi-colored ribbons trim the posts. Boyce, in his business, knows the right florist to provide flowers and greenery to soften the barn's wide-plank interior for the dinner and dance.

Outside, a combo plays a mixture of rock and country music. Eventually, Sharlene's cousin from Missoula stands up with a guitar. She awkwardly pulls the strap over her head and hits the mike with a thunderous clap that catches everyone's attention. She strums a few chords and then breathily sings a wedding song that she's written. It's hard to understand because she adopts a southern drawl as her melody line wobbles and she slides up and down between notes. She's belts out her words—

"They stand by a lake with a soda in each hand,
And they kiss mighty hard and gee, that is grand,
Sharlene and Jared, Jared and Sharlene,
He's the king and she's the queen."

Her song alternates between a blue-grass and western beat. Mercifully, it ends after five more verses and people applaud like it's the best show in town.

I stand next to Boyce's sister-in-law, Cassie, who quietly starts sniffling. I hand her a small packet of tissues so she can weep—hopefully, for joy.

Finally, the combo starts the wedding march. Somehow, the Miss America pageant melody spins through my head as Sharlene's six bridesmaids in rainbow pastel strapless dresses teeter down the gravel path in their stiletto sandals. During the short service, the girls make quick sleight-of-hand movements—as if they're choreographed—and jerk at their tight bodices before the dresses slip farther down.

Sharlene is strapless too, in a white crystal beaded gown. She wears a plastered smile as if she's dazed and in a trance. Her crystal tiara will be useful if she births a daughter who needs a Halloween princess costume. Jared is pale and shaky—his shoulders slump like he's on the Bridge of Sighs in Venice. His six friends traipse behind him in black tux and pink ruffled shirts. According to Arletta, the rainbow colors of the bridal party make some kind of a political statement, but Sharlene and Jared are unclear as to what it is.

Will Farmer Ahab to wear overalls? No way. He's in the marriage business. He walks from the barn, dressed in wedding garb—a long white robe and a satiny gold stole with bright red hearts. Around his neck are several heavy gold chains, the largest one centered with a shiny gold heart—

almost as big as the real one beneath his robe. He is a true Priest of Love. All he needs is a brazier of incense to offset the breeze blowing from the pig farm.

Ahab keeps his homily short. Grinning, he reminds the couple that oil and water won't mix unless they have a lot of soft soap. He reads a passage from Ecclesiastes—"Two are better than one....Also, if two lie down together, they will keep warm. But how can one keep warm alone?" He pushes his face closer to theirs with a wink and a grin, "Now, we all know what that means!" Everyone titters.

Sharlene and Jared's vows are even shorter.

"Jared, I promise that I will love you as long as the sun sets on Dolphin Bay where you first kissed me."

"Sharlene, I promise that I will love you and always celebrate the night we met at Finnegan's Bar."

Doxie, Jared's pet dachshund, wears a pink satin bow with the ring box tied to it. Jared's uncle releases Doxie and the dog, tongue lapping, runs and jumps up on Jared, as Sharlene draws back with a scream.

"I told you to leave Doxie home! He's spoiled everything!" Sharlene sniffs, lips trembling.

The ring box is retrieved as Jared's uncle leashes Doxie and leads him away. The dog barks in protest.

Farmer Ahab smiles again and mumbles something about "a first little challenge" and rushes through the ring exchange. He announces, "Sharlene and Jared are now husband and wife" as Doxie howls in the distance. Jared's best man, fainting, falls sideways as two groomsmen rush him into the cool barn.

Everyone applauds, glad to move out of the August heat into air-conditioning and a huge buffet. Cassie turns to me with reddened eyes and gushes, "Isn't this the most beautiful wedding you've ever seen?" She sniffles some more.

"Well, it's what Sharlene wanted—." What do I say— *unique* or *unforgettable*? I think of the song and Doxie's howls. "It is—unforgettable" That's entertainment.

Later, Arletta whispers that Sharlene and Jared left their options open, so their vows weren't rigid with traditional promises—"In sickness and in health" or "Till death do us part". Maybe it's just as well. Cal and I vowed a lifetime commitment, but it didn't work. Do promises mean anything now?

In the barn, I'm seated next to Arletta's deaf old uncle from Akron. Her sister's family is also there. We eat and rap glasses so the bridal couple can smother each other with kisses. The combo starts to play, competing with the crowd's jovial laughter. The music booms even louder. Young people must think if the sound level is LOUD, they're having a great time.

I finish my last bite of wedding cake—chocolate with raspberry filling. The noise is deafening like drums beating out a jungle rhythm. I get out of there.

At home, I sit on the patio and look at the fountain. The garden solar lights cast a romantic glow through the dark leafy foliage. I hear crickets and an occasional twig falls. I am alone, and lonely. Cal and I did everything right—with a church wedding, hymns, scripture, and godly vows. Is it fair that our marriage should end?

Sharlene and Jared seem to be a very oddly matched couple. She flits from one idea to another. Jared has a hang-dog look as if he needed a mother's care. They met when Jared applied to mow lawns for Boyce's company. Sharlene helped Jared fill out the form.

Will their marriage last? Time will tell. Two people make bizarre promises without any idea of what the future holds. Marriage is not rational—it can only be lived.

I no longer pray for my own marriage, but tonight I look at the full moon and bow my head, *Dear God, grant Sharlene and Jared a long and happy life. Hold them in the palm of your hand. In Jesus' name. Amen.*

It's all I can do.

Arletta and Boyce spend the weekend entertaining relatives. By Wednesday, Arletta drops by. The wedding is over, but the bills keep coming.

"Sharlene was upset when her Dad asked for her credit card which we've always paid." Arletta sighs. "Jared's parents asked him for the same. Now, they're mad at everyone."

"They'll get over it, especially when the photographer sends back their pictures." I assure her, "It was a beautiful wedding."

"I hope she doesn't hang on to her snit." Arletta looks at me. That's dangerous. "I need to keep busy. So do you."

I take a deep breath. I know my future will be her new project.

I head for Christ the Shepherd Manor. I'm anxious to see Irma and describe Sharlene's and Jared's wedding. I have snapshots in my handbag. Even if Irma doesn't know the couple, she may find the pictures interesting enough to recall her own wedding.

When I get to her room, an old man sits in her wheelchair watching a rerun of Jackie Gleason and Alice goading each other. I step outside and double check the room number. I stop a nurse's aide in the hall.

"Where's Irma?"

"She's gone," the young woman shrugs, "—left last week."

"Where?"

The aide calls over her shoulder, "Died. A week ago. If you want to know more, ask the Director," and rushes off.

I stand at the Director's door, heart pounding. "I'm here to see Irma. She's not in her room."

The Director points to a chair. "Do sit down. I'm sorry to report that Irma died a week ago on Saturday."

That was the day of Sharlene's and Jared's wedding. "I—I didn't know. I was fond of Irma."

The Director continues, "Services were held here on Monday and her ashes were sent to Ohio where her uncle and aunt are buried."

"I wish I had known."

"There was a small notice in the newspaper. Only a few residents knew her. Our chaplain gave a brief homily. We recognized her life."

She reported Irma's death without emotion, like a room that had been cleaned and the door locked. Then the key was thrown away.

"Next time, I hope you notify other Partners when a patient dies. We do form an attachment." It's a criticism cloaked in a gentle tone.

The Director stands up. "That's a good suggestion which we will certainly consider at our next staff meeting. However, you realize that privacy laws must be considered as well as staff time." She extends her hand.

I clasp it briefly and mumble a "Thank you." My interview is over.

Returning to my car, I feel a peculiar emptiness and a heavy sadness. Things won't change as far as notifying anyone. I wish I had been there to hold Irma's hand when she died.

Perhaps Aunt Cleda is lonely like Irma was. How would I know? I've been too deeply wrapped up in my own sadness. I dial her number.

"Aunt Cleda, I want you to know how much I love you. I've not said that enough."

She answers in that cheerful voice. "Oh, Tara, how good of you to tell me. I love you, too. I've wondered and worried about you. I feel so helpless. Maybe I should insist that you move to Naples."

"No—no. Your reassurance is all I need."

"You have your Dad's grit and your Mother's intelligence, so I feel you will manage well. Just hold on. I'm sure that Cal will come home soon."

I assure her that I'm doing well without him. In fact, I'm not sure that I want him back. It's nice to make my own decisions without consulting him.

Since Irma is gone, and Aunt Cleda isn't nearby, I volunteer to serve lunch to the OWLS (Only Wise Ladies Society) at the Senior Center. I feel almost as old already. Used up. Wise? Never. The older I get, the less I know. Arletta doesn't agree. She wants action..

"Soon, autumn will be here. You can't sit in this house all winter and mope. You must do something!" Arletta frowns as she considers possibilities.

"What have I ever done? Worked in a library back in the dark ages—that's all." I'm tired of plans. I live day to day. "I could update my teaching degree. Go back to school, but I don't fit in anywhere."

"You defeat yourself before you start. Look for a job—."

"Be a clerk? Stand on my feet for eight hours? Slave away at a computer somewhere? I don't think so."

"Find something part-time."

"Possibly."

"You need a counselor. There's this young woman Leslie who is a friend of—." Arletta explains how she's found a counselor for me. I half-listen and take the card, promising that I'll make an appointment with Leslie-whomever.

Part-time work intrigues me, but where would I start? Instead, I call Leslie's number at *Collage* and make an appointment. I'm to see her Thursday at the mall site.

A wise sage said *to err is human, to forgive—divine*. I'm human. Forgiveness isn't in me, so I'm being punished. How many light years did it take for the sun to zap me this afternoon? I'm burning up. Maybe I'll have a sun stroke and

90

die at the mall. That would be a relief. My hands are clammy cold. The gods think I'm crazy. No, Cal does. He says that I need a psychiatrist. I think the same about him. Meanwhile, he sits in an air-conditioned office and Anne buys sandals in a far-off Salamanca plaza, and ignores street urchins who beg for coins. Or maybe she listens to a Spanish guitar, played by a dark and handsome matador. No, they fight bulls, but they flirt. And they would find her. She's very pretty and smiles with that perfect American girl smile. I know what that smile cost.

Years ago the developers planned Richfield Mall with a European plaza and small trees softening the hard lines of square gray buildings. Now tiny red crabapples fall on the sidewalks, splitting open so their pithy hearts are smashed as people trample them. I know what it is to have a smashed heart. The apple skins shrivel and dry up in the hot sun. Maybe, I'll wither away, too.

Heat waves radiate from the parking lot. My feet burn through my thin sandals as I leave the car. It will be an oven when I return. Perhaps some young thugs will smash a window and give me instant air conditioning. There are too many thugs around. Or better yet, they'll knock me down and grab my purse. Leave me flat broke or with a broken nose. Put me out of my misery. Where is a security guard if I need one? Don't tell me to pray. I pray often enough and nothing happens. God is faraway. He doesn't listen to me, either.

It's a true August day. The sun bears down as a reminder of its power. Now, it sends the heat that it will take away in December. That's power. I have no power now. Once I had faith—so much so that I could move from Hartford to Denver—or was it Lexington?—without complaint. Now my faith is shaken, maybe lost. Nothing is forever—certainly not my marriage.

I stand under a domed green and white striped awning. It looks like the entrance to a French restaurant in order to impress women and consume them. The awning name spells *Collage*. There's a heavy walnut door—also fake. It's not real walnut, merely a wooden slab stained a rich brown color. My future's inside if I push hard against the door, but that takes effort. I don't push hard anymore. Let someone else ache from strained muscles. I squint at the brass plate:

COLLAGE
A new Life Spa
A new Vision for the New Woman

I don't know what it will cost to become a new woman. The old me paid a high price, but I'm a mark-down now. Used. A new vision is impossible. My eyes aren't that great. Once I had a life, but it washed away in a January rain. I need a new life. I need to start over.

I'm here because Arletta tells me to do something. She's sure that I'll wither away like a zinnia at summer's end with dry mildewed leaves and orange petals that get brown and crumbly. The stem weakens and leans toward the sun for some last sustenance. Instead, it gets zapped with more heat. It dies. The sun shows no remorse. No escape—not for the zinnia, nor for me. Biblical Shadrach, Meshach, and Abednego walked in a fiery furnace. I'm in one today, too, but deliverance is before me.

Beyond that walnut door is my guru, a Life Coach. Arletta found her and tells me this is a great First Step. At least, you'll explore—maybe find what you want to do. She thinks that I need a job or a new purse or a trip to Cancun. If I file for a divorce, I can buy red strappy sandals, don a bikini and a whole new me will emerge. If I step inside the spa, I want a signed paper that I will become someone else—without a broken heart.

Who else can I be? I was born near Muscatine, Iowa of Norwegian stock? We were surrounded by Swedes, so I didn't fit in there either. I should have been named Karen or

Ingrid or Signe. Instead my mother named me Tara. It fits. I fell down on the slick sidewalk last January like a rotted column on a southern mansion in my own Civil War, except I didn't know I was in one. The Rebels didn't win. I didn't know how to fight, and I lost my husband. Total defeat for me. Cal can claim his freedom any time.

A large woman comes up behind me. She's impatient. "Is the spa closed?"

"No," I shrug, "I'm waiting for a friend." That's what I need is a friend—a lot of friends, except they would tire of my story like Arletta—well-meaning as she is.

"Well, get inside away from this heat," she orders and stands aside, waiting for me to enter first. I walk in. The first shall be last. The last shall be first. Promises. Promises are empty. Meaningless. *I promise to love, honor and cherish you for the rest of my life.* Once Cal said that, but it's a lie. I believed him and shyly buried my head in my bouquet of yellow roses. The roses dried, withered, crushed like fine ashes. When I lay in sand—face down—on our honeymoon, I didn't see a thing. Not too smart. Even with a B.A. from McNaughton College, I didn't know it all.

Inside, the cool air revives me. The spa walls are a subdued sage green with antique floral prints in gold frames. Glossy magazines stand in a rack. On the covers, rock stars with spiky hair and leather jackets stare at the reader. These are the new gods with their pouty jerky gestures. Yo-yos with guitar strings. It all began A.W.—After Woodstock. A long time ago. My era.

Other women wait to be redone. There should be some kind of MRI machine where we'd be rolled into a magnetic field and come out with a new dye job, massaged, twenty pounds lighter and a clever brain, but with no heart, no feelings. The trainers are here to help us—young gods with sun-tans and muscles in the right place and the vestal virgins with their Collage pastel outfits to make exercise "more fun."

This is a two story building. The lower level is filled with gym equipment. Set up for yoga, ballet, aerobics, dance. Movement. Get going. Maybe, I should run—out the door. Upstairs, the hair salon extends over half the space. Cubicles for aroma therapy, massage, astrology, hypnosis, and whatever else to take the rest of my money. Perhaps I really need cranial-sacral therapy or a DNA diagnosis—Doing Nothing Anyway.

A receptionist at a computer asks, "Do you have an appointment?" She wears a wire halo with a mike. This won't be cheap. Arletta didn't tell me that.

"I'm to see a—a Leslie at two o'clock." I'm nervous. I've never had counseling. I knew it all, but not enough. I pull out a business card. Arletta made me take it.

The receptionist scrolls her screen. "Oh—Tara?" She frowns, "You're late. Leslie's waiting upstairs. Take the elevator. Third door on your right."

I'm four minutes late by the wall clock behind her. I don't keep track of time. Every day is too long. Nights are longer. I take a deep breath and open the door. A young woman rises and extends her hand.

"I'm Leslie," she says. "Do sit down." She seats herself and swivels around to her desk. A large white plasticized card with fairly large script is centered there. Leslie is a plump young woman with short dark hair. It has a distinctly purple cast. Her eyebrows are perfectly penciled arches, so she looks like she's permanently surprised. Her eyes are dark brown, too. Her glossy mauve lipstick curves around a large mouth. She wears tan cotton slacks and a matching tee shirt, a little tight over her ample torso. She's the daughter of a friend of a friend of Arletta's who doesn't know Leslie, but thinks I should.

A large gold framed certificate hangs on the wall. It's from some institute in Florida. Not a good omen. That's where I burrowed face down in the sand one time and tanned perfectly. Back in the hotel room, I tingled as Cal caressed my golden spine.

"Oh, you've studied in Bonita Springs?" I ask.

"Actually, I did my work by computer." She smiles uneasily, "—but the work was INTENSE. We had assignments—I took a client through all the steps."

Her credential is from a diploma mill. That cost her Dad a lot of money. I won't tell that to Arletta. Leslie picks up a form and a clip-board. At the same time, her forefinger grazes a button. The meter's running. I shift uneasily. If I remain her client, this will cost me plenty, too.

"Well, let's get started. I'm anxious to hear ALL about YOU. This will be a great relationship." She widens her smile to reassure me. What she really wants is a great relationship with a handsome gym trainer downstairs.

I don't want a relationship. I don't have successful relationships. Ask Anne. She's in Spain for the summer, bumming through cathedrals (never for worship) and castles. Soon she'll return for her senior year at Northwestern.. She blames me for everything.

"Mom, wake up!" Anne says. "You're too nice. NO ONE thinks like you do any more!"

I thought marriage was forever. I was sure that mine was Gibralter rock-solid, but it was really a sleeping Vesuvius that finally erupted. My mistake. I wish I'd been buried in the lava.

Leslie wants to know about my name. "—So unusual."

"My mother read *Gone with the Wind.* She decided *Scarlett* was too racy, so she settled for *Tara.*" It's a story that I've told many times. Who knows why parents choose a certain name? A sound? A friend? Politically correct? Anne was named for Calvin's mother at his insistence. "How long have you been a counselor?"

She hesitates. "I don't call myself a counselor. Counselors look backward. I help a client look to the future. I'm a COACH—a Life Visions COACH. I'm here to help you find

DIRECTION, but you CHART your own COURSE. You will not be defeated, you will be MOTIVATED! You will MOVE FORWARD?" She sounds like a training tape. Or a cheerleader.

I rise and look closely at her certificate date. "What did you do before you became a coach?"

"Retailing. I was a personal shopper and then in the credit department. I decided business wasn't for me—." She shifts uneasily in her chair.

THAT means she was fired. Instead, I'm nice. "It's good that you like to work with people."

"I do! I do! Now let's finish this background material."

When I tell her that I've lived almost a half-century, she goes tsk-tsk as if I've said a naughty word. "You have LIFE EXPERIENCE!"

"My husband Cal—Calvin—and I separated last winter." She wants to know more, but I won't tell her about that awful morning when he just walked out. That's not right. He sped away. I stumbled on an uneven sidewalk, hidden by a puddle. Fell. Almost knocked myself out. When a passing motorist stopped to help, I told her that I was jogging. One lie leads to another. Why do I keep reliving the details? I've got to stop.

Leslie looks at her plasticized card. She follows a list of questions. This will be like an *I'm okay, You're okay* session back in A.W. days. We sat in a circle and concentrated on mood colors—green or purple or yellow and decided what we were. I said, *Brown* and the others shouted, *No, you're pink!* Classroom angst. I resented tuition money for a worthless course by a teaching assistant, Psychology 201. What goes around, comes around. Except now, it's via a Life Coach.

"Have you considered OPTIONS?"

That's Arletta's buzz word, too. Tara, you do have options. I want to crawl into bed and pull the covers over my head. Maybe sink with the TITANIC again tonight. Stouffers or Encore on a tray. Maybe both. Arletta tells me to use a linen napkin for a placemat and add a pink rose to Aunt Cleda's Waterford bud vase. Live like Martha S.

Leslie hasn't a clue. I have to help her.

"Maybe I'll go back to college," The idea just popped into my brain. "—Update my teaching certificate. I never taught, but I was certified back in A.W. days."

"Is A.W. like—in Wisconsin? Wyoming?" Leslie wonders. "—Appleton, Wisconsin?"

I stare at her. "Woodstock. After Woodstock. There's B.C., A.D., B.C.E., C.E. and A.W. I'm of the A.W. generation."

Leslie doesn't get it. She's too young. She really hasn't a clue. She writes slowly, "Ohhh—After Woodstock. There's a Woodstock in Illinois, but that would be A.W. IL. Right?"

Right or wrong, she knows nothing. Don't be logical. I say, "I mean A.W. is Algoma. Wisconsin." We did live there once, but who cares? Nothing makes sense. After A.W. the world went to pot. Literally. I tried to escape with Cal. He went corporate. I followed.

Leslie yawns and smiles with those perfect teeth. "Well, it sounds like teaching might be a very good OPTION. You EXPLORE. You TRY SOMETHING. If it doesn't work out, it DOES NOT mean failure. It means that you've eliminated one option. Then you concentrate on other POSSIBILITIES." She emphasizes key words. Are they on the plastic card?

Comfort words. My marriage is a failure. I want other possibilities. *Coach, you tell me. Should I change my name to Scarlett and dye my hair to match?* Leslie's hand grazes the button again. She stands up. The introductory-offer interview is over. In every way, I'm finished.

"This has been a great beginning," she grins. "You have my card—."

"What about another appointment?"

"That's the beauty of Life Visions! We're not restricted to any time frame. You can call me anytime—day or night.

We coach by phone. Our computer system tracks the calls. Your monthly statement reflects the charge for the time you use."

We shake hands. I walk out into the glaring sun. I have Leslie's number in my purse. I won't call, but I'll tell Arletta that my time was well spent. I know the lingo—options, life vision therapies. I don't need acupuncture either. My nerves already throb from a thousand tiny unseen needles.

I drive slowly back to my Victorian parlor

Arletta drops by. Her expectant eyes reflect her enthusiasm for my effort. She hopes I had a fantastic afternoon with Leslie. I won't disappoint her.

"It's a really fancy establishment," I say. "—Ah—very fancy"

"You deserve the best." Arletta sounds like a cheerleader. I was one, too.

"Jump as high as you can. Let the fans know we'll win."

Cal said that. I didn't intend to be a cheerleader, but the others wanted me because I was thin and wiry. I could top their half-time pyramid with ease. I jumped down and twisted my ankle, but I smiled through the pain. I clapped my hands in rhythm, swinging my royal blue pleated skirt as I swiveled my hips. I smiled so wide my white bunny ear muffs almost fell off. The bitter cold wind deadened the pain that crawled up my leg. Keep smiling, Keep smiling. Cal loved to see me out in front. He boasted to other seniors. "That's my girl!" When I cried with pain, he hugged me. "Just think—we won the conference title!" Did he care about my pain?

"What did she say?" Arletta asks.

I feign answers. "Oh—not much really. She asked basic information—name, age, husband—ha!—Anne. We talked about the—the future."

"Good! Like what?"

I try to think hard. What advice did Leslie give? "Oh, she thought it was a good idea that I go back to college this fall and update my teaching certificate."

If my own daughter thinks I'm hopeless, why will any high school class listen with their lip beads and charcoal tattoos? All they need is a jungle, swinging vines and apes. Tarzans of the new millennium. I gave up being a flower child—long paisley skirts and love beads—when I married Cal. An adolescent fantasy that I could change the world with love. Me and Jesus. He was hung on a cross. I'm in an empty house. I'd be laughed out of high school with my raccoon hair and trim slacks and cashmere sweaters. I have nothing to teach. I know nothing about life, except it hurts.

Arletta beams. "—Back to school? I think that's wonderful! A real first step."

"I can't concentrate on a book—."

"Of course, you can! You read more than anyone I know—."

"That's not the same as study—." It scares me think about registering for classes. How can I fit in anywhere? My self-esteem is gone. Maybe Anne and I could bond as students. She's away, but when she comes home, we might discuss classes or share observations about that sub-ethnic group of homo sapiens—professors. If I sit in a university class, maybe I'll be a New Woman with a New Vision. Of what? "—I won't fit in."

Arletta frowns. "That's your trouble. You defeat yourself before you begin."

"It takes tuition money."

"—Get it from Cal."

"I don't talk to Cal." I don't tell Arletta that all week Cal has left messages to return his calls. I haven't and I won't. I'm afraid of what I might say. No. I'm afraid of what he might say. *Divorce.* I'm not sure that I ever want to see him again. Ever. Yes. I do. I want to know why he left last January.

"Well, if you get a divorce, the judge will make him pay tuition money so you can support yourself. At least that's what happened when—." Arletta chatters about Dorrie or Rosemary or Daphne or some other woman or relative or neighbor who has survived divorce.

I don't listen, because I can pay my own tuition—thanks to a generous income from my parents trust. But the thought occurs that Cal might pay—a lot—just to be rid of me, money that I could use to benefit others. Maybe build wells in Africa or a couple of schools in Peru. Cal owes me that much to keep me out of the funny farm.

Can I sit in class on a hard chair in a college classroom? Maybe chairs are better designed now. It might be nice to consider the works of Shakespeare again or Angelou or Tyler. Cross the square to the Student Union. Watch a beefy football player hustle a date with a stringy-haired coed, pimply with silver acne and nose beads. I'm cynical about everything. Give the tattooed kids a chance in their academic jungle. They don't know much and I know even less. A perfect fit.

Arletta brings me back to reality. "You still have time to register."

"I don't have a catalog. I don't know what courses I need—."

"That's one call to a counselor's office," She smiles. She's happier now that she's arranging my life. "Let's have lunch tomorrow. The library has catalogs. You can even register on-line. I'll help you."

"I don't want to teach."

"Then take something you'll really enjoy. Lit. Drawing. Music Appreciation. Computer Science."

"Try Logic and Philosophy, too." I look out the window. Already a few green leaves are withered in the summer heat. Time is fleeting. "Maybe Art Appreciation. I always thought I'd like to work as a museum docent. Keep those squirmy kids enthralled with Monet."

Arletta's eyes warm with approval. "You can do it! Find a morning class. You must get up to get there. No more old midnight movies and sleeping too late in the morning. It's time to move past your sadness." She picks up her purse and heads for the door. "We'll arrange the whole thing tomorrow afternoon."

I shrug. "You arrange it. I'll go. I'll kill time on the campus—like the kid who doesn't want to work for his Dad, so he goes off to college."

The phone rings. I let it kick into the answering machine. It's Cal's voice again. He says he MUST talk to me. I ignore the machine. I wish Arletta wouldn't listen. She may find out that Anne called last night. She said her Dad had called her in Salamanca. He wants to talk to me, so would she please get me to answer my phone?

I ignore the answering machine. "I'm still not sure about classes."

"You don't have to be. I am." Arletta waits. "Aren't you going to answer?"

"No," I shrug, "Cal walked out. He can come here if he wants to talk."

"Boyce heard he dined at The Continental last week with some other guys. That's a good sign." She stops abruptly.

"What does she mean a good sign? Does she know something that I don't? Boyce has contacts all over town and hears lots of gossip.

"Maybe he's afraid that you won't listen to him," Arletta continues.

"Don't sympathize with Cal!"

"I'm not. It's just that if he has second thoughts—."

"Cal never has second thoughts. He always knows what he wants to do—like last winter. He left without warning. Said he would be at the Hilton in Atlanta. Except he wasn't there. I called and he wasn't registered. Why didn't he tell me the truth?"

Arletta stands at the door. "Maybe there was a reason. You could forgive that one mistake. I'll see you tomorrow at eleven. We'll shop for your college wardrobe."

She's made my decision for me. I'll register for the fall semester.

I listen to the answering machine again. Cal's voice has a pleading quality. "Please Tara. I know you're angry, but we have to talk. You set the time and place. You can even leave a message on my machine. Please, please, call."

His voice is insistent. Of course, we have to talk. I've postponed it. He wanted to see me two months ago. I changed to an unlisted phone, but he got my new number from Anne. Cal gets what he wants.

I punch his number. What's his apartment like? A studio? Never. Cal likes space. That's why he insisted we live in this big English number in the Windsor district. Does his sublet overlook the lake? Is there a pizzeria nearby? I always did his shirts because he never liked the Chinese laundry near the station. Where does he take them? Did he buy a new wardrobe for summer? I have a hundred questions that I'm afraid to ask. No—only one question. Why did he leave?

"Hello—this is Tara," I say slowly, carefully.

"Thank God, you've called back. Where've you been?" His voice is strained.

I think hard a minute. "I've been at the Library," I stammer, "—I picked up a university catalog. I may go back to school this fall."

"Oh, really?"

Quickly, I add, "—That means tuition—"

Cal ignores this. "Look, Nana's coming to visit. She wants to see you. May we come out this week-end?"

Not here, Cal. To see you sit here would be too hard to bear.

"I'm going away for the week-end." I'm not, but he doesn't need to know.

"Who with? Are you seeing someone?"

Who wants a leftover wife with reddened eyes? No, I've finally quit crying. "That's my business!" I snap.

"Don't do anything foolish."

I'm not sure that I hear him correctly. He sounds like my father when I went on my first date. I don't want a scene. If we're surrounded by noisy students, I won't cry. If we meet on the campus, he and Nana won't have much time. They'll be brief.

"Well—next Monday," I say curtly. "Noon. I'll be at the Student Union after I register." Not true. Arletta's making sure that I register tomorrow. "I won't have much time."

I hunt for a quick explanation. There is none. I have lots of time. Every drawer is perfectly in order. Things are polished twice a week. The closets are cleaned out, except for his. It's a pleasure to step into a well-ordered house and know the newspapers won't be thrown on the floor, or Cal's tie dropped on the hall table. I no longer bear bruises from the drawers he's left half-closed. Maybe I've adjusted to living alone, but I'm not sure I like it. Well, maybe I do.

I dress carefully to see Cal and Nana—beige slacks, a matching beige sweater and an autumn leaf scarf around my neck, the ends flaring casually over my shoulder. I slip on my wedding band which belonged to Cal's grandmother. I have new leather flats, too. I'm overdressed for a campus, but I intend to look like I'm doing well without him. Which I am. Since Arletta and Leslie think that college is a great solution, I think it is, too. I look forward to losing myself among new people—young people. Maybe I'll understand Anne. She's vague about her future plans. She's been in environmental studies because she wanted to save whales. When we talked last week, she said she's changed—she intends to work with immigrants. Will she stay with that? She's positive that she doesn't want to be a nurse because she'd have to draw blood samples.

Anne, be a travel agent. Or sell sports cars. I can't help you anymore.

If my marriage is to end, the campus is an appropriate place. That's where our our romance began. I worked afternoons in McNaughton's Library. Circulation desk. Cal stopped by three afternoons in a row. Each time, he tried to check out the same reference book, an old green *Notable Americans 1900-1925. Volume I.* Frayed at the edges.

"We can't check out reference books," I said very seriously each day.

On the third day, I said, "Are you interested in any special American?"

He leaned over the counter with a cocky grin and said, "You!"

Surprised, I said, "What do you mean?"

"Look, I've been here three days in a row. Notice me. You treat me like any other dumb guy trying to check out this old book. Very distant. Give me your great smile and say you'll meet me at the Union."

I saw the head Librarian behind her glass window watching us. Students were lined up behind Cal for check-outs. I glanced at the clock.

"I get a break at three-twenty. I'll come outside then."

That was my fatal mistake. I should have gone to the staff lounge instead and sipped a coke alone. I was an idealist in those days. I wanted to join the Peace Corps, or teach in a missionary school, or run programs for inner-city kids. I would make the world a better place. Help Jesus or President Kennedy save the world. Instead, I married Cal.

We married in June after graduation. I carried yellow roses and then we moved to Philadelphia so he could get his

MBA. I worked in an old library building and typed his term papers at night while he studied. Our little apartment wasn't as big as our first living room. But we were crazy about each other and saw only glorious days ahead. We lived on hope.

I had one long white satin nightgown that I carefully washed and ironed. We were glad when the snow fell and we could stay warm, locked in each other's arms. A crowbar couldn't pry us apart.

"Oh Cal, what happened to us?"

I call Aunt Cleda and tell her that I've consented to see Cal. "I'm sure that he'll ask for a divorce. Nana will be with him to provide support."

"She's only there because she wants to know what you expect from him—money, that is."

"I don't expect anything except his decision. I'd file myself, except I'm unsure of what I want to do."

"Don't do that! After any traumatic event, don't take any action for a year."

"A year? I'm tired of waiting for him to make up his mind."

"Cal may regret that he walked out. He has so-o-o much pride. Maybe he wants you to beg him to come home."

"I'm over my tears. I'm ready to move ahead. I've signed up for two university classes, so I'll be very busy this fall."

"Good for you! Keep smiling and don't do anything rash." Aunt Cleda hangs up.

I'll get through this meeting with Cal and start classes. I feel stronger and a bit excited to be back on a campus.

I push through the heavy plate glass doors and look around when I hear Cal's voice.

"Tara—up here!" Cal stands alone beside a window on an upper level.

This is a good place. There's only a smattering of students around since classes start next week. We can hear each other without shouting. I walk—not too quickly—to the table and make sure that it remains between us.

"Where's Nana?" Has he lied to me about her desire to see me? Don't try an embrace. No meaningless kiss. Spit out a request for a divorce and leave.

"She and Wendell just stayed overnight. They flew to Banff. She sends her regrets." Cal says. "You're looking good. You've done something new with your hair."

"Oh yes. Elena updates me like a computer—a tint to match the season." I pat my hair, changed now to a light brown with a reddish hue. "Don't you have a new cut?"

Cal laughs self-consciously. "Well, mine's thin on top, so Rafael—I think that's his name—suggested a longer length. I've got to move with the times. Look young—mod." The tension eases. Cal adds, "You're thinner too. I hope you've been eating okay."

"Arletta sees to that." I don't explain. Arletta suggests an early lunch after the fitness workout. She still drops by a plastic container with a ticket to a bridge benefit, although I'm a lousy card player as Cal knows. I notice a stain on Cal's jacket. Maybe, he eats in too many restaurants now. If he were home, I wouldn't let him leave the house with that spot.

There's an awkward silence. Once we were so close. From a long glance, a touch, a nod, we knew what the other was thinking. Now, we only stare blankly at each other.

"We can go somewhere else for lunch," Cal suggests.

"No, this is fine. I'm not hungry." That's a lie. The smell of grilled hamburgers fills the area. I see students munch away and poke French fries into catsup puddles. As soon as Cal's gone, I'll indulge myself too. "What do you want?"

Cal makes circles with his car keys on the plastic table. He takes a deep breath.

I brace myself. I know what's coming.

"Anne wants us to meet weekly for lunch," he says quietly, firmly, searching my face for my reaction. "You never answer my calls. I want to know what you think."

106

I want to lash out,—So, it's my fault?—but I'm careful. Very careful. I'm back in our kitchen in winter, immobile. I'm not sure that I hear him correctly. I scarcely breathe. My heart's beating too fast, and I might hyperventilate. Does he want to come home?

"What do I think?" If he's serious, I want to laugh. "I'm to tell you what to do?"

"My apartment isn't too far from here. At least you could stop by sometime."

I shrug. "It's your decision. You left."

More silence. Cal's always been so self-assured. He doesn't look quite the same. Older. Tired. Maybe like he's caught between a rock and a hard place.

Cal looks away. "I left because things piled up at work. A lot of changes in the office. I had to make a decision. I needed time alone. To think."

I've adjusted to being alone—at least a little bit adjusted. I'm not sure that I want Cal back, even if he gets down on his knees and begs. I think I'm moving on. "I'll be busy with classes this fall. I won't have time to meet weekly for lunch."

Cal shrugs. "You always liked to study. You were a better student than I."

Angrily, I should remind him that he owes me something. Doesn't he remember that senior term paper that I typed for him? The spelling that I corrected, the sources I properly annotated? He got an "A" and I got an engagement ring. He said he would make a million dollars by the time he was forty. I was impressed. Well, he got his million—and more—and I got a broken heart. I keep my thoughts to myself.

"You've always kept up with books—plays—things like that." Cal continues. "I only read the Wall St. Journal and fall asleep when I try anything else."

Cal's forefinger twitches when he plays with his key case. I know it does that when he's nervous. Maybe he isn't well. He should be in the prime of life. He doesn't know how long our bed stayed unmade—just as he left it. His black

Allen-Edmonds were still askew beside the bed where he kicked them off. I shut the door and our bedroom stayed that way until Arletta insisted that I straighten up everything. I must be careful and keep my anger under control.

He interrupts my memories and repeats. "My apartment has a lake view. I wish you could see it. You can use the place if there's an ice storm and you can't drive home this winter."

Is he being generous and clever, so I'll be soft and agreeable when he asks for a divorce?

"I don't want to see it." I look out the window at the leaves drifting to earth. Summer is over and so is my marriage. "Tell me the truth. Did you have an affair? Is there someone else?"

Cal reddens and hesitates.

Now, I know the truth. There was—or is—someone. Who is that someone? A new office intern? No, Cal wouldn't look at the young bimbos. He wants someone intelligent like Diedre. Ah, now she's a possibility. Convenient, because he could have a total wife to join business and home together. No changing roles when he goes home at night.

Some men dream of a Venus arising from the foam. Others search for a sensual siren, a mystical Eve to keep them perpetually excited. There are women who pretend they fulfill a guy's need. Diedre could be such an office tigress who pursues her boss and then destroys him. Or a female pirate who steals her boss without any guilt—the kind who's sure that illicit love is blessed because God is LOVE, a modern permissive Eros.

Does Cal remember Vera? She was a new vice-president in south Boston—or was it Hartford? No, south Boston. She was a frizzy-haired redhead in the era when her hair always looked like she'd just showered. She aimed for the glass ceiling and that's where Cal's office was—with huge windows looking east toward the Atlantic. She intended to be there, too.

Vera was a divorcee, capable and direct. At the annual Fourth of July picnic, she said, "I've been alone long enough. I intend to remarry." She looked straight at me. "Men tire of their old life and want something fresh and new."

For a moment I felt a double whammy—a blow to my chest and a rapier thrust between my shoulder blades. I almost stopped breathing. For the next year, I felt I was in a duel, as Cal spent long hours with her, reorganizing that plant. She never hesitated to call him, even late at night. If I softly protested, Cal said, "She's my number-one support."

Even after Cal was transferred, Vera called for several months. At Christmas, when I opened cards, I realized her swimsuit picture and personal note were meant for Cal. I threw both in the kitchen trash. Then I retrieved them. That evening I gave them to Cal and said loftily, "Vera has put on weight." Cal barely glanced at Vera's picture and tossed it away, along with the note. I felt better.

Cal's in the land of indecision. Does he play games? Suddenly, I am totally calm. Cal can never hurt me again. For many years, Cal depended on me to be there for him, but he was never there when I needed him. This time I'm the one who will walk away and leave him standing there—alone. I won't ever care for him again—not if he offers me a diamond bracelet and a five pound box of Salzburg chocolates. Well—maybe for the chocolates. Not likely.

Cal frowns, "Tara—please understand! There are lots of rumors—things are mixed up at work—lots of pressure. There's one other thing—."

I brace myself for the word *Divorce*.

"—Maybe we could have dinner on Saturday night? Catch up on things?"

I give an exaggerated sigh. "Oh, I am sorry, but I do have plans." I don't, but I'll invite Brad and a few choir members for a backyard picnic—a grill-out, complete with Berkley's fountain, and bug spray. "I want to be ready for classes on Tuesday." I walk away.

"Wait a minute!" Cal says. "Be careful around the campus. Always park in a fenced lot with a security guard. Things happen. You can't be too careful."

"You do the same." I hurry on quickly without looking back.

Cal calls, "Come and see my place sometime—."

I bump into a tall broad-shouldered man in blue jeans and a navy sweatshirt. I look up and our eyes meet. He carries a briefcase that almost bangs my thigh as he steps aside.

"Sorry," I mumble and head for the door. I feel his eyes and Cal's watching me for any misstep. I get through the plate glass doors without stumbling and head into the brilliant sunshine. For the moment, I'm still a married woman, but I don't need a husband, I need a future. Perhaps I'll find it on the campus.

Actually, I don't have classes on Monday. My classes start on Tuesday—Intro to Contemporary Poetry and Modern American Masters. I've lost touch with everything. Maybe the university will help. Forget my feelings. Find my brain?

Anne returns from Salamanca just in time to begin her senior year at NU. After her summer study, she toured Spain to soak up history and enjoy the old cities. She stayed there as long as possible because Cal and I aren't together. Somehow, she still hopes we'll reconcile.

"It's impossible, Anne," I say. "It's been too long. My trust was broken. He must beg to come back. You know he will never do that—not in a million years."

"—But if Dad wants to come back, you must forgive him."

I turn away. She doesn't understand hurt. She thinks she was hurt when her boy friend dropped her for her roommate last year. She doesn't know real hurt. Fickle boy friends are quite replaceable. Husbands are different and I doubt if I will forgive him. That gives me real trouble because Jesus was physically crucified with all the agony and pain of an unjust punishment. Yet, he prayed that God would forgive those who persecuted him. How can I do less? I don't want to answer that nagging personal question.

Anne drives back to Evanston early Monday morning. I spend the rest of the day in anticipation of tomorrow's classes. What lies ahead? This time I'm no wide-eyed eighteen year old. I'm old enough to know better—about what? Hopefully, the difficult days of sadness and melancholy are behind me. Who said, "To those who feel, life is a tragedy—but to those who think, life is a comedy"?

I've felt badly for too long. I'm ready to "think" and laugh at life. The university is a great place to do both.

ACCEPTANCE,

N. THE ACT OF ACCEPTING, OF THE STATE OF BEING ACCEPTED; FAVOR; APPROVAL; BELIEF; ASSENT; AGREEMENT TO TERMS, WHETHER EXPRESSLY OR BY SOME ACT CONSTITUTING A VIRTUAL ACKNOWLEDGMENT, AS OF A CONTRACT.

I arrive at Eisenhower Hall early, the first one to enter the classroom. I sit in the back and watch students filter in. A perfect fit with my hair dyed—this time, tawny brown—and my cell phone in hand. They're sophomores and look so terribly young. However, there is a difference. They think they know it all. I'm smarter. I don't know much—and what I do know, I wish I didn't.

One young woman is pale-faced, with puffy circles under her eyes. She wears a new tee-shirt with a rock star logo and worn jeans. As she turns her back, two frayed slashes open beneath her buttocks. Has she custom-cut them for a provocative peek, or are they sold that way? A box of tissues rests on top of her notebook. She frequently sniffles and wipes her nose. She looks like a waif. I want to hug and comfort her.

Others saunter in. Jeans and tee-shirts. Cookie cutter sameness like convent uniforms. Doesn't anyone dress up anymore? I'm glad to sit behind them. I'm too well-dressed—a past generation—in gray slacks and a Norwegian sweater.

Next, our professor pads in on moccasin-clad feet and dumps his heavy briefcase on the desk. A big man with a hooked nose profile, he's in jeans and a tee-shirt, too. He nods to some familiar faces and sighs. He's tenured, so this is old stuff. Mark off another year until retirement. I study his face. His tired eyes peer out from bushy gray brows and a broad forehead. Balding, his remaining hair is long and pulled back in a braided pony-tail. He says we're a larger class than he expected.

A student murmurs, "Why not? It fills a requirement."

A brief look of disappointment crosses his face. "My name is *Windfeather*," he says. "The catalog may list me by another name, but that is the dean's error. Hopefully, this course will expand your horizons. Perhaps you'll find some new insights through ancient sagas and creative writing. I want you to love poetry so much that it's necessary to your existence." He looks doubtful. He pulls out a sheet for roll call.

I want to be there. I'll read twice as much as he assigns. Jack Kerouac, Allen Ginsberg, and Sylvia Plath were big names in the sixties. I know nothing of present poets. I'm here to learn about Galway Kinnell, Billy Collins and Robert Pinsky. I'll consume them all. Have a poem-by-poem romance with Wendell Berry. His wife will never know.

I scribble notes as he outlines the course and I stash his handouts in my new notebook. The hour goes too quickly. I file out behind everyone and head to the Student Union for coffee, until it's time for Art 303. I look around, and realize I'm not alone. There are other mature students on campus. Some are even older and retired. I relax. I'll blend into the campus, unnoticed.

In the Fine Arts building, Modern American Masters meets on the second floor. This time the class is smaller. We sit in straight oak chairs. A large screen is rolled up above a chalkboard at the front of the room. An old slide projector and overhead machine sit in the back row. I move into a rear seat near the projector and find myself isolated. Most students are in the first two rows. The same coed with the slashed jeans wanders in, sniffling, with her tissue box in hand. She sits near the door, ready to escape.

The professor enters. Where have I seen him before? He is tall, rangy with the easy gait of a confident racehorse. I glance down at my notes. The light is dim and the print is fine. His last name sounds Danish or Finnish. It doesn't matter, because a dark-haired junior says, "Hi, Gunnar!"

"You—again?" he laughs. "I should have flunked you last spring."

"Credits!" the student banters back. "Easiest way to graduate!"

Others titter. I study Gunnar. Then I realize that I passed him last week when I left Cal in the Union. His steel blue eyes gaze over the class with amusement although his sandy graying hair curls around his head like a cherubic halo. I wonder if it's a natural curl.

"—And Mattie!" Gunnar nods to the slashed jean-clad waif.

She shrugs, "Hi. This is a Fine Arts requirement for me, too." She turns away with a distinct grimace.

Now, I know her name. I'm curious about her distaste for him.

Gunnar outlines the course briefly and says that he illustrates most of his lectures with slides. He'll test on the recognition of artists that he presents. Papers are required on two artists of our own choosing. Grades will be based on attendance and tests.

He looks down his sheet of names. "And you must be Tara," he says, nodding at me with his penetrating gaze. His eyebrow lifts, expectantly, as if to say *You and I are of the same age. We understand each other. These kids are mere babes.*

"Yes, I'm Tara." I'm glad that I've worn slacks and a Nordic blue sweater that makes my blue eyes seem more intense. I'll show him I want to be here—listen carefully, and write two papers—even a half dozen—to prove I can still conquer a course. Once I knew Matisse, Grandma Moses and Andy Warhol. *Gunnar, tell me about contemporary artists. If the others don't care, I do. Pay attention to me.*

He hands out a syllabus, noting articles reserved in the library and a list of artists to consider for our term papers. Strange names—new to me. I feel happy—inspired. Maybe I should have opted for academia instead of marriage. Too late.

As I walk out, I follow Mattie too closely and stumble on her heels. She turns around and stares at me.

"I think we're in the same classes together. Modern American Poetry and—," I say.

"Oh. Yeah." She moves on without a smile.

116

I think, *Mattie, please talk to me. Don't turn me away like Anne does.*

"Look," I stammer, catching up with her. "I haven't been on a campus in ages—over two decades. I need to get a handle on things. Could we talk?"

Mattie stares at me through narrowed eyes. "What are you—a Psych major, back for your doctorate? You need to interview me?" She's a born skeptic. "I've got nothing to say—except if I don't do IT by twenty-one, my life is over."

I want to reassure her. "Oh, you have many years ahead." What is IT? I want to find out. "Look, could I buy you a coke—or a burger? Chips?"

She weighs the offer. "Yeah—with salsa."

I guess she wants taco chips. We head for the Union. She keeps her head down. Her left ear holds a sliding scale of silver rings. Does she sleep on them?

In the cafeteria, she takes a tray and I follow. She grabs all three choices—coke, burger, and chips with salsa. I pay for our orders. She finds a table where two other coeds sit. I follow with my iced tea and salad and take the fourth place.

"Mattie, do you like our art professor?" I ask. "You wrinkled your nose when he came in."

"He plays favorites. You'll find out. Leave it at that."

"How?"

Mattie gives me a long hard look. "You'll see."

Her friends giggle at Mattie's response. They understand something that I don't.

"It's been so long since I've been on a campus," I begin. "I don't understand your—your talk—the IT." The girls look at each other and laugh loudly. I'm twice their age, but I feel like I'm a hundred years old and know nothing. "I'm so out of touch with—with things."

Mattie's friend says, "Oh, Gunnar will get in touch with you real soon—real soon."

"Don't give Gunnar away!" Mattie gives a half-laugh and coughs to keep from choking.

I listen to a conversation that I don't understand. I finish quickly and leave. I really don't belong in the Student Union. Another day, I'll eat off-campus in a back booth, alone with Dante's *Inferno* since *Paradise Regained* is an impossible dream.

My classes are on Tuesday and Thursday. Arletta comes by on Friday morning for a report on my first week on campus. She doesn't ask, but she really wants to know about my meeting with Cal. Somehow, she seems to know a lot about Cal—maybe more than I do. Is that through her husband and networking?

"I sit in the back row and keep quiet," I say. "The kids seem so terribly young."

We laugh over how I paid for Mattie's meal and whether folk art would qualify for a term paper in art class.

"And Cal—have you ever seen his apartment?" There's a hint of sympathy in her voice. "I thought he might ask to move home—."

"Look—," I remind her with some irritation, "Cal's a grown man. He left. He's taken care of himself for nine months. He can keep right on doing it." I hear the anger in my voice. "You forget I'm the one that suffered a broken heart! I'm not his foster mother or his housemaid anymore!"

Arletta is surprised at my outburst. "Well, if you really feel that way—."

"I do!"

"I thought you'd have a little more sympathy for Cal." She looks at me sharply. "Did you talk to Cal about—about his work—and stuff like that?"

I know too much, but I don't want to talk about him. "Cal lives his life. I live mine. That's it!"

"—But is it enough?"

"I'll make it enough."

118

The choir director calls to remind me that practice resumes on Thursday evening after the summer vacation. I weigh whether I want to sing again. Will I relive that rainy night after practice when the golf clubs weren't in the garage and I found a terse note from Cal that I must sleep alone? I decide I want to sing. I can never be that deeply hurt again. I promise that I'll be there.

I'm on the campus Tuesdays and Thursdays. I watch the bulletin board for afternoon lectures or recitals—anything to lengthen my day away from home.

On Monday and Wednesday nights, I go to the mall. Or the local library. I thumb through magazines. I read newspapers. I linger in the small library gallery for local artists until I soon recognize every name. I study the bulletin board as well, carefully reading announcements—yoga classes, community band practice, an autumn house walk, two art fairs on the weekend.

There's a notice for a part-time job in the Library. I linger at that, remembering my college days. I pushed away thoughts of working when Cal left me. Now, I head for the circulation desk and ask for an application.

"You'll have to get that from the Administration office," an assistant says. "It's open from nine-to-five Monday through Friday. Or you can call and leave your name and address. One will be mailed to you."

When I get home, I call the Library and go through the hoops of voice mail. I'm told to push one and then, three. After the beep, I leave my name and address. A part-time job is a convenient way to avoid lonely evenings. When the application form arrives, I fill it out. Work experience? "Library Aide—McNaughton College; Two years— reference assistant at a branch, Philadelphia Public Library." I don't add that was twenty-five years ago. I scribble, "—Can work part-time evenings and week-ends". I drop it in a mail slot. I won't be hired with my old employment record.

I'm still upset with Cal, but I keep busy with classes now. I've gone through enough sadness. I tried to bargain with God who doesn't listen to me. Others tell me that I've accepted my situation and am doing well. Will I ever have closure? I doubt it. I still hurt a lot.

I sit in Windfeather's class and wonder if I made a mistake. He suggests we try basic poetry forms. I don't write poetry, but it doesn't matter to him. He expects at least a haiku or a limerick, inspired from nature for the next class. That'll give me something to do this weekend. I'll scribble away on a limerick and read about haiku—maybe I can rearrange another poet's lines. Other students cheat. It's their way of life. I can, too, but I won't. My conscience is still governed by Luther's Catechism and his phrase—*captive to the Word of God.*

I hope Gunnar doesn't expect me to paint a picture. His eyes meet mine once or twice, but otherwise I could be a rag doll in the corner. I take notes as he lectures, and wonder why I'm there. I'll never be a docent. I don't like modern art. I like Rembrandt.

When class is over, I bypass the Student Union and head for a nearby shopping area where I can wander along, killing time as I glance at displays of tee-shirts, cameras, and cell phones —all attractively presented. Their bright colors demand attention. A tattoo parlor is jammed between art supplies and a sports store. That's what I need. A tattoo on my cheek that reads *Used.*

At the book store, the entrance is crowded. Nevertheless, I pause at a half-price stall filled with a varied selection— *Witchcraft for Today's Consumer, Be Your Best You, Find God in Yourself, Midnight Laughs for the Newly Married.* I should browse the poetry section inside—maybe find a book of limericks that I can crib to get me started. I like to read, not write.

As I look through the plate glass window, I see Gunnar surrounded by several coeds—a guru with his disciples.

Quickly, I turn away and follow the crowd. Across the way, a rap record from a music store blares its garbled sounds above the traffic. This is a true university street.

The next block has several restaurants. What do I want? Moussaka? Pancakes—twenty-four hours a day? Spaghetti? I walk into the Chinese Palace—a small place crammed between a Swedish bakery and an Asian spice shop. A few tables center the room with dark booths along two Peking red walls. Large brass dragons and painted lotus blossoms add to the Oriental atmosphere.. The hostess, a short middle-aged lady with almond eyes and a tired smile, motions me to sit anywhere. I choose a back booth and glance at the menu. I'm never hungry. I eat to avoid a lecture by Arletta—*You must keep up your strength.*

I tell the waitress that the sweet-sour chicken is fine. I pull out my pocket calendar and wonder how I can fill it with anything beside classes and choir.

"Do you study art with that much concentration?" asks a deep voice.

I look up as Gunnar slides into the opposite seat. "May I join you?" he adds.

I smile, "You have already."

"I noticed you through the book-store window. I think you saw me, too. I escaped the young ones and followed you."

"So I see." I'm not sure that I want him there. I haven't been alone at a table with a man since Cal left. Gunnar looks good because he's terribly attractive with his warm voice and relaxed manner.

"You're having—?" He raises an eyebrow along with a sly grin.

"—Sweet-sour chicken."

"No, you're not. I'll order for you." He waves to the waitress. "Cancel the lady's order. We want two dim-sum, number seven and one number three, beef. And she'll have almond ding chicken."

It feels good to hear a man take charge, but I don't want Gunnar to take charge—not now. As the young waitress crosses out my order, I speak directly to her. "I don't care for the almond ding. I intend to have sweet-sour."

Gunnar lifts his eyebrow again, "I'm defeated. The lady will have sweet-sour." As the waitress turns away, he gives me a slow captivating smile, "You'll be sorry."

"I make my own decisions—."

He studies me. "—Very well, but I know this place and every chicken dish. I've tried them all. I ate here when it was *Edith's Home Cooking* with red-checked cloths and plastic daisies. He touches the lone pink carnation in a glass cylinder. "At least, this is real—," he pauses "—like you."

"Oh, I'm very real—an authentic middle-aged woman. No, make that a mature student."

He studies me through narrowed eyes. "You're really a reincarnation of the white Tara from Hindu belief. She is the Star goddess, the female aspect of the greatest god."

"Wrong! I'm not even the six-armed green Tara of Buddhist, Jain, and Tibetan Lamaism—a celestial boat woman who ferries people from the world of delusion to that of knowledge." I look at Gunnar and return a sly smile. "Years ago I took a course in symbolism and ancient mythology. My classmates were also amused by my name."

"—You may not have six arms, but you're very attractive."

"I'll remember that on a gloomy day." I need to change the subject. I glance down at the paper mat, covered with signs of the Chinese Zodiac. It's a lifesaver. "I think I'm a Boar—spelled B-O-R-E."

"Never!" Gunnar grins, "—Guess what I am."

I study the possibilities "I hope you're not a Snake or a Rat."

Gunnar makes a quick calculation and answers, amused. "I'm a Monkey."

I read, "You are very intelligent and able to influence people—."

"—Like you, I hope."

I continue. "You are easily discouraged and confused. You are to avoid a Dragon or a Rat."

"Then I don't have to worry because you're both a student and a lady. I'm glad you joined my class."

"Don't be too sure. We moved around a lot. I haven't kept up with the art scene. That's why I'm a student." I'm cautious, but I'm suddenly happy, too, to sit there and spar with Gunnar.

The waitress brings two dim sum—plum dumplings—with a pot of steaming tea. Gunnar pours, his long fingers gracefully curving around the twine handle.

He glances at my hands. "Are you're married?"

I won't tell him about the separation. "Cal—my husband—is with a large corporation. He's in the city every day—."

He doesn't believe me. "—How nice that you're free."

I look at him sharply. Free? I wish I felt free. "We have a daughter Anne at NU in Evanston. She perfected her Spanish at Salamanca this summer."

"—So you're filling time?" He chides me with his inquiry.

"No!" I protest. "I may update my teaching credential. I worked in a library for several years after we married—until Anne was born. That was a long time ago." It took two sad trials and three months of confinement before Anne came. The nurses said I would forget all my sadness after she was born, but I never have. The early losses are locked away deep down. "If I become a docent at the Art Museum, I want a better background." I rush on as Gunnar studies me. "It's necessary to keep informed about current trends—." I stop. "I don't know exactly why I'm on campus. It just seemed a good thing to do."

"You're no different than half my students. I'm not even sure why I'm teaching."

Suddenly, I relax. It's pleasant to be there with him.

Gunnar reaches across the table and pushes away a strand of hair that touches my cheek. "Lovely," he says. His hand glides down to my chin which he gently lifts. "You have a classic face—a perfect oval—the kind that Renaissance painters wanted for their portraits of royalty. You could have been the model for a portrait of a duchess."

"You're teasing me!" My cheeks warm from his touch. Carefully, I move my face slightly away. "Thank you for the compliment. I'll remember that on a dull winter day."I stab a bite of plum dumpling and somehow get it to my lips with a steady hand. Inside, I tremble. It's been a long time since Cal touched me. Once I read that babies die if they're not touched and held. I want to be held. I change the subject. "How did you get here?"

Gunnar leans back. "Actually, I'm from Ohio. I wanted to make it big in New York, so I graduated from Columbia and married too soon. My first wife was a ballet dancer. She slept all day and danced all night. I painted all day and slept all night. It didn't work I moved to San Francisco and married a Hawaiian coed—a really beautiful girl. I painted a whole series of canvasses using her as my model."

"Do you have any left? I'd loved to see them."

"Actually, she became homesick and went back to Maui. So I spent several weeks, cleaning off my canvasses." Gunnar laughs as if his marriage and pictures were a huge joke.

"You weren't devastated? I mean—to lose your wife and all your work—."

"Oh, I still had the canvasses. They were more important. Preparing a canvass is a lot of work. Someday, I'll tell you about the process. We'll lunch together again. Often, I hope."

"Well, I have a busy schedule, so I won't promise." I change the subject. "So you came here——." I taste the sweet-sour chicken. Gunnar was right. I should have ordered the almond ding dish.

"Yes, and gained tenure. I'm at the university for life! That's a lo-o-ong sentence," Gunnar cracks a half-smile.

I notice his wedding ring. "—And you remarried?"

"—More or less."

"More or less is an impossibility!" I protest, but that's my marriage, too—more or less.

"My wife Carmela works for a corporation in Houston. We have a good marriage. She comes back every other week-end or I fly down there. It leaves us both free—to pursue our own affairs." He studies at me with a questioning smile.

Is there a double-meaning to *affairs*? I look away.

Gunnar continues, "With her away, I have uninterrupted time for painting."

"Do you specialize in oils—prints—pastels?" It's a dumb question because he would be familiar with all mediums.

"You must come to my studio sometime. I share one with Reggie Gibbons who is also in the art department. He sculpts. Our place is away from the campus where we have space for really huge works. I do things the hard way—make my own stretchers and prepare my resins. Sorry—I get technical."

"It's interesting. I never thought about preparation——." On purpose, I glance at my watch. "I've got to go." I signal for my check. "It's been very pleasant," I add primly.

Gunnar is amused. He knows that I'm unsure of myself. Inwardly, I argue that there's nothing wrong with a middle-aged professor and a middle-aged student lunching together. Why am I so skittish? Nana and Jill would laugh and call me *a prude.*

He pushes a fortune cookie toward me. "You first."

I snap it apart and read, "—*You will take a long trip*. How odd! I read one like that when my friend and I dined at the Bamboo Hut. And yours?"

"—*Eat, drink and be merry*. I can't do that alone." He lifts his mug of tea. "Here's to us."

Outside, I hurry back to the campus parking lot. I'll go home and take a cool shower on this warm autumn afternoon. I'll tell Arletta about my classes, but not about lunch with Gunnar.

On Sunday morning, the Pastor stops me as I hurry to robe for choir. "It's nice to see you smile. How are your classes?"

"Fine. In Poetry, I have to write something about nature. For Art, I'll study a sunset and find similar hues in a modern painting. What will I do if there's a thunderstorm tonight?" I laugh.

"Look at an Edward Munch painting," he grins.

During his sermon, the Pastor mentions Adam and Eve. My mind wanders. I decide they're a topic for a limerick— the garden, the snake, and a couple flitting around a la natural. I can't wait to get home. I'm glad that Arletta and Boyce are tied up with a football party.

It's a gray afternoon. I pull on my old purple velour robe and settle down with a yellow legal pad and the TV remote nearby. I glance at the football game, so I can converse with Arletta tomorrow. I won't show her my limerick.

Between fumbles, passes, and turnovers, I spend the afternoon, but the limerick doesn't happen. Instead, a stream-of-consciousness poem takes over. The verses flow until I almost have a story. Have I overdone the assignment? I don't care, because for three hours I haven't thought about Cal or Anne or even Gunnar. I type my lines on the computer and stash a copy in my notebook. I can't wait until Tuesday—to show it to Mattie and the others.

On Tuesday, Windfeather listens as other students read their verses with reactions from titters to boredom. I'm surprised when he calls on me.

I apologize. "I intended to write a limerick, but it turned out to be something else."

"By all means, let's hear it."

Shakily, I read aloud my poem.

ЈUBURBAN WIFE

A gray fog snugs her indoors
Haloed street lights will mark his way home
A *Welcome* mat lies before the blue door
Where a straw wreath with white daisies
And a gold ribbon hangs from a brass knocker.
She waits   restlessly paces
Stares through the bay window
Watches for his quick stride
Up Colonial Drive—a twenty-five
Minute walk from the station.
Last night he said so little.
She bites her lip—should she meet him
Have a laugh on the way home
Talk about jogging a yapping poodle
A late garbage pick-up   a telephone survey?
She waits   lights a cinnamon candle
In his aunt's antique silver holder
Remembers his gift—*Passion* perfume
Frantically dabs ears wrists cleavage
An aroma more pungent than the candle.
She hears the grandfather clock tick-tock
Twelve minutes past seven a distant
Harsh whistle as the commuter train arrives
Slides fast away down a hard metal track
Where two rails side-by-side never meet.

She waits   wipes troubled eyes
As the candle burns lower
Snuffs it out with wet fingers
And closes the chintz draperies
Against the murky night.

Other students look at me as if I were an alien from another planet. Then someone laughs, "That wife's a loser". Another, "—a real headache for the guy."

Windfeather says, "That's not exactly using things in nature, but your poem is a good example of the creative process. The brain begins with a vision, but your imagination creates something entirely different."

A coed interrupts. "I find Tara's poem really difficult. I'm a born-again Christian. She paints a very dismal picture of marriage which is very sacred. The wife needs to find JESUS. She should pray that HE will save her marriage as well as her soul."

I stare at her. "Maybe the wife does pray, but—." I stumble, searching for a gentle response to the girl's outburst.

Windfeather interrupts, "The relationship between a man and a woman has been a problem since the beginning of time."

"I witness to what I believe!" the coed thrusts her face forward. "I am for JESUS! HE can save her if she will only pray to HIM. She needs faith."

There are groans and titters around the room. The coed glares at some students behind her.

"You've made your point," Windfeather nods. "Let's move on and hear some other poems."

I want to witness that I'm a Christian, too, but I remain mute. Do I challenge her that praying to Jesus doesn't answer problems, but gives a person strength to meet a problem? Others look for my reaction. I turn the other check. I study my notes. I want to listen to other young women and Mattie so I can understand Anne better. As we leave, the ardent young coed rushes by me as her low slung jeans ride down and her shrink top pulls up, revealing a silver ring on her navel..

Now I know—good manners are out. Silver rings are in.

I follow Mattie at a safe distance and head for Gunnar's class. I take my usual place—center rear row. Today an old projector is behind me, so I move away. Gunnar darkens the room. He pushes a button and a screen slides down. He stands beside me with the control in his right hand. How many times has he done this lecture? His voice lazily points out the contrasts of Warhol and Wyatt. It's hard to stay alert in the darkness and warm room. After the attack in Windfeather's class, I feel drained. My eyes half-close.

I feel a gentle touch on my right shoulder. Gunnar's left hand rests there casually, as if it slid there without realizing that it is my body instead of a chair back. His hand stays there, the warmth spreading through my knit turtleneck. I hold my breath. Do I move and embarrass him as he realizes his mistake? Or do I sit there until he clicks another picture? I stay motionless.

During the presentation, Gunnar occasionally massages my shoulder with his left hand. Finally, I hunch forward as if I'm intent on the slides. Soon, he finishes and class is over. I almost walk past him when he calls, "Tara—may I have a moment?"

The others leave. I stand there, waiting, like a first grader with a smudged paper.

Gunnar slowly takes his time, filing his pictures. "Let's lunch together."

I hesitate. "Will I be safe if a table is between us?"

He grins, "What happened? You looked tense when you came into class."

"Well-l-l, I had Poetry today. The class didn't appreciate my attempt at blank verse."

"They're too serious about some things, but never the right ones. You needed a shoulder massage. I wanted to help."

"That's dangerous with a student and more than I expect from an art class or a professor."

"Don't limit my concern for you. There's another thing—how do you keep that cool reserve? You really remained quiet for a long time."

Should I tell him that my life is on hold? My doctor tells me not to cry. My Pastor tells me to be grateful for each day. Arletta tells me to enjoy life. I don't know where I'm going or what's ahead. I'm here. That's all.

Gunnar breaks into my thoughts. "You haven't answered, but I'll find out. I have a proposition for you."

"If you want me to invest in a North Pole gold mine—no. If you want idle chatter—yes. I'm very good at that."

He looks at me with an impish grin. "You're more than idle chatter—a lot more. Let's get out of here."

His hand grasps my elbow and points me to the door. His touch feels so good.

Gunnar's studio is in the warehouse district—above a graphic design business and a wholesale lighting company. Gunnar unlocks the street door and we climb a dim stairway. Once inside I can see why he likes the place. Large windows with good north light face an urban landscape. The campus seems far away.

Two empty easels are in the center. A tall shelving unit holds art books and paints, jars, brushes, boxes of pastels, charcoal sticks, pencils—all the items necessary for a serious artist. Posters from the Louvre and a series of Japanese prints are tacked on the east wall. On the south wall, a large charcoal nude lies on her side—stretched out with her back to the viewer. I wonder if I should study it—or count her vertebrae—or if I should comment. I pause at a large unfinished canvas on the west wall. Great splashes of dark blue on

130

a grey background could represent a coming storm. Is it a *work-in-progress* or is it finished?

"Don't say anything—," Gunnar says with a cocked smile. "It's something I started, but lost interest. This is my area," he says, pride in his voice as his hand sweeps the room.

He nods toward another door. "We'll look at Gibbons sculptures."

I follow him and see a red clay figure of a baseball pitcher as he leans forward with a ball in hand. It's a good sculpture, but nothing unusual.

"Gibbons has a commission from a doting grandparent who wants a statue of his grandson in college." Gunnar smiles. "That's bread for what Gibbons really likes to do— elegant and whimsical birds which are later cast in bronze."

Gunnar takes my arm again and nudges me toward a third doorway. There is a worn flowered sofa, a large tweedy rust chair, and a second-hand table with three old scarred school chairs, A counter with a sink and microwave runs along one wall. A small refrigerator stands at the end.

Gunnar waves his hand again. "Here we have all the comforts of home. Sit down. I want to talk business with you." He microwaves two inscribed mugs—*Life begins at Fifty,* and *Mardi Gras—Wow!* With a flourish, he sets them on an upturned wooden box, a substitute coffee table, and hands me a green tea bag and a cookie tin. He pulls his tweedy chair closer to the sofa. At least, it isn't a brown recliner.

"You have my curiosity," I begin, a bit uneasy in a strange place. I tell myself there's nothing wrong in being alone with my professor in an isolated studio

"I've been adrift. I don't know what I want to paint." Gunnar says earnestly. He leans forward, "When I saw you in the Chinese Palace, an idea struck me. I should attempt a series of paintings of every era—from the old masters, impressionists, through the abstracts until today."

"That's a big project."

131

"Maybe do a modern Nativity—Mary and Joseph getting off a bus in Las Vegas."

"You've got to be kidding! I don't find that amusing."

"No?" He laughs, "I think it makes the old story—relevant!"

"—Ridiculous!" I snap. "I don't think sacred things should be mocked."

"Everyone goes to Las Vegas. It would place those ancient travelers in this era. However, I see the Nativity as a folk tale."

"I see it as Biblical truth." I turn away

"—Maybe, we should change the subject. I don't want to argue with you," he grins. "Don't be upset with me. Hear me out."

I offer a small smile in return. "I won't argue with you either. Now, I only argue with God. I lose every time." I stir my tea. "Anyway, we were talking about your project—."

"It will keep me busy for several years." Gunnar adds, "—Maybe, a lifetime."

"Where do I fit in?"

"I'll begin with the Renaissance. I want you to be my model."

I'm speechless. Slowly, I warily ask, "Just what is involved—?"

"—Sitting. Twenty minutes—a half-hour—between breaks—whatever rest you need."

"I'm flattered, but—"

"Gibbons and I shared the nude on the wall. He sculpted while I drew." Gunnar's voice deepens, "But I need a model with your classic face. You're a natural."

"—I hardly know what to say." I sound like a fifteen year old. "Renaissance? What would I wear?"

"I'll borrow a Shakespearean dress from the drama department—something with jewels. You can pose as Queen Elizabeth—."

"—Obviously, the First."

"—Of course! You don't have four children like the present Queen, do you?"

"No, but Elizabeth, the First, didn't have any—so I'm the wrong model. I have one daughter."

Gunnar waves this away. "Here's the bargain. I'll paint you. If it sells, you'll get a percentage. You'll be as famous as Mona Lisa."

"I doubt that." I grin. "How long will this take?"

"—As long we want it to last." Gunnar shrugs. "It'll work. We'll be good together." I hesitate. Is there a double meaning is his words, *As long as we want it to last...we'll be good together*? A bit primly, I say, "I'll think about it."

We both know—he has his model.

.

Anne calls from Evanston. "Have you seen Dad this week?"

"No."

"Well, you might show some interest. I know he invited you to see his apartment. Please stop by sometime. Take some pictures. Promise? Soon?"

I think, *Oh, Anne, you must be a romantic to think there's any hope for your Dad and me. I'm making new friends—at least one, Gunnar. Your Dad is past history.*

I say, "—Well, maybe. I'm awfully busy with classes and all—."

"You could take pictures of his view and send them to Nana. He won't. He doesn't like cameras. He never gets things centered. He always argued with you and finally, you snapped them."

"Anne, I have other things in my life now—." Gunnar doesn't teach on Fridays, so I sit for him in the afternoons, unless he flies to Houston for the weekend. I haven't even told Arletta yet and I won't tell Anne. Instead, I add, "—But I'll take some pictures if that's what you want." I won't call Cal, but I'll casually drop by his lakeside apartment.

I insist that I meet Gunnar at his studio. That way I can make a quick exit if I don't like his set-up. I'm excited. I know I'll be in a heavy velvet costume, but I take a leisurely bath as if every pore must be scrubbed clean for his brush. I dab on a spicy perfume. The stairs creak as I climb to the second story. I rap lightly at his studio door.

"Come on in!" Gunnar yells. "Don't stand on ceremony!"

Why do I think of Daniel in the lion's den? Gunnar grins and helps me out of my jacket. Quickly, I move away from him.

"You're skittish," he teases. "Don't be nervous, it's only preliminary sketching today."

"I'm not sure about this arrangement. I've never modeled before."

"We're even. I've never painted you before."

"—But you have painted. You have the advantage." I shiver in his cool studio.

"Let's have something to warm up," Gunnar says, walking toward the kitchen. I follow like a lamb to a sheepfold. We sit on the sofa. Our hands grasp steaming cups of cider. "I should offer you a hot toddy, but Gibbons can't handle alcohol, so we don't keep it."

I follow him into his studio room. A French baroque chair is there now. A wine red velvet dress is casually thrown across it. Gunnar motions, "Your place."

I pick up the dress. "Do I put this on today?"

"No—," Gunnar moves the chair, so I must face the north light. "—Sit," he orders in a firm masculine voice like Cal does when he's in a restaurant. I like Gunnar's tone, his imperial manner. In some ways, he's a lot like Cal, but I think he must be different.

I slip into the chair. Gunnar pushes my right shoulder back, so I'm half turned against the gold brocade background. He lifts my hair and lets it fall casually away from my neck. I feel his soft touch and wonder if his hand rests a moment too long. I move ever so slightly even though I want to feel his touch. It's nice to be with a man—hear his voice, see his stride, feel his hand even for a moment. I miss Cal.

I see the amusement in his eyes as he studies me behind his easel. I breathe easier. The silence continues, only broken by the occasional scratches of his charcoal sticks. His concentration is so deep that I think he doesn't really see me. I grow tired and my neck hurts from sitting in one position. I move my head for relief.

Gunnar glances at the old wall clock. "I'm so sorry," he apologizes. "It's time for a break."

"Let me see the sketch."

"No way," Gunnar replies, dropping a cloth over the easel. "—Not until it's done. You might quit. I want you here. I like you here."

"I like it here, too. It's a new experience."

We go back to the kitchen. I sit on the sofa, but I wish I'd taken the tweedy chair instead. Gunnar hands me a mug of jasmine tea and sits beside me as his left arm rests casually behind me. Warily, I wonder what his next move will be. Finally, he hands me a sketch book with studies of various students through the years. A lot of them are coeds. Like trophies? How many have been invited to his studio? I'm treading in unfamiliar waters. I turn the pages and am impressed with how a line drawing can portray a mood.

"Tonight, I'm flying to Houston. Usually, I leave on Thursday night after classes, but I needed to get started with you."

Should I be flattered by his attention? "We could have waited another week."

"May be you could, but not me." Gunnar takes my hand. "You're my inspiration for the most important project of my life." He holds my face toward lamplight. "—A lovely face." He leans forward as I quickly turn away. He drops his hand and laughs, "That's what I love about you—a real queen—untouchable!"

"I'm married." I don't add—at least, legally.

Gunnar gives me a sharp look and laughs, "—So am I!"

"I can't get involved."

"There's no involvement here. Life should be enjoyed. Don't you agree?"

I search for his logic. "—Only if the circumstances are right." I stand up. "I'm tired. This is too new for me. I must go."

Gunnar studies me. "—But you will come back?"

I should say *No*, but I say, "Yes."

I feel happier than I have for a long time. It's Saturday and I decide to see Cal after all —for Anne's sake. I should call, but I decide to drop by casually with the camera. No big deal. Didn't Cal invite me visit him sometime?

I stop at the supermarket and buy daisies for Cal's apartment. No pot of mums—just a simple bouquet in a paper cylinder. I drive carefully—not too fast, so I'll arrive relaxed, able to greet him as an equal with interests of my own—like my studies and posing for Gunnar.

I drive to *The Stanford*, a high-rise on the lake. A low-slung black sports car pulls into a parking spot ahead of me. I find a space at the end of the lot. The other driver, a young woman, walks hurriedly through the heavy plate glass doors as I follow her at a distance. .She walks with a confident stride. Although I can't see her face, I know she must be smart and savvy because she wears a beret at a jaunty angle. She carries a white orchid covered by a plastic sleeve.

I follow her through the entrance and watch as she bends over at the long apartment list and blocks my view. She is a tall dark-haired brunette, wearing stiletto-heeled boots with her faded jeans and black leather jacket. Where have I seen her before? I pull at my green head scarf and wish I didn't wear these protective outdoor glasses to save my eyes.

She punches a button and leans to the intercom. "Cal? It's Diedre." Pause. "Okay, I'll be right up." There's a harsh buzz and she opens another plate glass door. She turns and gives me a dazzling wide scarlet smile, showing perfect teeth and warm brown eyes. "—Sorry I took so long." She heads for the elevator inside.

Like a statue, I stand there rigid with shock. I, too, peer at Cal's apartment number just where her fingers were. Six-eighteen. I hurry to my car and study my daisies. There's a trash container across the street. I could drop them there, but I'm too cheap. Slowly, I drive home, past a bus stop where an old lady stands in a shelter. Her hair is caught in a dark green scarf, too, and her black coat is buttoned up against the cold wind. She hugs a bulging grocery bag as a worn black purse dangles on her left arm. I jump out of my car and thrust the daisies at her.

"Have a good day!" I call over my shoulder and speed away because my day is not so good. I wonder, Is Gunnar having a great time in Houston? No doubt, Cal is happy in his apartment. Did Diedre come for lunch? Will she fix an omelet for him? Or will they share an intimate back booth at some trendy bistro? He ruined my life. I hate him.

Thanksgiving is next Thursday. Arletta calls, "We'll celebrate with Boyce's family in Branson and see all the shows. Come with us."

"No," I say, "I have other plans." Instead, I'll call Jill and invite myself to California. I add, "I haven't seen Jill for almost six months."

I know it's late to book a plane, but I'll catch a night flight. I dial my sister's number and suggest that she invite me.

Jill rushes her words, "I'm sorry Tara, but I'm off to Ixtapa for the holiday. Let's plan on Christmas—for sure." She pauses, "—But what will you do?"

I tell a lie. "Oh, friends have asked me." I don't know what I'm doing. I never know.

I'm surprised when Cal phones. "Anne is flying down to Guadalajara with me. We'll spend the holiday with Nana and Wendell. I hope you have a happy——."

I hang up. With Gunnar also gone, I just won't celebrate. Why should I? What have I to be thankful for? A distant daughter? An errant husband? A lonely house? Sleepless nights—although they are waning?

After Sunday services, the Pastor asks me the same thing. I can't evade him. "I don't have anything really definite for Thanksgiving." I wish I could think of an excuse.

"Well, you're invited to our place. My wife always fixes too much food. We've asked some foreign guests. One's a young Chinese engineer, here for six months. Also Kjersten, a Norwegian student—you may have seen her at church." He speaks with finality as if he's made my decision. "Oh, Clyde and Ingrid Thorson will join us, too."

"That will be nice," I mumble and turn away. I don't want to go. At least, Arletta will be relieved by my Pastor's invitation.

Last night I sang with the joint choirs at the ecumenical service on Thanksgiving Eve. It was a nice service, but I look forward to Matins at Trinity this morning. Later, I'll cross the parking lot to the old parsonage where Pastor and Regina live. I've only been there once—when we first moved here. Anne and I attended the Christmas open house held annually by Pastor and Regina. Anne was a senior in high school and moody because she, being new, wasn't invited to high school parties. Occasionally, she substituted when a ringer was absent in the bell choir. It was a relief when she left for Evanston the next September. I joined the senior choir. Trinity became important to me.

About fifty of us filter into the sanctuary for Matins. The brilliant autumn sunshine streams through the stained glass windows which gleam with radiant color. There is the deep sapphire Nativity scene with a star and Bethlehem in silhouette. Other windows portray the life of Christ, leading to the cross and resurrection. The Pentecost window is filled with deep reds and gold. Over the altar, the window is a mixture of interlocking symbols—bread and wine, circles, a dove, palm branches and *Alpha* and *Omega* Greek letters, along with two dark crosses for the crucified robbers. The great Jesus cross hangs high above the altar. I love to meditate and discover some new meaning each time. Sometimes, I think I was meant to be a contemplative nun in a desert convent. At this point, Cal might agree.

After the service, I wait in my car until I see Pastor cross to the parsonage. It's an old three-bedroom ranch house on an adjoining lot, built when the first unit of Trinity mission was erected fifty years ago. The small church had an altar in one end and a fireplace in the other, so both worship and fellowship activities could be held there. The parsonage was built next door for a Pastor's family, but the basement had an outside entrance and used for Sunday School classes.

Through the years, later Pastors wanted to buy their own homes, so the church gave them an allowance and used the parsonage for youth activities or immigrant families..

After I joined Holy Trinity, I heard brief references to Pastor's predecessor, "The Rev" Pete and his wife, Bunny. It seems the church treasurer embezzled funds, which was discovered during The Rev's sabbatical study. The Rev Pete was supposed to be in Arizona at a retreat center. Instead, someone met The Rev and Bunny on the ski slopes at Vail where they had rented a condo for a month with the rental and other perks paid from the Mission and Endowment Funds. The Rev Pete resigned and the treasurer was jailed, sentenced, and put on probation. Some prominent members left the church.

Pastor and Regina arrived and consented to live in the old parsonage until the church recovered from the financial losses. He cleaned up the financial mess and gave the congregation new hope. Regina cleaned up the parsonage which was repainted and the plumbing fixed. It's in poor condition and will be torn down after Pastor and Regina retire. Probably a family education building will be erected.

I ring the bell and Pastor greets me.

"Ah, it can only be Thanksgiving with that special aroma of turkey and cornbread dressing drifting through the parsonage," I grin. I see the dining table is perfectly set with silver, china and crystal. It will be a pleasant experience to eat on china again instead of a green plastic plate in front of the TV. I feel relaxed, ready to enjoy pleasant conversation and the mum centerpiece. I also feel happier than I expected to be.

I smile at Zhigang, the Chinese engineer, and greet Kjersten with a "God Dag!" which is the only greeting I know. She's savvy enough to accept my attempt at "Good Day" and flashes an appreciative smile—one that would melt the Geiranger fjord.

Since her college dorm is closed, Kjersten is staying with Pastor and Regina during the Thanksgiving break. Is she another of Regina's "waifs" as any unexpected guests are called? Kjersten shows pictures of her family to Zhigang and then he fishes in his pocket for his snapshots. I pull a chair closer to Clyde as Ingrid disappears behind the kitchen's swinging door to help Regina. I try small talk. "You must be very busy this month. I read about an outbreak of flu—." I knock on the lamp table for good luck.

"It comes around every year," Clyde smiles. "Actually, I've wanted to talk to you about the congregation's mission trip."

I need a quick excuse so I can decline. I don't intend to go anywhere, now that I'm on the campus. Besides, Gunnar will still be working on my portrait as an English royal. I don't need to lie. I don't speak Spanish, but Anne does, so I can be truthful. "Anne knows Spanish, I don't."

Fortunately, Regina stands in the doorway and announces dinner. Along with the turkey, Regina serves a sweet potato casserole, creamy mashed potatoes with rosemary, green beans au gratin, a cranberry and orange salad plus a relish tray.

"Awesome!" Kjersten grins with that perfect smile. I hope she gets back to Oslo before an agent hands her a modeling contract.

Everyone agrees the meal is a perfect Thanksgiving dinner. The general conversation drifts to living overseas. Regina asks polite questions and I study her. I don't know her well, and I wonder if anyone does. No doubt she knows a lot, but she doesn't gossip.

The pumpkin pie is met with "Ahs" and "Great". Somewhere, I read that Chinese people aren't too fond of sweet desserts. Politely, Zhigang takes several bites and pushes aside his pumpkin pie. He nods at Regina with an apologetic smile.

"It's nice that you've invited us. I assume your own family couldn't make it this year," I say to Regina.

"Oh, they're too busy—." She responds, sounding edgy.

Pastor frowns, "Now, mother—."

"Well, it's true! Tell it like it is! Our son Edmund lives in Burbank—he's a director in television. He owns a condo on the big island of Hawaii so he takes his friends there on holidays." She pauses, "And our daughter Beth and her family live in Orlando. She's in the legal department and her husband is a hospitality executive at Disney World."

I say, "Oh, their children must love that,"

"They're bored with Disney World! They vacation in Maine. In fact, our grandson will go to Bowdoin after he graduates in spring. He hopes to live in Maine someday and own a tackle shop." She looks away. "Maybe we'll retire in Maine, close to him."

Ingrid asks, "So you'll head for Orlando for his graduation?"

Regina and Pastor look at each other. "—If we're invited," Regina says flatly. "We hardly know our grandchildren. They live so far away—."

The Pastor interrupts, "Well, our children were raised in Fargo. They're strangers to this area. We don't provide any excitement," Pastor adds in a wistful tone, "Beth says there's not much reason for them to vacation here."

I think, —*Only to visit their parents and grandparents.* Will I be in a similar situation with Anne someday? Pastor and Regina have been modern nomads like Cal and I were. Did their children hear too many sermons? Did they have to deal with too many parishioners? Did they move too many times? Did their parents live too frugally? Will Anne reject visiting me with some lame excuse?

Regina's face is flushed with embarrassment because she's said too much. Brightly, she explains, "Well, we moved on to Grand Forks, and Aberdeen. Then to Montevideo and Hibbings." She jabs at her pie. "All the moves took their toll. But now, we're here!" She sweeps her hand in a circle. "Now, you're our family!"

I feel a kinship. We're sisters in spite of the age difference. She doesn't belong anywhere and neither do I.

After dinner, we're too lethargic for much conversation, so we settle into chairs. Seated by the fireplace, Zhiang rests an *erhu*, a two-string stick fiddle, on his lap. His instrument is round-shaped, closed at one end with a python skin resonator. He moves his long bow horizontally across the strings. A thin poignant melody filters through the room. I'm surprised how it calms and moves me. I close my eyes and feel that I'm praying in some ancient temple in the far Orient. Somehow, it seems a fitting closure to an unusual Thanksgiving afternoon. I feel totally relaxed. Suddenly, I feel happy, too. I'm no longer concerned about Cal's actions. I know I can manage my life very well without him.

Before I leave, Clyde pulls me aside. "About this trip to Guatemala—we'll do some educational, medical and church work. If Anne is free, we'd love to have her as an interpreter. You, too."

Anne—on a mission trip? I am doubtful, but I say, "Well, that might be a possibility." Who knows what spring will bring? Or what will *grab* (her word) Anne?

Then he adds, "You should think about it for yourself."

"Me? Teach the Mayans about modern art? That's about all I know," I laugh. I don't remind him that I may be in divorce court by spring. I'm ready for closure with Cal. Gunnar has made that possible. A live affair to replace a dead marriage, even if my conscience does plague me that I'm still a married woman. Well, like Gunner, sort of married—except he likes it that way.

What about our promises? *"For richer, for poorer? In sickness and in health? For better, for worse—till death do us part."* They were made a long time ago. Maybe they're not meant for my life anymore.

I return home. As I pass our dining room, dark and empty, I am nagged with the thought. I have this beautiful room, designed by Ursula. Why didn't I have a festive Thanksgiving dinner here and save aging Regina all that work? I'm full of "should haves" these days. Maybe, I'll invite them at Christmas, but I know I won't. Instead, I'll give them a gift certificate to Gustav's restaurant tucked into their Christmas card

I go upstairs and snuggle in my bathrobe—the old purple one that Anne gave me five years ago. One holiday has past and I managed it alone—well, maybe not alone. As the Pastor said months ago, *"Friends will help you."* True. And foreigners, too.

I wonder if I should phone Anne in Mexico. No, because Nana might answer and I don't want to talk to her, or Cal. I can't call Gunnar because he's with his wife. I dial, "Aunt Cleda? I want to wish you a happy Thanksgiving."

"How nice to hear from you! I dined with friends at a Naples hotel. No one wants the work of a real Thanksgiving dinner any more." Aunt Cleda sighs, "How about you?"

"I'm moving on." I want to tell her about Gunnar. I no longer care what Cal does since I have a new man in my life. "I love my classes at the university and I met—."

Aunt Cleda interrupts, "—Now, you must promise me that you'll give yourself a year before you date. Don't fall madly in love with a salesman. I don't want you to do anything foolish on the rebound—like become a cougar!"

"—A what?"

"—A cougar! That's when an older woman takes up with a younger man. So, don't date an eighteen year old freshman. Promise?"

I mutter, "I promise" about the freshman. My fingers are crossed. Aunt Cleda is too late. I'm involved with Gunnar. He's a panther circling his prey and I'm as silly as a fluffy kitten. I like it more and more.

Arletta stops by on Monday after Thanksgiving. I expect a lengthy account of her week-end with Boyce's family. She's never cared for his brother's family. Instead, she holds the business section of The Herald.

"Look at this headline," she says, pushing the paper at me.

I stare at the bold headline, **COLTON INDUSTRIES GAINS CONTROL OF MIRRON/MOLTEN**. In smaller type, the caption reads, *CEO Promises No Major Shake-up.* I take a deep breath. "I remember—Cal mentioned this possibility several months ago. He won't be affected." I hope this is true. He will always drive himself too hard—either in a company or corporation or now, a conglomerate.

"Are you sure about his job?"

"I'm not sure about anything anymore." That's the truth.

"How long has he been with Mirron?"

"Twenty three years. He started with Mirron before it absorbed Molten—long enough for us to move plenty of times—." I shrug, "—Long enough for Cal to have at least one affair like any other middle-aged guy who's afraid of growing old with a middle-aged dull wife." I struggle to keep bitterness out of my voice.

"Now, don't be hard on yourself!" Arletta points to the headline. "Keep me posted, if there's any change with Cal."

I know that he won't be fired. He's a long-time executive and too smart.

The final classes of this semester resume. On Friday afternoon, Gunnar hands me the heavy wine red velvet dress again. I slip into it behind a screen. He carefully arranges the skirt in graceful folds, across my lap. He props a pillow behind my back to keep me erect. He fusses with the stiff lace collar, his fingers touching my skin, his warm hand more firmly on my shoulder. It lingers there. Then he bends over close to my face and presses my head close to his own for a correct position.

"Hold that," he says softly in my ear.

I know it is only a matter of time until I yield to his possessive moves. I am hungry for a touch, an intimate smile, an appreciative kiss, a shared memory. We are alone in his studio. Who is to know what will happen? Tick-tock. Tick-tock. Only the wall clock breaks the silence.

Flirtation is so pleasant because I convince myself that it isn't adultery. Or is it? How do I explain this emerging affair to myself? And to God? Because now God, not Cal, is my problem. I know the commandment. "Thou shalt not commit adultery." which seems an ultimatum when spoken in old English. Straight from God. Shall I pray, *Excuse me, God.*

After this one time, it won't happen again—I promise! I mean it! Amen. Okay?

I smell the oil paints. I study Gunnar's movements. He peers around the easel at me and then back to his work with deep concentration. Sometimes, he mutters to himself and dabs the canvas quickly with a turpentine rag. He even hums. Have other women posed for him and yielded to his possessive hands?

Suddenly, he stops and studies me with his eyes burning like a gas jet's blue flame. "That's all for now. Come, let's rest." He pulls at my hand.

I want to resist—make an excuse to leave—but I'm weak. I follow.

We head for the sofa. We sit down just as the door opens. Gibbons walks in and drops his old gray parka. "It's hot in here," he says.

I don't know whether to laugh at his truth, or cry with relief. Gunnar's spell is broken.

"I didn't expect you," Gunnar growls at Gibbons. "I'll fix some tea."

"It's been a long afternoon," I say. "I'm going home." I change clothes. Carefully, I walk down the worn stairway, suddenly feeling free. From what? Have I been rescued? Was I on a perilous path descending down into an unknown canyon with rocky rapids, rushing toward a plunging waterfall? Do I care? Was Gibbons arrival only a coincidence? That's scary.

The Bible says, *God works in mysterious ways.* That's even scarier.

It's time for Christmas shopping. Anne calls from Evanston that she'll be home for Christmas after all, although she considered a two-week cruise to Buenos Aires. "Call Dad. Ask him to come for Christmas Eve," she says. She doesn't give up.

I don't tell her that I don't want to see him again. "I rejoined the choir. We sing at midnight services. He won't come because He doesn't go to church." She doesn't buy my excuse. I'm glad she doesn't know about Gunnar because I don't know what to tell her.

"We three can have an early supper together," she says. Anne can't accept that Cal is gone forever. I bite my tongue. Divorce is now inevitable, even a relief. I'll ask for one after Anne goes back to Evanston in January.

I shop the malls. Gifts for Anne are easy—perfume, a sweater, and a book of Neruda poems. I'll add a generous check. Should I give Cal a little black book with Diedre's number and a note, "Room for more"? If he drops me, he'll drop her, too, someday. Even faster. It's easier the second time around.

It's dusk as I leave. The security police have two large men spread-eagled against a wall. The newspapers are full of thefts and pickpockets. I hurry to my car and dismiss those problems—or so I want to believe. Another ten days, and my first semester will be done.

After Thursday's classes, I drive directly to Trinity for choir practice. Brad, the organist and director, asks me to sing an alto solo line. It's the first time he's chosen me since last January when I bowed out after Cal left.

In four-part harmony, the choir begins,
   May my meditation be pleasing to him, as I rejoice in the Lord,
   Praise the Lord, O my soul, praise the Lord.
The organ responds with a majestic trumpet melody.
The choir continues,
   May the glory of the Lord endure forever,
   May the Lord rejoice in his works—,
The basses respond,
   He who looks at the earth and it trembles,
The tenors follow,

Who touches the mountains, and they smoke.

An organ interlude soars into the empty nave. Brad nods to me and I respond with the firm warm alto line,

I will sing to the Lord all my life;

The soprano's notes rise in clear high tones,

I will sing praise to my God as long as I live.

Then the choir joins together for the last verse,

May my meditation be pleasing to him, as I rejoice in the Lord.

Praise the Lord, O my soul. Praise the Lord.

With a triumphant flourish, the organ ends the anthem.

Brad is pleased. "It's coming together nicely. We'll be ready by Christmas Eve." He quips, "Please, stay healthy. No flu. No chicken pox. No trips to Bermuda."

He may be prepared, but I think of Gunnar and I wonder—Will I be ready by Christmas Eve? How can I sing praises and have an affair with Gunnar?

This Christmas God is my problem.

CLOƧURE,

N. THE ACT OF CLOƧING; AN END OR CONCLU-ƧION; THAT WHICH CLOƧEƧ OR ƧHUTƧ; AƧ IN *CLOTURE* (FR.) TERMINATION OF A DEBATE, UƧUALLY BY CALLING FOR A VOTE.

—AND BEYOND

Choir practice lasted longer than usual, because we also practiced an anthem for Epiphany as well and rehearsed a special Christmas liturgy. It is late. I'm tired and I look forward to a cup of tea and a warm bed. When I pull into my drive, a police car, lights flashing, pulls up behind me.

The officer gets out. "Does Calvin Irwin live here?"

I stiffen, wary. "Well, this is his address—sometimes. What's wrong?"

The officer is beefy, impressive, big. I don't want to tangle with him. "This address is listed on Cal Irwin's license. He's been hurt."

My hand covers my mouth. "Oh no! What's happened?"

"He was jumped by a couple of thugs tonight in the Richfield Mall parking lot. They plastered a flyer on the car's rear window. He left the motor running and got out to remove the paper. Someone jumped him from behind. After your husband fell, the other thug backed the car over his left leg. The security cameras caught the whole thing. Your husband was rushed to Community Hospital. Do you have someone to go with you?"

"Yes-s-s. No-o-o. I'll call my best friend from the hospital." My mind whirls. "How badly is he hurt?"

"You'll have to ask the staff." The officer looks at me more closely. "Are you sure that you're okay?"

"I'll leave immediately," Scared, I get back into my car and race away. I drive through a changing caution light and another driver leans on his horn. I don't stop for the yellow light, but he, also, rushes too quickly into the intersection. We're both wrong. A crash is narrowly avoided. I take a deep breath and drive more carefully through the dark night.

I dash past the parking attendant through the Emergency Entrance door. Inside, a receptionist sends me to a waiting lounge on the fourth floor. I'm caught in a maze of elevators and halls. Signage arrows mark various directions. Finally, I stop at a nurses station and hope it's the right one.

"Is there any information about Cal Irwin? I'm his wife."
How easily the words slip out. At the moment, I'm still his
wife.

The plump nurse in a Hawaiian print smock and scrub
slacks turns to her screen. "He's still being examined. The
lounge is at the end of the corridor. Wait there until some one
can see you."

I walk down the hallway, past closed doors. I remind
myself that it is night, so all should be quiet, but I'm apprehensive. People are brought here to recover, but some die.
What is ahead for Cal?

The lounge is an open area with windows on three sides.
I can see the lights of distant office buildings above the dark
silhouette of trees. Two men huddle in the corner and mumble in hushed voices. An older woman glances my way and
nods, a coffee cup in her hand. She turns and stares into the
night. I sit, my head cupped in my right hand, elbow on the
chair arm, trying to absorb what happened to Cal.

I thumb through well-worn magazines as the wall clock
spins an hour, two hours. I call Arletta and realize, too late,
that's it's one a.m.

"I wanted you to know. Now go back to bed."

Arletta promises, "I'll be there the first thing in the morning."

More time rolls by. I inquire from a night nurse, "Doesn't
anyone know anything?"

No one does.

Cal's somewhere nearby, in this medical complex and I
have to wait until someone can bring him back to me. I pray,
"Dear God, don't let him die. I need—," I stop. I'm not sure
that I need him, but Anne does, *"—because Anne needs her
father. And I need to let him know that I'm no longer angry
with him. In Jesus' name. Amen."*

At four a.m. a young intern asks if I'm Cal's wife. "He's
in Room 416. Before you go, you must know—your husband

151

is badly injured. When the young punks jumped him, they really roughed him up. His whole left side is badly bruised. Maybe a cracked rib and probable broken leg. We think they beat him with a flashlight. He's not a pretty sight."

"But he will live?" *Dear God, Cal's too young to die.*

"I think so. We'll assess any brain injuries later with a scan. He's stabilized for now. He has a pretty deep gash above his left temple." He adds, "He's heavily sedated, so he can rest."

"I'll just sit there. I must see him." I hurry down the corridor.

I open the door quietly. In the darkened room a machine connects Cal to sprawling tubes and bags. Something emits a plopping sound every minute. Dimly, I see his bandaged body with a head wrapped like a mummy's large white odd-shaped skull. His left arm and shoulder rest motionless as his right hand twitches on the blanket. He is silent. His right visible cheek is puffy and bruised. I want to cry out. I'm not prepared for this.

Tears silently slide down my cheeks. I quietly pull up a chair beside the bed and take his right hand in mine. I lay my face against it, as my tears continue. It's been a long time since I cried.

Dear God—I said I wished Cal were dead, but You didn't have to kill him.

Arletta comes mid-morning. We drink coffee in the cafeteria while the staff attends to Cal and gurneys him off somewhere.

She pushes back a strand of my hair. "You look tired. You must get some sleep. Come home with me."

"I can't leave Cal. He may leave me, but I can't leave Cal. I just can't."

"He's not going anywhere."

"—But if he wakes up—."

"He's really bad," Arletta says softly. "You'll have a lot of days to be here. You need to think of yourself, too. What if he comes out with terrible headaches, or loses a leg——." She stops abruptly. "Oh, I've said too much." She reaches for my hand. "You've got to be strong for Anne, too. She idolizes him."

"How well I know! She always defends her Dad." I've slowly let go of my anger, but sometimes it lingers beneath the surface.

"Well, she's unsure of her future. She needs the anchor of both parents."

I remind Arletta, "I stayed married for better, for worse, for a long time. I guess I must be here for him—at least until he's stable and functioning." I push away any doubts.

She leaves as the Pastor walks in. I start to cry. He embraces me.

"I've been so angry with Cal, but I never expected this."

The Pastor hands me a tissue. "The prince of darkness is a gentleman," he says with a wry smile. "That's Shakespeare—from King Lear. It's too bad that Shakespeare and The Bible are *politically incorrect* because many students and others would have some help when the unexpected happens."

"I want to believe in God," I blow my nose, "but He seems so far away."

"Well, then, his helpers are nearby. We were there when Cal left you. There's a verse, God puts those who are alone into families. Whatever is ahead, you know that your church family is here to help in anyway we can."

His presence calms me and his prayer means even more. *"Oh, Holy and Eternal God, we come to you broken and sorrowing. Calm our fears and give us strength for the days ahead, through your Son, Jesus Christ our Lord.. Amen."*

I murmur *Amen,* too. He leaves with a promise to return and see Cal later. I slip back into the visitor's chair—a green plastic one—next to Cal's bed and begin my vigil. I hold his free hand, close my eyes only to rouse long enough to see a nurse monitor his machines. Cal and I are again together in a bedroom—even if it's a hospital room—after many months. Is this an omen?

He sleeps and I doze.

In late afternoon, Cal rouses enough to realize that I am there. "Tara," he mumbles through swollen lips.

"I'm here." I lean over to kiss him lightly on his right cheek, a spot not covered by bandages.

"Don't leave me," he whispers with effort.

"I'll stay as long as you need me." The words slip out before I realize I've made a new commitment. When my right hand tires, I slip the left one in its place, although it is more awkward. My back begins to hurt. Finally, Friday night comes. I return home, drained and ready for a long night's sleep in my own bed. I've been gone for over twenty-four hours since I left the house for choir practice last night.

I think, *Cal, we both hurt together. Can we bind up each other's wounds?*

The phone rings as I enter the house. It is Gunnar.

"Where've you been?" Gunnar snaps. "I waited all afternoon at the studio."

I realize it is Friday. "My husband was attacked last night—I'll tell you about it later. I stayed at the hospital all night and just came home. I forgot about this afternoon."

"It's too bad he's hurt, but what about the painting?" His voice is sarcastic. "Your husband will get well, but my picture is on hold until you come back. That delays me! The art department is scheduled for an exhibition at *Stefano's* after the holidays. I want your portrait to hang there."

"Surely, you've painted my face by now. Get another model to wear the dress—."

"You know nothing about portrait painting or your commitment to me!"

Commitment? I stifle a laugh. What does Gunnar mean by commitment? An open marriage with an affair whenever the mood strikes him? What about his wife? How often does he think of her? Suddenly, I see him clearly. I have had a great longing to be loved, but it's a serious mistake to believe that he cares for me. In many ways, he's like Cal—only devoted to his art in the same the way that Cal is devoted to the Mirron/Molten corporation. Gunnar is also wrapped up in himself. It makes me angry. Why do men think their work is so important and that women should so easily accommodate them?

I snap back, "My husband's recovery may take a long time! I won't be there anymore, so find someone else!" I hang up, before he can slam down his phone. I feel relieved and free.

I call Nana in Mexico. When she flies in, she'll expect to stay with me. I brace myself for a long December with meeting Nana's many demands. She likes to look young. I must admit it works for her. When I'm with her, I always feel tired and middle-aged. And I never want to look in a mirror.

"Hello—this is Tara," I say, a little too loudly to bridge the many miles. "I'm calling with bad news. Cal was injured last night in a parking lot. A couple of thieves jumped him and stole his car. He's in Community Hospital—."

Nana answers, "He should have parked in a lighted area. I always park under lights. I hope he's not too serious."

"As a matter of fact, he was badly beaten—"

"—But he will live?"

"I think so." I wait, but Nana says nothing. "When you come, I want you to stay with me—." That's a lie, but where would she go? I'll drive her everywhere like Wendell does because she expects to be served.

"Tara, that's sweet of you, but I can't get away just now. I need a couple of tucks under my chin. Even though my plastic surgeon was booked solid in December, he slipped me in next Wednesday—," Nana's voice rises with excitement. "—you know, a new woman for the holidays!"

"But Cal is hospitalized—."

"I just saw him at Thanksgiving. I really can't do anything for him right now. I'm sure that he'll get the best of care. You'll see to that. You always manage everything so well." She pauses. "I'll come after the holidays when he's up and around, so give him my best. Oh yes, will you buy a poinsettia for me? Be sure to put *'Love, Mummy'* on the card. Bye." She hangs up.

I recall Nana's words—that I don't sparkle. During the holidays, she will sparkle with her taut skin, plastic implants and dangling earrings. I wonder—what will my holiday bring?

I wait until late Saturday morning to return to the hospital. All is quiet as I enter Cal's room. He's still heavily sedated. His eyes are closed and he lies there immobile. I pull up a chair and kiss his hand. I lay my cheek against it again to signal that I'm here.

His blue-black lips are swollen and a bruise has spread beneath his visible eye. He mumbles, "Tara?"

I lean close to his face, "Yes. Don't try to talk. I'll stay with you."

Cal, silent, tugs at my hand with a weak effort. My vigil begins again. As I sit here, I realize that in a matter of minutes two thugs—strangers—completely changed my world. I am uncertain about the holidays. What will they bring? Christmas Day in this hospital? If Cal returns to our house, will I make daily trips with him to a rehab center? I've been so free to attend classes, but Cal's needs may change that. What is ahead for me? Silently, I pledge to myself that I will make my decisions without pressure from anyone else.

After lunch break, I stop in the hospital gift shop and buy a red poinsettia and write,"Love, Mummy" as Nana instructed. As I turn a corner, I see Diedre stride into Cal's room, holding a huge orchid with cascading white blossoms. She wears a dazzling smile on her scarlet lips. She's tall and slim with stiletto boots and a designer knit poncho. I follow behind her. She abruptly stops when she sees Cal, so bruised and bandaged, sleeping.

"Oh! Is this the right room? Cal?" She looks around, unsure about the strange figure, silent and connected to tubes.

"Yes, this is really Cal," I answer as she turns around and stares at me.

Unnerved, she runs her hushed words together like a mouse in a closet. "Oh. I'm Diedre. I'm—I'm one of his—co-workers. We work together on the same team at Mirron —I mean, Colton. We were all shocked to read about his accident." She holds out the orchid. "I wanted to bring this in person."

She stands away from the bed as if Cal's ugliness might reach out and grab her. She's young, unacquainted with pain. She doesn't realize that a long vigil is a weary task and a longer recovery will be even more demanding.

I feel strong. "I'm sure he'll enjoy the orchid. When he wakes, I'll show it to him." I set Nana's poinsettia beside the plant. In the dim light, Diedre doesn't recognize me from the Christmas party a year ago. My hair is no longer gray, but a warm brown, with bangs and a longer cut that flips up around my ears. Arletta says that I should keep it this way.

Cal still has his eyes closed. Diedre studies him. "I want his bed raised so he can talk to me," she snaps, as if she's an executive directing the janitor to empty a wastebasket.

I protest, "I can't tell the nurse to do anything."

"You brought the poinsettia. Aren't you a hospital volunteer?" Diedre asks.

"I'm Tara, his wife."

"Oh."

She doesn't expect me to be here. She's not sure what to say. What did Cal tell her about me? Did she hope that I was a slow-witted nag, hard as nails?

I hold his hand again—a possessive move which is my prerogative as a wife. Softly, I give her the whole dismal picture. "The doctor's worried about Cal's cracked rib and the possibility of pneumonia. When Cal's released, he may have several months of rehab. His left leg is broken in two places. He may need to use a cane. Fortunately, his right hand was spared. It's unclear when he can return to work."

Diedre looks at Cal, so discolored and so quiet. Perhaps she wonders—when the bandages are gone—if Cal will look like the same hard-driving executive with the sharp ties and salon hair that she once knew. I know when he recovers, he will have aged. He'll be more gray, balding, with worry lines across his broad forehead. Possibly with a limp. Or recurring headaches. His life won't be the same. Nor hers. Nor mine.

Like Cal, Diedre's in shock, too. Cal's body can't be fixed with an executive order, a fresh invoice, a balance sheet. His future can't be programmed like a big advertising campaign with clear and specific goals. He's a human being—no more—no less—with a frail mortal body. This is different scenario from her business world where she has some control. His accident isn't in her long-range plans. She's still young and smart. She can't comprehend what abrupt changes life may bring in the blink of an eye, but she'll learn.

"He's been my mentor at work," She tries to explain, "We work very closely—"

I step aside. "—Would you like to speak to him?"

Cautiously, Diedre moves closer. "Cal—it's Diedre," she says in a whispery voice.

His eyes stay closed, but his right hand rises off the sheet in a brief wave—his only acknowledgment. He tries to speak. "Tara—where—are—you?"

Diedre steps back, as I sit down and hold Cal's hand again. "I'm here." I know she wants out of here. I lean closer and purposely murmur again, "I'm right here, dear."

"I'll call to find out how he is," Diedre says. She wants to put this shock, the dark room, and the injured figure behind her. She leaves—maybe for The Coffee Place and a latté with friends.

I'm still here.

Anne comes home from Evanston. She's through with finals. She's not unlike Diedre when she sees her Dad. There's disbelief that his injuries can be so severe. He's even worse than she expected. She finishes a box of tissues before she can compose herself. She holds Cal's hand as he wakens.

"Anne—." Cal mumbles.

"Don't talk, Dad. I'm here with you."

I watch them—so much alike. Cal has always been confident and sharp. Anne has that same air of sophistication. Will I have my family with me for Christmas Eve after all? A week ago I thought that was an impossibility. I don't want to dwell on this situation, but even in dark circumstances God may work in some inscrutable way.

It is Christmas Eve. Cal remains in the hospital, but Anne and I attend the midnight service. Blue banners decorate the nave. Tiny lights are strung in flowing curves between the wall sconces, also marked with brass French horns. In the chancel, a Nativity scene with manger and straw is below the vigil light. The altar is banked with white poinsettias, wrapped in gold. All is special and festive. The bell ringers accompany the choir as we process singing, "Enter His gates with praise—." I bow my head. I am in a sacred place. I see Anne seated alone in a side pew. She is hunched forward, head bowed, as if in deep prayer. The worshipers are also in a seasonal mood, as they join with the great organ in familiar hymns. When the choir sings, I solo my anthem line with calm joy.

I also offer a silent prayer of thanksgiving. My cup overflows tonight with my daughter home and my marriage still intact—well, maybe.

The pastor's sermon is titled *"Keeping Watch—."* He says simply that Christmas always brings hope. As Christians, we must follow Jesus' example during our life—our *Keeping Watch*—on earth. The congregation moves slowly forward for the precious sacred meal. Anne edges herself into the choir line, so we can kneel at the altar together. Worship ends with the church darkened as we light our candles and sing *"Stille Nacht, Helige Nacht"* in both German and English.

When we arrive home, I realize that Anne has been crying. We sit in silence by the fireplace, drinking hot cider.

Carefully, I comment, "It was a lovely service tonight. Very moving."

"I didn't expect to cry, but I did," Anne says, somewhat defensively. "It isn't right that Dad isn't here."

"You're tired from finals and the shock of the accident. Also, you didn't expect to find your Dad so injured—."

"—But alive! I'm so grateful—utterly grateful to see him alive!" Anne bursts into tears again. "But it's more than that, Mom." She stares into the fire. "What will I do with MY life? I'm such a failure—" She sounds like some coeds I met in September.

"—At twenty-two? Don't ever say that! Your life's just beginning—"

"I said I wanted to be a doctor or nurse, but I can't stand the sight of blood. Then I thought maybe embassy work. It sounded exciting, but who knows where I might be stuck? Some distant post in the south Pacific? Then I was sure I wanted to be like Dad, in business. Fly all over the world on company jets. I took one business course, and hated it."

160

I want to comfort her. She's too old to hold in my lap, and stroke her hair. However, I know what she says is true. What will she do with her life? I reassure her. "You'll find something."

"I want to make a SIGNIFICANT difference. After graduation, Eileen will organize women and children who work in Taiwan's sweatshops. Rachel has a grant to study the mating habits of some Amazon insects. What will I do? No one cares about my future."

"I do!" I reassure her.

Anne wants to believe she is a person of worth. In this age of celebrity, the false face with a doubtful talent—carefully groomed by hucksters—has replaced any authentic voice. Once the united family sustained a young person with a father and mother who, together, spoke respected truth as they were taught. That old assurance is gone—perhaps for Anne, too. Deep down, she's spiritually hungry for a reality she can trust. For me, it is God. I hope it will be for her, too.

She gives a wry smile. "Naturally, you're my Mom and you care, but I don't even know where I want to live. Minneapolis? San Francisco? Salamanca?"

I try for a light touch. "Make it someplace warm." I threaten, "I'll visit you during snowy January,"

"That's easy for you to say. You fit in anywhere." Anne sipped her cider.

I don't argue, but years ago I felt like an extra piece of luggage. "I know Dad's moves were hard on you. Your friendships ended too quickly." I think about her and about me. "Friendships take time and effort. They were difficult when we moved so often." I don't add, that maybe that's why Diedre became important to Cal. They worked together every day—spent time, effort and had a lot of contact with each other. What's that called?

Emotional adultery. During the week, Cal and I spent only a few hours together in the evening when we both were tired. Sometimes, he made other business calls at night. Why didn't we realize this?

Anne's voice is sad. "I was always the new girl in the class. We lived in houses, but did we ever really have a home—a place where we belonged?"

I tried to make a home for them. I fall silent with the memories—Hartford, Lexington, Chatham, Seattle, Hartford. Again. Even eighteen months in Golden. "I liked the Denver area even if it was for a brief time."

"I remember Algoma, Wisconsin. I was in second grade and played the Witch in Snow White. You made me a wonderful costume with a wig of stringy hair and a black peaked hat." Her voice drifts off.

"Algoma wasn't much fun with your Dad going back and forth to Milwaukee twice a month." I sighed. "Twelve moves in eighteen years. I remember when we lived back in Massachusetts, I drove you to a camp in Maine. You stayed a month so I could pack for our move from Lexington to—to where did we go next? You brought home that poster of the staff, signed with all the scrawled names—."

"—Taylor, Cass, Shirley, Dave, Hank and a dozen others—in heavy black script. What a summer that was. All the girls had such a crush on Hank—or was it Dave? That camp poster's packed away somewhere." She adds, softly, "I hated that camp—bugs and all."

I think of all the basement boxes, still sealed, filled with memories of so many different places. My New Year's resolution will be the same one—to sort through old clippings and pictures, the report cards and starred homework. Why did I hang on to all of it? I wanted to hang on to our life together. Maybe Anne will understand someday.

"You didn't object too much about moving to Colorado because you hoped to ski every weekend." I want her to recall the excitement that came with each move.

"—And the first time I tried skiing, I broke my leg." Anne falls silent with the memories. "How did you manage it all?"

"I did it to keep us together. I really tried." How was it possible? I smile. "I always found a congregation ready to welcome us and give me strength."

"Will I ever get married," Anne begins, "and move all over the country like you?" She gives a wry smile, "Although I'm not very good with recent boyfriends—one enlists in the Marines and found another girl. The other gets engaged to my roommate. So much for MY successful relationships."

Anne's more thoughtful than before. Maybe Cal's accident has caused her to rethink her priorities. I want to sound convincing. "You just haven't met the right guy."

"Remember Travis? You never liked him. Why?"

"Well—," I hesitate. Travis had pit-bull eyes and a selfish demanding manner. Anne needed to be very strong, and wary of possible future abuse. "—I didn't know him that well. We never really talked much." I remember Clyde Thorson's query. "I spent Thanksgiving afternoon with the Pastor and Regina. A group from Trinity will go to Guatemala in the spring on an educational and medical mission. Clyde Thorson wondered if you were available as an interpreter."

"Really?" Anne brightens. "—For how long?"

"—A week, plus a couple of traveling days."

"That's a possibility, especially if it matches spring break." Anne asks, "Are you going?"

"I'm unsure". Divorce court still hangs over me like a Damocles sword. "—It depends on—on things—." Why am I hesitant? I know why. I'm concerned about Cal. Old habits die hard. I ought to be here to encourage his recovery, but maybe Diedre will take care of that. Of course, if Anne asks me to go on the mission trip with her, I'll go. She won't.

"—Will you bring Dad home when he gets out of the hospital?"

"No. He'll go to a rehab center. There's a fine one close to the hospital. Otherwise, he would need someone to drive him to therapy." I turn away. "I don't take care of him any more. Certainly, you can understand that."

Anne ignores what I've said. "—Mom, you've always been here for us. It's so good to be home. Dad will want to come back—I know that for sure!"

"I doubt it. He's moved on with his life, too." I think of Gunnar. Even if my tie with him is gone, will there be someone else in my future? "There might be other people—."

Anne doesn't want to hear me. "If the three of us are together on a mission trip, it will seem like old times"

I want to tell Anne that nothing ever again will be like old times. Love does take time and effort. I don't have enough of either one left for Cal again.

Anne has another idea. "If I could, I would take care of Dad. It would give my life some meaning for awhile," she sighs, "but it's back to school if I want to graduate.."

I change the subject. Slowly, I suggest, "If you really want to do something with your life, pray about it. Prayer isn't to find an answer, because you have free will. It's to assure yourself that you are not alone. God cares, too."

Anne gives me a crooked little grin. "You can say that," she shrugs. "Oh well, I might try. I sure can't figure out anything by myself."

"—Just be careful what you pray for." I know from experience. I wanted Cal back, but I didn't expect him with a broken body.

I turn out the lights and we climb the stairs. It is early Christmas morning. Through the darkened windows, the stars seem very bright. I remember the beautiful chant at the midnight service—.

My soul magnifies the Lord,
And my spirit rejoices in God, my Savior.
Quickly, I fall asleep.

It's Christmas day. After the midnight services, Anne and I intended to sleep late. A few hours pass and I hear the phone ring. I jump up, afraid that it's a nurse—Cal's condition has changed—we should get to the hospital immediately. The frantic thoughts stop when I hear Arletta's voice.

"Merry Christmas!"

I stare at the lighted clock. It's after six and still dark. "Merry Christmas to you, too." I yawn.

"I have some wonderful news—Sharlene and Jared are having a BABY!"

"Now?" It's a dumb question, asked in my half-awake haze.

"No—sleepy head—in late June. They told us last night. It's our Christmas present."

"Congratulations, Grandmama!" I yawn again and stretch.

"I'm making plans already. I told Boyce we'll give a huge block party on the Fourth of July with fireworks and a Texas-style barbeque so everyone can meet Tummikins. Isn't that the cutest name during pregnancy—?"

"It's certainly—ah—unique." Memories wash over me. *Moonbeam* was the name Cal and I gave our unborn child. On a summer nights, we sat on a park bench. Cal talked about his new challenges and I clasped my growing girth with maternal pride. We watched boys on the monkey bars and girls swinging higher and higher. Who would Moonbeam be? It didn't matter. Already, we loved Moonbeam with deep unconditional love.

Arletta rushes on, "—It means lots of changes for everyone—."

Maybe I should apply for Sharlene's job and help Boyce temporarily. "If Boyce needs help—."

"That's the beautiful part," Arletta says. "Sharlene has a little morning sickness, so I'll fill in for her until she feels better. Then when the baby comes, she can drop little Tummikins off with me in the morning and pick Tummikins up after work."

"—How convenient—." Expecially for Sharlene during the next eighteen years until the kid goes off to college. At last Arletta has a fulfilling project. "—Is Boyce ready to pass out cigars?"

Arletta hesitates. "Actually, Boyce is a little miffed. Jared wants to take his paternity leave with Sharlene while she's on maternity leave. They say it's important to bond as a family. Boyce growls about their plans. June and July are such busy months. I assure him that we'll work everything out."

"I know you will." Do I feel a pang of jealousy because Arletta won't have time for me? Whenever we walked into our house, she always straightened any picture slightly askew. She helped me find my keys. She called me on lonely midnights and told me to turn off the TV and go to sleep. She supported me during the worst year of my life. I will miss her gentle support.

"It's such a joy to see Sharlene and Jared make plans. Sharlene will diaper and feed the baby on Monday, Wednesday, and Friday. Jared will do the same on Tuesday, Thursday and Saturday." Arletta likes to have things organized.

"What about Sunday?" I ask.

"They'll take turns. Of course, some weekends Tummikins will stay with us while Sharlene and Jared go away to keep their marriage alive"

"Is it in trouble?"

"Oh, no! But they'll need to relax from all the responsibility of a new baby. They must try to bond like other young couples."

Bond? Cal and I bonded the moment we married. Nothing could separate us. We were raised by Depression parents who taught us to accept responsibility because we would live and work in an adult world. We "put away childish things" when we married.

166

Arletta hesitates. "There is one other thing. I may take signing lessons this spring. That's the new way of communicating with babies." She sighs, "I won't have much time for lunching out. I hope you understand—."

"I do I do!" I remember that Arletta told me life goes on, and it does.

"We're such good friends, I wanted you to be the first to know. 'Bye."

I must brace myself for monthly ultrasounds of Tummikins' fetus sloshing around and Sharlene, in profile, with a bulging belly. In July, we'll traipse into the media room for a bizarre video of Tummikins' birth, surrounded by chattering families and the Missoula cousin twanging away on her guitar.

How can I skip the big blowout? I'll go feed penguins in Antarctica. No, I won't. Instead, I'll cut watermelon slices and pour lemonade and skip the video. I'll celebrate Arletta's first grandchild with everyone and stifle a pang of envy. With a grandchild, Arletta has a future. Will I be like Ingrid and Clyde Thorson without a grandchild? Even if Anne marries, will she remain childless? I wonder. A career seems more important than a family for many young people—a computer better than a kid.

I long for simpler days when storks delivered babies.

I fix ham and cheese crepes and a fruit cup for a brunch by our Christmas tree. Anne gives me gifts that she's saved from last summer's Spanish travel—a large pottery bowl from Toledo and a gold cross, heavily etched. I give her my presents and her eyes widen with my generous check. She gives me a quick kiss on my cheek.

We muse about other Christmas celebrations when she was a child. One was spent on the big island of Hawaii. She jumped the surf on Black Sand beach and I watched green turtles waddle across the sand while Cal golfed—another world gone forever.

Anne gives a secretive grin. "I did pray last night as you suggested."

"That's good. I hope it helped calm your spirit."

She pauses. "It did more than that. It gave me hope, but I won't tell you what my prayer was about." There's a triumphant tone in her voice as if her prayer will be answered, according to her wishes.

I know her too well. She prayed that Cal and I reunite so that the three of us can be a family together again. Even that is too much of a miracle for Jesus to manage, but I'm silent. I won't spoil her Christmas day with the cold hard fact—our marriage is over.

Time slips away. Anne and I hurry off to serve Christmas dinner to the homeless at St. Jude's community meal, an ecumenical effort. The long tables are decorated with plastic fir boughs, red satin bows and white plastic angels. From a sound system, carols float through the room.

Anne serves pumpkin pie with a warm smile and "Merry Christmas." I push along an expectant mother's tray while she holds a wiggly child on her hip. Her three older children are close behind her and manage their trays from experience. People keep coming—two Latinos in clean jeans and navy sweatshirts, a man in a bright yellow plush coat, a wrinkled old woman clutching a bulky plastic bag. I offer to hold her bag while she gets her tray. Instead, she clutches it closer to her breast and angrily glares at me.

I ask, "May I hold your tray while we go through the line?"

She hesitates, then nods. We follow along as servers load her plate with turkey and all the trimmings. She holds up two fingers for bread and two slices are added to her tray.I start down a row of tables, but she stops and points to an end chair. She doesn't want to sit near people. She eats quickly as other helpers bring more diners to fill up her table. She doesn't look up, but wolfs down the food and wordlessly leaves as quickly as she came.

I wish she would talk to me. What brought her to this situation in her old age? Does she have a family somewhere? Was there an unresolved quarrel years ago that was never healed? Somehow, my marital problems with Cal, my tensions with Anne, even my flirtation with Gunnar seem very shallow and stupid compared to the real loneliness and poverty of the homeless. There is no answer as to why I am spared and that homeless woman suffers.

By twilight, we leave for the hospital. Anne's in a happy mood. She says, "Let's fix Dad a chocolate sundae."

"It'll melt by the time we get there."

Anne insists, "—Not if we keep it in the little ice chest with the cold packs."

Anne is like Cal—ready to execute a plan in spite of obstacles. I'm amused as she assembles everything. She drives a little too fast, but traffic is light. We enter the hospital and wait for the elevator which always seems too slow. As the door opens, Anne rushes in, and almost bumps the tall young brunette woman who hurries out. Diedre sees me and looks away. I join Anne and the door closes behind us. At least she's gone, and we three can celebrate together.

When we enter Cal's room, I notice a tall glass vase with a dozen red roses. While Anne awkwardly hugs Cal, I glance at the card, *As ever, Diedre.*

Cal smiles, "Oh, those are from my office staff."

I shrug because Diedre isn't a concern of mine. She is his problem. A smaller bandage covers his head and the bruise on his face has receded. He, also, is in a good mood.

"I thought you'd never come," Cal says, and holds out his right hand to me. I lift his hand to my lips.

"I wanted to buy you a round of golf at Boca Raton, but I brought you this instead." Anne, laughing, opens the chest and holds out the sundae.

"Oh, this is the greatest. I'm so hungry for chocolate," he adds, looking at me." Maybe we can have a Christmas dinner together on Valentine's Day?"

I say nothing, but tuck a napkin under his chin. I want to match their banter, but Diedre's visit has momentarily left me uneasy. I'm wary of Cal's sincerity. Then I think of the old bag lady at St. Jude's. If I'm unforgiving, will I be like her when I'm old and wrinkled?

"We can talk about that later, if you ever get out of here."

Anne is confident. "We'll celebrate! We'll have turkey in the dining room. I'll set the table myself with crystal and china. We'll do it up right! Won't we, Mom?"

I murmur, "—Whatever you want."

She flashes me that expensive smile, "You're the greatest!" with a thumbs up. "Isn't she, Dad?"

He nods and grunts through his painful mouth, swallowing ice cream. I hope he means "Yes".

In January, Anne goes back to the university. I pick up the mail at Cal's apartment. Everything is dull and dusty. I can tell right away that his cleaning lady is sloppy. His old brown recliner sits here, covered with a gray film. I've always hated that ugly chair—the bulkiness and dark chocolate color. Cal insisted on buying it for the den. When he took it last spring, I was relieved. Soon, Cal can sit here again in his pain and let a day worker take care of him. I will be freed from daily visits to the hospital. On the surface, nothing has changed except for Cal's injured body.

I enter Cal's room and he's sitting up, looking better than he has for many days.

"The doctor thinks I can get out of here at the end of the week."

"—Really? That's great."

"I'll start therapy several days a week."

"I'm sure that can be arranged by the staff."

Silence.

"I have to go somewhere—either to a rehab center, or my apartment, or—or home."

I didn't want to hear that last possibility. "True."

Cal takes a deep breath. "May I come home? Tara, please can't I come home?" His anguish is genuine. "I don't want to go to a rehab place with all the other patients. If I go, I'll never get out of there. I know I won't."

"Well, I don't know—I must have time to think—." Which is a lie. From the night when I knew he would live, I've wondered whether he would come home. Why do I hesitate? Anger? No I've let go of that. Pride? Possibly.

"I'll make it up to you." He waits for me to answer, but I'm mute. "—Just until I can get on my feet again. You won't have to drive me to rehab. I'll get a taxi—." He grabs my hand, holding tightly as if it were a life-preserver.

"Oh, it's not the driving—it's the arrangements with your bedroom upstairs. How will you manage that? Do you want a hospital bed delivered to the den?"

"No! I'll have my brown lounge chair brought back home—." He searches my face for an answer. "I can sleep there. I've drifted off in that chair lots of nights in the apartment."

I stifle a smile. I thought I was rid of that horrid chair, and now it will be back in front of the TV again.

I hunt for any excuse. "It's all the meals. I—I don't cook much anymore."

"I'll hire a cook."

"No! I don't want another woman in my kitchen. Two people in there—it won't work."

"I'll get Della's catering service to deliver meals—enough for both of us."

"Della sold out to two young men. It's not the same quality as she had." I shake my head. "No, Della's is out of the question."

Silence.

Cal looks at me with pleading eyes. "Please, Tara. I won't cause trouble. I swear I won't. I can get up at night as long as I have my walker nearby. You can still go places with Arletta. I won't ask for anything more. Just let me come home."

Slowly, I say "I guess it will work out—just for as long as you're in rehab."

Cal grabs my hand and holds it to his cheek. "Oh, Tara, you are the greatest!"

"That's what Anne says, too." I turn away so he can't see the tears in my eyes "I'll see you later." I leave.

As I drive home, I mentally plan our first meal—something simple like chicken crepes, sun-dried tomato and fresh thyme tatines. For dessert, coconut crème brulee. And yes, a stop at Annetje's for her hand-dipped chocolate strawberries—just for a welcome home. Nothing overdone, of course. Tomorrow, I'll run out to Fontanini's Italian Grocery for spiedini, alla Romana, and also some prosciutto. That should bring color back to Cal's cheeks. Not that I need to fuss, but he does need good food. That's what I'll tell Arletta if she chides me that I'm trying too hard to please him.

Wait! Arletta's right! I don't need to make that effort again. Cal's only home until he fully recovers. Instead, I stop in the deli for a rotisserie chicken and a strawberry-spinach salad. Then I hurry into Klopfer's for rocky road ice cream.

That's enough.

Cal comes home, a year after his quick exit last January. Our den has replaced his hospital room. His walker leans against a small table. He sprawls in his recliner like a piece of crimped paper—legs propped up by a pillow and braced by the extension. He rests easily at a comfortable angle. I put the TV remote beside him, along with the daily paper and a soft drink.

"—All the comforts of home," I say in a pleasant voice, but without a smile.

He reaches for my hand, "It's good of you to do this."

I turn away. "I try to be good. I've never believed there was an advantage in being otherwise."

"The doctor thinks I can go back to work in maybe three weeks." He watches for my reaction. "—Well, maybe—at least—for a long morning."

"Let's take one day at a time." *I learned that from you, Cal. When you left, I lived from day-to-day. Now things are different. I'm not the old Tara. Honestly, I wish I could be. I'm not sure that I want to take care of you anymore, but I'll manage it for a few weeks. If home is the place you go when there's no place else to go, then you're home.*

Gradually, Cal takes over some responsibilities. He pays some bills on-line. As I file others away, I notice the phone bill. Lots of calls to Diedre. I argue with myself—why not? She's on his office team. Cal wants to keep informed about business, but frowns over a few quick changes at Colton. "It's not the old Mirron/Molten corporation," he says soberly with our afternoon coffee.

I pick up The Herald which he's dropped on the floor, pages askew. He hasn't changed, but I have. I want to be rid of his papers, the drapes, everything. Start anew.

During late January, the stores immerse us in red hearts and Valentines. I dismiss them because my days are filled with Cal's needs. By the time I help him into the car, drive to the therapy clinic and return, it's early afternoon. I give him a quick lunch. He naps for awhile, as I sometimes do. Then I fix a light supper and we watch Larry King, or a basketball game. I close the drapes and place a fresh water glass beside him, as well as a bell, if he needs me in the night. His cell phone is there also. Often he talks to Diedre after I go to bed. Sometimes they have long conversations. Last night, he was still on the phone when I turned off my light and dialed the classical music station. He can do what he wants to do because he can't hurt me any longer. I look forward to spring and the mission trip to Guatemala. I told Clyde Thorson that I'd go. Anne is still unsure.

Cal progresses to a cane. His accident has kept him away from work for almost two months and he's anxious to return. He circles Monday with a red marker and makes his plans. The limo will pick him up at seven-forty and take him into the city. He'll return during the evening rush hour. That works fine for me, because I have a Garden Club meeting that day. Boyce, who has a lawn service spring, summer and fall (snow removal in winter) will be guest speaker. Often, Arletta and I linger over dessert and coffee.

Today—Monday—is a raw day with a pounding gray rain, a melancholy morning to match my apprehensive mood. Snowdrifts slowly melt, leaving black gritty mounds. A few crocus and daffodils emerge beneath the evergreens under the picture window, a hopeful sign of a new season. I wish a bright sun blazed across the sky to welcome Cal back to work.

He is dressed in a gray suit with a silky sheen. I straighten his striped navy and gray tie and smooth his shoulders as in the old days. I move to kiss his cheek and then pull away. It is meaningless because he will soon move back to his apartment. He is anxious to return to his "old routine" as he told me last night.

Slowly, he climbs into the limo with difficulty. He stoops slightly as I push his cane across the seat. He grabs it, attaché case in his left hand. With a nod, he signals me a "Goodbye" and the limo pulls away. Maybe Diedre has organized his team to meet him at Colton's entrance. A picture in Sunday's Business section showed installation of the new **COLTON** signage in bold block letters on the old Mirron/Molten building. No doubt, the old logo has disappeared from every corporate door.

I straighten the den and fold up the newspaper that Cal carelessly left beside his recliner. I study Cal's ugly brown recliner. Soon, it will be gone again when Cal returns to his apartment. I will miss hearing his slow step-by-step climb to our old bedroom. Whatever he does, he will make his own decision. I like sleeping in the guestroom. It's become my space and that's MY decision. We will never be together again.

Nevertheless, I'm uneasy. It'll seem strange not to have Cal around—not to give him mid-morning coffee with his newspaper. He is better than houseplants—and more work. He makes noise—male noise. I like the sounds—his rich baritone voice as he sings in the shower—the way he slaps his right knee in amusement—even the heavy tap-tap of his cane on the kitchen floor. Someone is here with me. Maybe I should get a dog when he leaves. The house will seem so lonely, but a dog will be more work than a husband. No way—I would have to walk the dog. I prefer to play cribbage with Cal and win! That's much better! Those fireside games of cribbage will be over, too.

I sit on a hard straight chair at the Garden Club meeting. Some vague premonition stays with me while Boyce instructs everyone on reseeding damaged lawns. I half-listen, because Cal will—no, I'll—contract with Boyce to care for our yard this season. After Anne graduates and settles somewhere, I'll buy a condo and be finished with lawns and gutters and trimming bushes. Home ownership is overrated. Been there. Done that.

My mind wanders as I try to imagine Cal back in his office. Will people pat him on the back with words of welcome? Have there been any changes on his floor since Colton Industries moved in? What if his office has been relocated to a different place? Will he have the same team with Diedre, Clifford and the others? What if he really doesn't fit in with

175

a new management style? He was trained in old F.A. Mirron's philosophy of team cooperation and hard work.

That faint premonition tells me that I should hurry home. I open the front door to an eerie stillness. I head to the den and find Cal in his brown recliner—silent, immobile, staring into the gray afternoon. The room is almost dark, without lamplight.

"Cal?"

He stares at me with troubled eyes. "I'm fired. Just like that—fired!" His voice is choked, flat, sad.

"What happened?" I snap on a sofa lamp and see him slumped and defeated with an ashen face and puzzled eyes.

Bitterly, he turns away. "Everyone was so happy to see me return. They slapped me on the back in the elevator. Said things would get done now." He looks at the window. "Ten minutes after I sat down at my desk, Kendall from Human Services marched in, accompanied by a security guard. Kendall told me there's been a reorganization and Colton has eliminated my position. He gave me ten minutes to leave."

I'm stunned. "—Just like that?"

"—Just like that!" Cal repeats, snapping his thumb and forefinger. "Then Kendall goes through severance details. I was so numb I barely listened. Our future is in this!" Cal throws an oblong navy blue case, filled with papers, across the room. "The security guard cleaned out my desk as if I can't be trusted! A final insult!"

As I look at my broken husband, I know I must be very careful. Slowly, softly, I respond. "You were president of—of how many small firms? Each new position meant a move. And then you managed the whole southeastern division in Atlanta."

"I was the glue that held everything together!"

"—You built a very capable team. They can't get along without you."

Cal attempts a wry smile. "Colton will get along very well without me. It has a new strategy of reorganization and

176

confusing titles. At Mirron, we believed in teamwork. From the beginning, we built an *esprit de corps*–worked together. That's what old F.A. told us when he started Mirron——." His voice trails off as he remembers those early and exciting days. "Teamwork! Teamwork! Teamwork! It was like a litany every day."

Cal rambles on. "The proudest day of my life was the last time I saw F.A. when he was dying of pancreatic cancer. Franklin Archibald Mirron. Took my hand and said, 'Cal— you're the one I'm proudest of. No one believed what I saw in you, but I knew—I knew you would grow! I could throw any challenge at you and you'd make things right! Just keep at it, son, and you'll be on the Executive Committee yet.' That's what he told me! THE EXECUTIVE COMMITTEE—that elite group of UNTOUCHABLE ONES—the EXECUTIVES that provide LEADERSHIP and STRATEGY for the company." His voice growls with sarcasm, emphasizing certain words with heavy anger.

I want to remind him that the old man has been dead for eleven years—shortly after Mirron expanded and purchased Molten. Cal would never be named to the Executive Committee. I realized that a long time ago because Cal is a traditional nuts-and-bolts guy—like a good repair man. He fixes companies, but can never envision them. He's not a wheeler-dealer or the creative visionary that the Executive Committee wants or needs, but I will never tell Cal that. He would say that I don't understand, but I know the new word is *Innovation—think outside the box*. Or better yet—create the box. Come up with unusual products that fill a need. Invent. Re-create. Sell a million.

I applaud Cal's strengths. He should be satisfied with his reputation for analyzing difficult problems. I remember the high absenteeism at Algoma. He studied the situation and closed the plant for the first two weeks of hunting season. Machinery was repaired and the small factory put in order. His workers returned with glowing stories of deer they stalked. The women employees loved the head start on the holidays. Then absenteeism dropped to nothing.

That success led old F.A. to send Cal to Hartford where the company was being robbed blind because of sloppy management. The Board wanted to sell that company. Cal put in security checks and got rid of cubicles so office workers were in one big room with their computers. His own office was behind a glass wall. He was first to arrive in the morning and parked in the employees lot. Before long, things changed. Old F.A. beamed when production surpassed its goals the first year. Years later, he was sent back to Hartford to oversee construction of a fine new automated plant. That was when Anne had a crush on that Yale student. It was a big relief when the plant was finished and we went to Chatham. Or was it Denver?

Somehow, Cal wanted greater recognition. Now, he's too deep in memories and anger to listen to me. I never needed a husband on the Executive Committee because I loved Cal for his own earnest qualities of integrity and hard work, and his ability to make things right. And I guess I still love him—in a wistful way—even if our marriage is over.

Cal glares at me with steely eyes. "—And old F.A. insisted on excellence when Mirron took over Molten with its confusing matrix philosophy where every department overlapped some other area and paper was shuffled between cubicles. Quickly, F.A. made changes and cried, 'Teamwork!' He pounded the table so hard it jumped!" Cal growled, "Now, Diedre and the others are *Client Advocates*—whatever that means—off to San Francisco. She's a new *Cluster Coordinator*. The CEO's new title is *Proactive Director*—another UNTOUCHABLE! Things are done under the mantra, *Management by Objectives*—more buzz words!" He mumbles sarcastically, "It will never work—never work."

Did Diedre sleep her way to the top? That's no concern of mine now. For some reason, I'm relieved. San Francisco

178

is across the country. "You trained Diedre very well."

"—Too well. I think she's known about this for a long time. She played games with me," he adds bitterly. "Cliff saw me in the hallway and said, 'Too bad, old man, that you won't be with us in 'Frisco.' *Old*—he called me *old*." Cal shudders. "I took a taxi to my apartment and sat there a long time. I thought about everything. I gave my life to the Mirron company. I helped it grow and expand. Did the same for the Mirron/Molten corporation." Silence. "And this is what I get—termination! Out!"

He murmurs, almost in a trance, "I did everything anyone asked. Who took Hartford and turned that sloppy little operation into a smooth stable company? I did! Whom did they send when Denver went up in flames? Me! No one believed that business could be up and running in three months, but I got it done!" He covers his eyes, deep in memories. "And South Boston was in a terrible state—ready to be spun off, but old F.A. sent me! Two and a half years before we were out of the woods. It was such a relief to leave my office every night and make the long drive back to you and Anne in Lexington. But I handled South Boston for the old man because he inspired me. We lost a giant when he died." He adds, "My days are over, too. I might as well be dead."

I want to soothe his pain. "Anne was always so happy to see you. You called her your *Miss Moonbeam*." I remember Lexington too well and how moody our teen-age Anne could be. When Cal came home, she was all hugs and kisses to gain his permission if I had denied her new shoes or a chance to stay up late and watch TV.

"When Mirron/Molten expanded overseas, who was sent to bring back an objective review of facilities and personnel? I went!" His voice sinks, "If I died tomorrow, they'd send a spray of lilies. No one would stop long enough to come to my funeral. I thought I was important. Now, to Colton Industries, I'm nothing. They want new ways of thinking. *Innovation. Open-source software. Voice recognition systems*. And

179

they have the private equity capital to make it work. I don't understand anything anymore." He repeats, "I am NOTH-ING! I'm nothing!"

I see the anxiety in his eyes. He's not afraid of death—he's afraid of life, of a future that seems so meaningless. He worked hard for—counted on—a seat on the Executive Committee one day. Now, that's gone. We sit in silence. I take his hand and hold it to my cheek. If we were in bed, I'd hold him tightly and let him cry.

"Somehow, I think you ought to feel relieved—no more hours, pouring over those operation problems and endless papers. Dull. Dull. Dull! You never had time to think of anything else. Often, I wanted to slip something else in front of you—just to give you a fresh perspective. Maybe an old Trollope novel—so amusing. Or an Agatha Christie mystery, just for fun. I even thought of Jesus' Sermon on the Mount—to give you something really challenging and thought-provoking to read. There's so much wisdom in those few pages and I always find some amazing new insight. Your business degree may have trained you for a successful career, but it sure didn't teach you about living a full and complete life!"

Cal rubs his chin and stares at me as if I'm a stranger. "I never knew that you felt like this. Why didn't you tell me?"

"You never asked!" I turn away, afraid of a latent bitterness. "Maybe it was just as well. At least we were together—sort of—when Anne was growing up." I move toward the kitchen. "I'll fix a little supper for us."

"Wait! Will you call Nana and tell her? I can't—I just can't tell her that I've lost my job." He's close to tears. "She's always been so proud of me."

For a moment, I wonder if Cal's drive for success wasn't a lifetime effort to gain his mother's approval. She has always flitted in-and-out of his life like an impatient wedding photographer. She kept pictures of Cal at celebrity golf tourneys, but ignored the ones from our family birthdays. Did she ever tell him that she loved him for himself?

I won't call Nana and be that kind of a wife any longer. "No, you can call her after we eat. She will understand." He'll be lucky if she even listens to him. Instead, she'll tell him about her latest bridge triumph or how people think she's a young fifty. "Don't be afraid. This, too, will pass. Things will work out —they always do." I must be very careful. Cal's world has collapsed. Mine has suddenly become more solid.

I think about Jesus' promise, *Blessed are the poor in spirit, for they shall see God.* Cal is now very poor in spirit, but seeing God would be a miracle for him. Once in a Psychology 301 course I read a book by Viktor Frankl, the psychiatrist. I remember that he wrote, *"Man is not destroyed by suffering alone, but by suffering without meaning"*. That's Cal. He can't find meaning in anything. He needs hope.

Through the window, the late afternoon sun breaks through. I see a rainbow.

Cal is depressed, listless, moody. He feels he's nothing now. He moves through his days, doing as little as possible. Often, he phones an old associate, chats briefly and hangs up. If I'm around, he says, "No one wants to talk to me anymore. I'm too old, out of the loop."

One night Diedre calls from San Francisco. Afterward, Cal turns wearily to me, "I told her to get on with her life. I have nothing more to say to her."

I leave The Herald's employment section near his recliner, but he doesn't read the ads. Boyce and Arletta come once a week for bridge. Usually, Cal and Boyce win, because I'm such a terrible player. Arletta doesn't mind, but Cal thinks I let them win to keep up his spirits which makes him more irritable. He doesn't want my sympathy. He needs more than that. He needs a job.

I remind him, "You can think of your severance package as providing for early retirement—live on Siesta Key and fish every day." He can afford a nice condo. Would I say *Yes* if he wanted us to start a new life together? It depends on the location. Not San Rafael—too close to San Francisco.

"—And do nothing?" Cal almost shouts. "Do you want me to sit and vegetate? I'm in the prime of life, but no one—but no one—believes that! I'm too old!" He limps upstairs and slams the door. I won't suggest early retirement again.

He makes an appointment with a head hunter. He dresses in a navy suit fresh from the cleaners and I hand him a subdued maroon striped tie. He folds up his collapsible cane and hides it in his briefcase. I drive him to the agency and he limps slowly to the plate glass entry, trying to walk erect.

Two hours later Cal limps lopsided to the car and pounds the pavement hard with his cane. I can tell that he's not pleased. I don't ask about his interview. I know.

As I pull away from the curb, Cal says, "You're looking at a has-been."

"I don't believe it! You have too much experience."

"I'm past fifty. Any corporation can hire a half-dozen young MBA's for what I'm worth. They can work them as hard as possible, and limit their vacations." His shoulders slump. "Let's go home and have a sandwich. I don't have anything to celebrate."

Cal sleeps too late each morning, because he watches classic movies all night. About three a.m. I hear his television's muffled sound. I peek into the bedroom and see him asleep as the Titanic sinks again. It's a rerun of my own nights last spring. What goes around, comes around.

I want to tell him to pray about his future, but he'd reject that because he's too proud. He doesn't need God because he believes that he can take care of himself. He thinks he makes only rational decisions based on facts. Anything else is irrational to him. However, there's another world of emotion and intuition and the spirit that can transform things and bring new vigor and hope to life.

He won't believe me because Cal thinks he's a realist. However, I'm the real realist. I know that tea and water are two separate entities, but when heat—which can't be seen, but only felt—is applied, I have a delicious cup of tea. Cal needs someone or something to transform his despair into hope. I've grown tired of my role as his nursemaid. When we watch TV, we sit like two worn-out bookends with a shelf of old family albums between us.

When I'm in the guest room, I pray for Cal. *"O Lord, you promised not to turn away from a broken and a contrite heart. Perhaps Cal isn't contrite yet, but he is broken. Have mercy on him. In Jesus' name, Amen.*

I realize that my anger and bitterness are almost gone. I leave Cal in God's hands and fall asleep.

Anne comes home for the week-end. She's excited, because she's opted to go on the mission trip. She'll miss only two days of study, due to the university's spring vacation which happens the week after Easter. She doesn't change her decision when I say that I've joined the mission trip, too.

"That's great. I'm the prayer partner of Jeanette—she's a surgical nurse—so I'll room with her." She anticipates traveling again. "I may take an extra year at the university and get a degree in linguistics. What do you think?"

Cal answers, "That's a real switch—"

Anne shrugs, "I've done all this work in Spanish, so that should help."

"That sounds very sensible," I wish that I'd said something else because Anne gives me an odd look. She isn't crazy about anything sensible. She must have Nana's genes.

"Well, when you two leave, I'll go to Las Vegas and play the slots, Maybe make a buck. Earn a living." Cal says, in an attempt at grim humor. He hated conventions held there.

Anne studies him, "Dad—come to Guatemala with us!"

"Me? On a mission trip? The Pastor would double-up in laughter."

I quickly add, "No, he wouldn't. You'd be a real asset."

Cal reaches for his cane, "—With my bum leg on that mountain terrain? Anyway, what would I do? I'm not religious. I know nothing about medicine, and I sure can't teach Spanish."

"You can help the children with simple arithmetic. Two plus two are four, the same as numbers in any language," Anne argues. "You can hand out vitamins."

"—I don't know. It's a long time to sit in an airplane. What if I get headaches or stumble and break my other leg?"

"You'll have a whole medical team to help. Dr. Thorson and Dr. Pagel are both going, plus an occupational therapist and two nurses." Anne puts her arm around him. "Please, Dad—for me—." She looks at me. I nod. "—For us. Really, we haven't been together for ever so long." She waits. "We could dine together every night." His silence continues. "—At least think about it."

"Maybe." He adds, "I'll talk to your mother."

Anne kisses him good-night and goes upstairs. We mull over Anne's suggestion.

Finally, I ask, "What's your real hesitation?"

"I won't fit in. I've never gone to church. I—I was really embarrassed about that when the Pastor called on me in the hospital."

"—And I don't know why you won't attend church. People always are glad to see you."

Cal hesitates. "Would I fit in? I don't think I've ever been baptized. My parents were divorced. No one was around to take me to church. I spent weekends with my Dad and he worked on Sunday. He said the church always asked for money."

"It does some other things, too," I say softly. "Our congregation is just one of many that sent work teams to help Katrina victims. Our youth group painted rooms at a teen shelter. Some men roofed the home of an elderly couple. What about the continuing food pantry and the after-school tutoring program for inner city kids? For years, the women have made quilts—hundreds of them—for refugees around the world. The church does more than ask for money." If Cal came to church, he would have a whole network of friends interested in him and his future, but I won't argue with him now. "Your Dad's been dead for a very long time. His accusation was a big mistake!"

"My mother never had time for church because she wanted to shop, or have some fun on the weekend as she phrased it. When I did go, I didn't get anything out of it—."

"—But that's the most selfish reason of all! I don't go to church to get something! I go to worship—to acknowledge that God is my creator. When I'm there, I'm reminded to serve Him and to help others." Cal's remark irritates me. "We worship whether we understand or get anything from the service at all. Worship isn't mental gymnastics, it's —it's about a relationship." I turn away. Maybe I've said too much. "I need to constantly strengthen my relationship with God."

Cal narrows his eyes and looks directly at me, "You really do believe in God, don't you?"

For a moment, I'm silenced by his question. "Yes, I believe." I add, "I pray to God to help my unbelief—my limited understanding. That's from scripture. I can't help myself, because belief has always been there. I was baptized when I was a baby. I loved to hear Mama assure me that I was a child of God from the very beginning. The Bible says *In my mother's womb, You knit my bones.* Belief is a part of me. I can't live without it. Maybe that's too hard for you to understand."

Cal is silent. "You're so fortunate. I've never had that assurance." He pauses. "I don't understand things, like the words *sanctification* and *salvation*. Such strange words mean nothing to me."

"Those are theological—church—terms. Don't excuse yourself because you can't understand the language. Every discipline has its own language. Look at business with *options, futures, margins*. Or art with *impressionism, cubism, perspective*. Or any science —*kinetic energy, atoms, magnetic fields*. Look at computers. I don't understand how they work, but I still use a computer."

Cal holds up his hand. "Okay. I hit a sensitive button. That big Greek *Alpha* and *Omega*, the *I* and other symbols— they're all meaningless to me."

"Well—you use a language that I don't understand. You say *SPC* to someone on the phone and I haven't the foggiest notion of what you're talking about."

"That's *Statistical Process Control—*."

"—And *AFP, AIX, Z-slash-OS*. I don't know what you mean, but I trust you. But if it were necessary, I'd find out!"

"Okay—the church has a right to a theological language. I just don't know it."

"Humph! If you're interested you can learn!" I catch my breath. "It might take your mind off Colton Industries because—face it—your future isn't there!"

Cal stares at his feet. "Once a guy buttonholed me and asked, *Brother, are you saved*? How do I know?"

"You should answer *Yes!* because that's the Lord's work. *Salvation* means that we're saved from our own human self-centeredness—our selfishness in many decisions. The life of Jesus inspires and commands us to think of others and—in humility—acknowledge our own weaknesses. *Salvation* is now. It happens daily for the Christian."

"How can you believe in God when everything goes wrong?" He pauses, "Prove to me there's a God and I'll believe."

"I can't and I won't argue, because you can't prove there isn't a God." I narrow my eyes and stare at him. "Prove to me there's such a thing as gravity."

"What?"

"I said *gravity*. You can't see it, hear it, smell it, feel it, or taste it. Tell me gravity doesn't exist, and we'll stay inside tomorrow. Otherwise, we'll fall off into space."

"At least, if I can't see gravity, I can see what it does—keeping buildings anchored on earth. Gravity is real."

"God is also real. If I don't see a visible God, I see how His Spirit changes lives. Think of Mother Teresa, or Martin Luther King, or all the saints—and even the Pastor."

Cal doesn't respond. There is a cold silence between us. I want to change the strained atmosphere. "How about a rocky road sundae?" Chocolate heals a lot of things. *Cal, if you bring me luscious chocolate turtles, I might forgive you forever.* That's a daily struggle for me. I'm sure I'm full of forgiveness and then a little bitterness creeps in.

He nods, "Sure." When I head for the kitchen, he stops me. "Do you want me to go to Guatemala? After all that has happened, I don't want to be a continual burden—."

I'm afraid of my feelings. I think I've forgiven Cal and then my old anger returns. I hunt for another reason. "It would mean a great deal to Anne if we could all be together, even in a strange place. Who knows where she'll go after she graduates—." I don't add —or where we will be?

Cal searches my face for a double meaning, but I turn away from him. "Will you call Dr. Thorson and ask him if there's room for a broken-down, unemployed old man?"

"No, because I don't know a broken-down unemployed old man, but you can call him tomorrow and ask if there's room for another volunteer who wishes to assist in any way he can." I soften. "How about some ice cream?"

"I'm too old to do much, but I guess I can hand out vitamins."

I scoop out a dish of rocky road and sprinkle nuts on top. "I'm going to bed," I add. "Anne will be up early to drive back to the University. She has a class at eleven."

Cal signals, "Have her wake me before she goes. I'll turn out the lights."

I kiss the top of his head. He holds my hand for a brief moment. It's become our nightly routine.

"Good-night," I climb the stairs to the guest room. Later, he will painfully climb the stairs to our bedroom. Neither one will ask the other to share a bed. Pride is even a bigger hurdle than hurt.

With assurance from Dr. Thorson that he can join the mission group, Cal tackles the trip as if he were developing a new product. Suddenly, there are books on Guatemala, a large map spread on the dining table, and medical appointments marked in red on the calendar. We go together for shots. He checks our passports. The trip gives him a new and different focus that postpones any lingering depression over unemployment. He reads constantly and shares an odd assortment of facts—eighty percent of the population live in rural areas and sixty percent are below the poverty line. The Mayans are considered socially inferior to those of European descent. That stops me.

"How can that be when the Mayans gave the world chocolate? We would be lost without rocky road ice cream!" I laugh with Cal and then wonder, "What if we are viewed as more ugly Americans?"

"I always smiled when I met someone overseas and bowed my head ever so slightly as if my host were from an ancient family." Cal continues reading. "If we see Mayan ruins, we'll be impressed by their advanced culture in ancient times." He looks up. "The military took control of the country in 1962. There was a Mayan rebellion in 1975 that spread to Mexico. The competing groups signed a peace accord in

1995." Cal also says that a couple of political leaders have formed their own churches.

I frown, "That's not right for politicians to use a church to gain more power."

Cal gives a half-smile. "Charismatic politicians always promise a utopia and use any method to gain power—religion, guns or butter—for their own purposes. 'Dirty politics' exist everywhere."

"Let's hope the peace pact holds. Too many innocent people suffer in a revolution."

Cal's eyes light up. "Call the high school. Maybe we can hire a senior to tutor us in Spanish after school."

I remind him, "Anne will interpret for us."

"—But we'll have a head start. Words. Phrases. Basics."

I wrinkle my nose, "Gracias, senor. Find some Spanish tapes instead."

So Cal comes home from the library with a complete set—Basic Spanish in Twelve Easy Lessons. We mouth words at lunch and dinner with an unknown teacher murmuring Spanish from a recorder that sits between us. That distance doesn't seem as far as in the past. We may communicate better in basic Spanish than English. When we're in a mountain village Cal can easily ask *Where is the nearest bank?* as puzzled natives stifle their smiles.

I will comment on the weather. *Gracias dias.*

When the phone rings, I'm surprised to hear Gunnar's voice. "Tara? How've you been?" There's undertone in Gunnar's voice that is brittle and angry. Perhaps he hasn't forgiven me for the abrupt end of our Friday afternoons together.

"Fine. Fine." Cautiously, I say, "What's new?"

"I want you to know that I finished your picture. Stefano's Gallery in the city will open a new show this Friday night. It's featuring works by the University art department staff. Gibbons will display his sculptures. I'll have a few other pictures along with *The Queen.* I'd love to see you there." His pleasant resonant voice lures me.

"I'm so sorry," I lie, "but Cal and I have other plans for Friday night. Maybe I can see it before we leave. We're going to Guatemala in a few weeks."

"Really? So, you've chosen to be faithful?" There's mockery in his voice. I can almost see the sneer on his lips. "The show will be there for a month. Do see it before you leave. 'Bye." He hangs up before I can.

Arletta consents to go with me to Stefano's Gallery late on Monday morning. She doesn't know that I posed for Gunnar. How will I explain my face in his painting.? I hope that no one else will be there that early. Surely, Gunnar won't be around. As we push through the heavy plate glass doors, we see a huge textile on the opposite wall. It is of multi-colored yarn strung through sticks, similar to a piece in Anne's apartment. Orange and yellow sequins within a large circle shimmer in the upper-right hand corner.

Arletta reads the name plate. "It's called Midday. Costs twelve-hundred."

"I suppose it's the sun shining through the woods, or—"

"—Or the prof had a lot of leftover yarn and sequins and she needed to use the stuff!" quips Arletta.

We study other textiles on exhibit. None of Gunnar's paintings are there. I look for my portrait and wonder if we're in the wrong gallery. Several of Gibbons sculptures are on pedestals, so Arletta and I slowly circle each one, noting the rough surfaces—almost an unfinished look—of children in various poses.

Architectural drawings fill a long hallway that leads to another show room. As we enter, I gasp. A huge canvas, entitled *The Queen*, hangs on the rear wall. The picture combines a short squat Queen Victoria figure with the plumpness of a stuffed doll. Her Picasso-like woman's face has a nose that is long and slanted. One heavily black lined eye is tilted upward while the other eye is closed. The chin comes to a sharp arrow point. Tousled black hair with bangs surrounds the chalk white face. On top of her head is a tiny gold crown. Only the wine velvet dress from the drama department is painted with the original splendor. The shining pearls are rich and lustrous.

Slowly, Arletta asks, "What do you think?"

"It is—ah, unique! I think the artist hates women!"

She grins, "—Or the artist hates his model." She squints at the price tag. "He wants five thousand dollars for his picture. He'll never get it."

"It doesn't matter. He'll clean off the painting and save the canvas." I smile, "After all, a good canvas can be used again and again—not like a model. Here today—gone tomorrow." How well I know.

Arletta studies me closely, but I leave before she can ask a question. She follows.

We lunch at Eddie's Bistro. Arletta wants to know more about the mission trip. I answer with a new lightness of heart. Thinking of *The Queen*, I know my past with Gunnar is truly behind me. I look forward to Guatemala with Anne—and even with Cal.

Arletta warns, "You'll come home different. No one visits a Third World country without gaining a new perspective." She fidgets with her fork. "After that long week-end in Buenos Aires last year, I came home changed."

"Changed? You're still the same person I've always known—and a very good friend."

"No—inside I'm different. One night as we walked to our hotel from the Theatre Colon, I saw a family search a restaurant's garbage bags for a little food. I couldn't sleep that night. That's why I volunteer at the Food Bank every week—and chair the Hunger Drive at my church. I can't throw away a half-eaten roll. And I abhor all the wasted food at banquets. I've been changed by that one little experience," she mused. "The family looked so clean, but they were so hungry—right in the middle of that big city. I always remember them when I pray, *Give us this day, our daily bread.*" Silence. "You'll be changed, too," she repeats. "—But don't forget, you're very special as you are."

I doubt it, but I don't argue with Arletta. I'm done with lust for Gunnar and anger over Cal. Suddenly, I feel happy because I feel free from anger and lust—free at last.

Thank God I'm free!

Late that afternoon, Cal answers the phone. I can tell it's a head-hunter. I hear Cal's responses and the rising enthusiasm in his voice. He hangs up and turns around.

"Guess what? There's a small firm in Silicon Valley that's interested in me. I'm to send my resume and maybe there'll be an interview. I'll fly out to San Francisco—."

Immediately, I wonder, Will he see Diedre while he's there? Instead, I say, "How soon? We'll leave for Guatemala in another week."

"Oh, I can still go. Things won't move that fast. I may not hear anything until we get back."

"—Just what kind of position?"

Cal hesitates, "It's not exactly what I've done. It seems the firm wants to open a small plant outside of Beijing. It needs a contact person—someone who's handled production and knows international markets—." His voice trails off. "Of course, the salary might not be quite what I should expect—."

I must encourage him even though I wish the offer were elsewhere. "Well, you certainly can pursue it—at least, find out what it's about."

"It'll feel so good to be working again," Cal murmurs. "The accident, the recovery—doing nothing—has taken too long." He smiles—the first happy grin I've seen in a long time. "Early retirement is not for me" He flexes his right hand. "I need to work—I really need to work."

I know that he doesn't want early retirement any more. It's really not an option for him. However, I frown. "Do you

192

really want the long flights, negotiations, long contracts, late nights, files, appointments, breakfasts for civic betterment—all those IMPORTANT things in life." I struggle not to be too sarcastic. I remember the death of our baby son—the loneliness when Cal was somewhere else. Was it Beijing or Hong Kong? He was too far—just too far away. I jump up. "You never took even a week-end vacation without your cell phone and your laptop. Go back to your world of airports and hotel rooms—if you want it!"

Cal stares at me. "Your attitude stuns me. Why didn't you ever say anything?"

"We've already had this conversation." I leave the room quickly, because I hear the bitterness in my voice. Did we—do we—really know each other? I fix a salad and quiche for a light supper. We sit stiffly across the table like jerky wooden puppets.

Cal says, "I never knew you hated my job so much."

"I didn't hate it." I shrug, "I knew Mirron/Molten was YOUR life. I grew tired of it. I thought maybe you would, too. I made a life for Anne and myself." I add, "That's all in the past. Let's just get through Guatemala next week. Then you can fly west to San Francisco—find out if Silicon Valley wants you. I'm sure it will."

Oddly, I get a call from the Library. The timing couldn't be better. One circulation employee will go on a three-month maternity leave during the summer. Would I be interested in such a short-term position?

"I'm leaving for Guatemala next week. I'll be gone ten days."

The secretary's voice was crisp and pleasant. "Do get in touch when you return. We'll set up an interview then."

I turn to Cal. "It looks like we'll both return to work. I have a job, too."

Slowly, Cal asks the question, as if he's stepping on hot coals, "Do you really want to stay here?"

"I won't move again. My friends are here, my church, and now, work. You'll move west and get on with your life." Maybe rekindle an old relationship with Diedre, but I don't add that.

Cal frowns, "Does this mean a divorce?" He's said the hated word—the one I never wanted to hear.

"I suppose it does, but let's settle it after the trip." I add, "We can't tell Anne right now. Let her enjoy our days together."

Last January I never foresaw a conversation when our marriage would end so calmly—not even a scream or a whimper. I walk out, but as I glance back at Cal, he sits with arched fingers against his lips, deep in thought. Divorce? A new job? I tell myself I don't care what he's thinking.

When the missionary group assembles to leave, the Pastor is there for a brief farewell. Before he prays, he says, "You may change the lives of native people when you bring medicine, and school supplies, and help them build a native church. However, you will be changed, too, in the process. You will never be the same after you experience their faith, their devotion, and their simple way of life. May God go with you."

Arletta told me the same thing. I can't change. I'm too set in my middle-aged ways. I made my last adjustment when Cal walked out. We'll go to Guatemala for Anne's sake and when we're done, Cal and I will wish each other well and go our separate ways .

Cal sits behind me. When I turn around our eyes meet. No one or anything in faraway Guatemala can change our plans. I only pray for a safe trip for all of us with the hope that Anne can accept our divorce as inevitable.

Anne believes this Guatemala trip will reunite Cal and me. I search my soul once more and find that I like to make my own decisions without Cal—or even Anne's—approval.

I don't need Cal for a full life. I can manage my own quite nicely.

There is a nervous laughter and banter as we head for the airport. Each of us is limited to one personal suitcase. However, we bring another suitcase filled with vitamins, school supplies, children's tee-shirts and shorts, and yardage for sewing projects. Someone quips that we really should charter our own plane. Another shouts, "—Next time!"

That's impossible for us—Cal, Anne and me. After this trip, the family will split apart. There is no next time for us.

We are tired and disheveled after the night flight from Chicago and land in Guatemala City early in the morning like a mob of excited and tired school children. After Clyde pulls out a sheaf of documents, the bored customs officials rush us through. They've already seen too many groups like ours—ready to help the natives build a better life, and leaving a bit of Americana behind when we depart.

Pedro, our contact, directs us to a transport which looks like a gaily painted old school bus without shock absorbers or air-conditioning. Our luggage is heaped on top like odd building blocks. Someone whispers too loudly, "Will it fall off before we reach that town of Panajachel?" We climb aboard for the long ride. Cal sits near the front with his cane between him and Anne. I'm farther back squeezed between Jeanette and Clyde. In spite of a bumpy ride, many attempt to doze after the long night's travel. Beside me, Clyde snores.

At last we arrive at Casa de Esperanza, a retreat center— our home for the next week. The compound is surrounded by a high wall of bamboo and stucco. It is called a *house of peace,* constructed to make us feel safe. Instead, it makes me sad. Thieves are the same all over the world and we build higher walls in fear of them.

As we enter through wrought iron gates, Brother Bill, our beaming host, motions everyone to a large patio inside. Within, the tropical flowers and lush foliage brighten our spirits and a scent of tropical blossoms surrounds us. Eventually, our luggage is brought in, too, and nothing has been lost to everyone's relief. Quickly, we are assigned rooms.

Cal notices a large three story building next door. He pulls me aside. "That's a hotel. I can arrange for us to stay there and we'll join the group in the morning."

What he really means is that we can have separate rooms, but that will look like we don't wish to share the simple arrangements like the others. The hotel will have a dining room while at the Casa we'll eat at nearby restaurants. Maybe Cal doesn't trust the local cafés or maybe he wants separate bedrooms.

A dozen scenarios cross my mind. Finally, I shake my head. "We came as part of this group. It's embarrassing if we don't stay here. I think we should tough it out."

Cal looks pensive. "We'll have to share a room."

I want to snap that *We did that for twenty-seven years until you took off*! I take a deep breath, and offer a wry smile, "Well, we've done that before."

Cal's lower lips trembles, "Thank you" and turns away.

I see Anne pick up her large duffle bag and walk off with Jeanette. She doesn't turn to check on us. Everyone will be asleep within the hour. I wheel my suitcase to our room and Clyde follows with Cal's bag as Cal limps behind us.

Our corner room has two windows. Both open to view high walls—with palm trees beyond one. The other wall separates us from the hotel next door. The furnishings are simple—a dresser and twin beds. The space between our beds is as wide as the Grand Canyon, for pride still separates us. Even if we wanted to, I know that neither of us will make a move to bridge that chasm. It is too late for that. Automatically, I lift the spread to see if the sheets are fresh without any hidden bedbugs.

Cal is amused, "You've read too many travel books."

"I always check bedding. Is this place well-managed? We don't know."

"Just don't insult the natives," he snaps.

His remark puzzles me. I think he's so critical. Do I come across that way, too?

We nap, and then meet for dinner at six-thirty. We're all starved, but in high spirits. Anne looks very rested and pretty in her white cotton blouse and white slacks with a silver belt. She's borrowed my blue scarf to catch her pony tail. She holds Cal's left hand, in case he stumbles on the rough cobblestones.

I walk behind them, turning my head left and right to assure myself that I'm really in Guatemala. The town surprises me because I hear amplified gospel music coming from somewhere. I expected a quiet sleepy native town. Instead, we're assaulted by noise, garish graffiti, and a mix of colorful characters.

A hippie guy passes, weaving in his cowboy boots, and whispers loudly, "Ready to smoke? Weed, here." Across the street, a cement block church boasts a big sign, "Come inside and find Jesus", as Anne translates for us. A dark-haired Mayan girl stands at the entrance passing out brochures. I take one and will attempt to read a few words later.

Posters and scrawled signs give a variety of addresses. One advertises a Taoist healing center. Others list folk medicine clinics with Indian head massages and herbal healing rites. Many are for lessons in Spanish, the national language which the Mayans must learn. There are competing pictures of Jesus connected with an array of products.

Something about the colorful mixture of people, graffiti, and noise recalls our Woodstock days when Cal and I were college students. I watch the speeding tuk-tuks careening around corners to the delight of young Mayans, cell-phones dangling from their leather belts and jeans. Young people are the same everywhere with their lust for speed, noise, and excitement in a search for happiness.

Before we leave, we will eat at a tourist café near the famous Lake Atitlan, whose sapphire waters reflect three distant mountains—dormant volcanoes. Can they erupt at any time? However, tonight we're directed to a neighborhood open air restaurant with a red tile floor and multicolored tile tables. The chairs have rush seats and wooden lattice backs, much like a colonial design in the states. Our group pushes some tables together to make two large groups. We sing a table grace in harmony as other diners stare at us—crazy Americans who have invaded their space. A few applaud.

Anne and Cal sit across from Jeanette and me. The server brings our order—the daily special of beans, rice, and *bef-stick* with a side salad. Just as Anne lifts her fork, she stops and frowns at three men who cross the patio.

"I think I know one of them, but I can't remember where—"

I turn around and look at the guys, *gringos* from the States. Two are middle-aged and the tallest one is younger. He has light brown hair and a ruddy skin. Obviously, he's out in the sun and wind a lot. He walks to a far table with easy grace.

Anne's traveled so many places, it could be anywhere. I suggest, "—Maybe at the Institute in Cuernavaca?"

"Um-m-m, I don't think so."

She takes a few bites and smiles at the stranger across the room. Presently, he stands beside Anne. "I think I know you," he says in a deep resonant voice.

"I think the same thing," Anne nods. "Where did we meet?"

"Yale?"

"No. Maybe Northwestern—?"

"—Never went there. I'm Dave McKinney. Years ago, I was a counselor at various summer camps—Outward Bound, Smoky Mountains, Maine—."

"That's it! Maine! Camp Evergreen?" Anne says, laughing. "I'm Anne Irwin. These are my parents, Tara and Cal." She gives Dave an even more dazzling smile. "I loved that summer—best camp ever! I was there just before ninth grade!"

I stare at Anne and almost choke on my salad. Only a year ago, she complained that she had a terrible time that summer. I had made her life miserable by taking her there. I say nothing. Mothers know when to keep quiet.

Dave recalls, "That's why we weren't sure we knew each other, because I was a counselor for the senior students. We did a lot of rock-climbing and overnights with tents. An outbreak of measles plagued us at the end. The parents were really upset."

Anne grins, "—Good thing that I left before that happened."

Dave looks toward his companions. "We're here, filming a couple of projects," he says. "When you finish dinner, why don't you three join us?"

Quickly, maybe too quickly, I decline, "We're still recovering from the plane trip. I think we'll turn in early."

Cal nods, "True. This leg is a bit painful tonight."

Dave says, "Don't worry about Anne. I'll see that she gets back okay. I'm at the hotel next door to the Casa." He goes back to his table.

Anne's face reveals a new excitement. "To think I came all this way and I meet someone from Camp Evergreen! That was eight years ago. I mean—no one will believe it when I tell them." She repeats his name like a mantra. "Dave—Dave McKinney! He's really great. To think—we found each other down here!"

Cal and I look at each other. I don't know Dave, but I nod, "I'm sure he's very great."

Cal frowns. Anne can't hold his hand when we go back to the Casa. That leaves me.

As we leave the restaurant, Clyde steps forward and says to Cal, "Here's my arm. You'd better grab it. We can give each other good support on these old stones."

I walk behind them, a little irritated that Clyde took my place beside Cal. And Cal didn't turn to me. Male bonding? Blah!

Everyone anticipates tomorrow when we head for the village of *Nuevo Refugio,* an hour away. Years ago, a flood destroyed the original village, so the natives moved their community to another hillside and called it their *new refuge.*

After breakfast, our mission team climbs into old two vans for the ascent to Nuevo Refugio. We already know that there are two speeds in Guatemala—fast and faster, but I'm unprepared for the narrow road that snakes up the mountainside with sharp curves around ever higher cliffs. A few others smile through clenched teeth and murmur about the beautiful vistas across deep valleys. I shut my eyes and white knuckle a sudden turn that seems destined to send us flying off a precipice into thin air. It gets harder to breathe as we reach a higher altitude. After forty-five minutes, our driver grinds to a halt with a cheery "Buenos dias!" I want to kiss the ground and thank God that we made it!

Quickly, we exit amid nervous chatter as our second van pulls up. Slowly, Cal climbs out, using the cane to brace his steps. I see the pain in his eyes. Anne talks to him in a low reassuring voice. I join them as we look around. We're on a plateau. A dirt road leads to the village farther up the hill. I match Cal and Anne's slow pace as we start to climb. Everyone ambles along in the higher altitude. I see a new patience in Cal's face. He's in a difficult and strange situation that others control. No need for an executive memo here.

The village does have a small store with the lone telephone to serve everyone. We pass a Pentecostal church and a community building where native women have their looms. One central well is their only water source. Often, it goes dry so drought is an ever-present reality. Someone murmurs, "I'll remember this well when my sprinklers turn on at home." Some else adds, "I'll never take water for granted ever again. Already, I'm thirsty. Let's bring more bottled water tomorrow."

They grind corn daily as it is their primary food, along with beans. It seems such effort to me, yet the women smile and chatter to each other as if they enjoy life. How do they manage with so little? I think of Leslie, my life-coach, and my struggle with plans for my future. No need for a counselor here. Maybe for these simple people, it's enough to be alive and take each day as it comes. Their lives aren't controlled by shopping malls and the need for the latest electronic gadgets and more *things*.

One-room houses are scattered around. I can't determine if there are actual lots or if the homes are perched on vacant land, taken by squatters rights. By our standards, there is poverty everywhere. No one seems to be around, but soon a few children emerge from somewhere, their bright black eyes staring at us *gringos,* dressed in our jeans and brightly colored tee-shirts. We are the first foreigners they have seen. In their puzzled eyes, we might be aliens from another planet. A few run back into their huts to hide. Clyde and Wil pass out chewing gum and suddenly a few little bronze-skinned boys follow us everywhere. They call out to others and the children come running from their huts with outstretched hands. We're American Pied Pipers in blue jeans with giveaways.

At a small cement block church, Carlos, the pastor, greets us warmly. He feels a kinship with us immediately because we're Protestants, kindred evangelicals like his own congregation. Forty-four percent of Guatemalans are now Protestant. This *evangelisto* church has a dirt floor and no windows, but boasts a single fluorescent fixture. An electric keyboard is near a plain table with a cross. I keep thinking that something is missing. Of course! I search for a clock. There is none in the church or anywhere around. I relax, as I realize I am going nowhere, and I don't have any appointment to keep. Outside, we see a circle of cornstalks, with a canvas flap over the entrance. That is their latrine.

Anne and Cal plus two others saunter on down the slope to the public school which has two sessions daily. Some students walk barefoot for several miles to attend school for only a half day. They're taught Spanish as the national language. What if Cal attempts his memorized phrases, especially the one about a bank? That's good for puzzled looks and giggles. Anne will be a good interpreter for him.

Clyde, Wil and the other men stop at the building site of the new church. They will lay foundation blocks, meaning they'll lug blocks up the hill from the pile near the pastor's home. The blocks are kept there because of theft—which happens even in this Mayan Shangri-la.

Plans for the new church are crudely drawn on a large paper, posted on the old church wall—not a blueprint, but adequate enough because the natives know what they want to build. When I think of the Mayan temples, why should I doubt that their church can be erected in such a direct manner? The Pastor predicts that when the new larger church is completed, it will be filled and overflowing with worshipers.

As Clyde and the men mix cement, some native boys want to help. They impress us with the way they lug the heavy blocks up the dusty hill. Some even put blocks on their heads. Since each block weighs about thirty pounds, the feat seems impossible and dangerous, but the small boys manage. Maybe they want more chewing gum. Have we introduced them to a poor habit?

I follow the other women to the community center for our sewing project. The native women chatter among themselves in their dialect which I can't spell, but sounds like *Kagchikel*. They fall silent when we enter. Finally, Pastor

Carlos explains our intention—to sew warm fleece clothing for their chilly nights. Although. Guatemala is close to the Equator, it gets cold in the mountains. The women accept the gaily patterned material for their children, but not for themselves. One or two wrap a large piece of fleece around their shoulders like a shawl, but they refuse any lightweight jackets for themselves.

We try to understand. Perhaps their own worn clothing was new when they married. Although their skirts and blouses seem almost threadbare, the intricate woven patterns reveal their own village, just as their local dialect distinguishes them, too.

As the day progresses, the fleece is cut and sewn for the children who now know we are there. A few women work at looms, weaving brightly colored runners or strips to become purses. One finishes a large square cloth in brilliant shades of blue, green and black. I want to buy it for a wall hanging, but where would I put it among my Victorian peonies and roses? I'll purchase it anyway and save it for my new condo after our divorce.

The sun is high in the sky. It is noon. I know this without our chiming grandfather clock. My watch will stay in my suitcase tomorrow—it isn't needed in Nuevo Refugio. Some students follow Cal and Anne from school. Beside Cal is a young boy who also limps. He must be about nine and uses a tree branch for a cane.

Cal beams, "Meet Benito or Ben—that's what I call him—my new friend."

Ben isn't too tall, but has the quick black eyes, a round flat face, and the jet hair of the Mayans. In a minute, I know he has judged me as a possible friend and trustworthy. My new sports shoes and designer tee-shirt don't impress him.

"Buenas dias, Ben," I say and hold out my hand. The child hesitates, then takes it shyly and moves closer to Cal who puts his arm around Ben's shoulder. I add, "This is a very beautiful place."

Anne translates and turns to me with Ben's answer. "He says it is more beautiful on the other side of the mountain where he lives."

That means he must walk at least a mile to get to school. I glance at his shoes—too small with the front cut out so his toes appear like little brown beads.

Pastor Carlos waves the children away when we eat the noon meal, prepared by his wife and daughter. This is a Mayan meal, but there is too much food—chicken, rice, beans, and salad—provided for us as guests. We've heard all the tales of the *tourista* malady, but we're excited and hungry. We ignore any restraint. Forget diets. Who counts calories at a time like this?

After lunch, we rest in the shade of corn stalks.

"The children are so happy," Cal says. "I don't see any hitting or fighting. They make up their games with pebbles and sticks. Look at Ben. The tops are gone from his shoes, yet he walks a long distance on a stony path to come to school."

"I feel that way about the women, too. I'm not sure they need or want what we have. I can't figure out which child belongs to which mother and which father. Everyone seems part of one large family." I am silent, thinking about this. I add, "You have a special friend. Ben clings to you."

Cal looks down at his leg. "We share a bond. We're both cripples."

I protest, "You're not a cripple! Your leg will be better someday."

"I doubt it. Anyway, my days of running to catch a commuter train are over."

"Maybe that's not too bad," I reply. I want to add that when God closes a door, He opens a window, but I'll save my corny wisdom for another day.

Young Ben—Benito—won't let Cal out of his sight. I leave them with Anne to take their siesta in the shade of tall cornstalks. I hike the trail that brings Ben and his sister to school every day. Surely, I can follow his path and see the beautiful valley beyond the curving trail and big boulders. I'm glad that I don't ask or need Cal or Anne's approval for my decisions anymore.

A stone spins underfoot. I grab at a bush to steady myself. A bird with brilliant blue-green plumage squawks and flies into the azure sky. It startles me and I realize how far I've wandered from the village. I can't see even a wisp of smoke. Suddenly a huge snake slithers across my path. With a sinuous movement, he lifts his head and stares at me with beady black eyes, his tongue darting out like tiny flames. I back away, staring him down. I realize that I'm alone, vulnerable to any wild creature in this Guatemalan Eden. I'm both repelled and fascinated by the snake. Maybe that was Eve's trouble, too.

Did the snake tempt Eve that she'd really be wise and happy if she ate the apple? I know now that other things—even family—can't make a person happy. My happiness must come from within, from the satisfaction that I'm true to my best self. Did I burden Cal and Anne with efforts to make me happy—just as I felt a burden to make them happy?I wonder.

The snake doesn't move. If Arletta were here, she'd take charge—cage the snake and give him to the Zoo in a presentation ceremony, covered by the press. Afterward, she'd serve her macadamia nut brownies and coffee. I envy her that talent. I wait for things to happen and usually, they do. I don't grin. I grit my teeth and bear it.

Slowly, I back down the path—silently as a Mayan in a tangled jungle. Perhaps this snake saved my life because I glimpsed a narrow ledge beyond the boulder. One misstep and I'd fall to my death. How did I get here? In the last year,

I wanted to die a dozen times through all the stages of grief—shock, anger, sadness, acceptance and closure.

Now, I'm beyond closure. I love my life. I'm glad that I want to go on! I want to live! I want to believe that Cal and I—and Anne, too—have a future. Will it possibly be together? I must not expect for too much.

Shaken from fear and this new emotion, I turn back to the village. When I arrive, Cal, Anne and Ben are still dozing. Anne rouses slightly, "Did you have a good nap?"

They never missed me.

By mid-afternoon, everyone is tired. We look at the two old vans and think about the trip down the mountainside. Release the brakes and slide the whole way. We'll really know how to pray after this trip..

Jeanette speaks in a low tone, "I hope the gears and brakes are working."

I close my eyes to nap which is impossible on the swaying ride. We pull up to the Casa's grillwork entrance. The gates open and we straggle through with tired aching muscles. I can't wait to flop down on a bed.

When Cal and I head for our room, Anne pulls at my elbow. "Oh, I forgot to tell you. Dave's taking me out to dinner tonight, so don't wait for me."

She dashes inside as Cal frowns, "I thought we'd be a threesome again on this trip."

Softly, I reply, "We may turn out to be a quartet."

We walk two blocks to a different restaurant. Tonight, I hold Cal's hand before Clyde can offer his arm. Along the way, we pass a shoe store. Cal hobbles inside to look at children's shoes. He holds out navy tennis shoes. "Do you think these will fit? His foot is a little longer than my hand." He stretches his fingers.

"Let's take them. We can always give them to another child and bring back an outline of Ben's foot."

Along with the large supply of new tee-shirts, we should have brought shoes since some children don't have them. Their feet bear many sores from the worms and parasites in the ground. Clyde says this also causes the children's intestinal maladies, as evidenced by their distended bellies.

The next morning we swerve and career again up the mountain to reach Nuevo Refugio. Ben waits beside the road for Cal. He must have arisen early to meet the van.

"My boy!" Cal hugs him heartily and hands him the tennis shoes.

"Zapato?" Ben's eyes widen as he motions For me?

Cal laughs and points for Ben to put them on.

Ben looks at Anne and rattles off some Spanish. Anne turns to Cal, "He wants to save them for his sister."

"No-no. Tell him, we'll buy his sister a pair, too."

Anne translates this and shyly Ben slips on the canvas shoes and walks around, feeling their newness and support. He comes to Cal and buries his head in his hands and starts to cry. Cal, like everyone, gets teary-eyed with the sheer joy of a simple gift of new shoes.

The driver frowns. "You should ask his mother first if you can give him a gift."

Cal and Ben limp off to find Ben's mother and get her consent. Will that gift set Ben apart from his friends? Cal thinks he's solved one problem, and maybe he's created a bigger one. Jealousy knows no boundaries.

This day almost repeats our first day. Now the native women smile more easily at us.Our midday rest is longer. No one looks at a watch. Time is suspended. Underneath the clear blue sky, all seems so peaceful. Cal, Anne, Ben and I lazily sprawl in the shade of tall cornstalks. Cal closes his eyes and dozes. Or is he quietly planning a project to outfit the village children with shoes? He needs something like that when he returns to the States. I want to say to myself, He's still a jerk!, but I don't really believe it.

Dear God, let him feel he's needed somewhere. At least, I can pray that much for him

I look toward the beautiful vista of purple-blue mountains which loom so large and rugged. All of our past troubles seem far away. A tiny piece of me wishes we could stay here together forever. Cal is really a fine man and Anne is a wonderful daughter, even if they irritate me sometimes.

I leave them to rest. Again, I follow Benito's path a little distance from the village. The ridge ahead is dangerous, so I turn around and return to Nuevo Refugio. It is too hard for me to climb to the other side of this mountain. I must be content where I am.

The rest of the week follows much like the first day. Each evening we return to the Casa, exhausted, but excited. Cal growls a little as Anne goes to dinner nightly with Dave.

Jeanette says a little tartly, "Anne's very quiet when she comes in late. I scarcely rouse. We do need our rest, especially in this thin mountain air. I hope she stays well."

How many people will come to our medical clinic today—Saturday? No one knows. In their own way, the natives spread the news. People have walked for miles, seeking our help. A Guatemalan doctor arrives to assist our medical team. He knows from touching an abdomen which child has worms. Our doctors and nurses happily see twice as many people than back in the States.

Jeanette quips, "What a relief—no paper work! No wonder, this goes so fast."

Dave has driven Anne up to Nuevo Refugio to film us at work, although he is so adept that many natives are unaware of his camera. I glance at him and see that often his focus is on Anne as she interprets native complaints to our clinic staff. Cal and I hand out vitamins and the nurses give pain medications. Again, Anne translates any medical advice.

A huge pile of knit shirts—rejects from an American company—are on a long table as giveaways. Soon, the youngsters are running around with bold words advertising a *Twelve Strike League, Run for your Life*, and *Eat at Dugan's Diner*. Such simple things as a new logo shirt make them so happy.

Sunday's schedule turns out differently from our expectation. We have a Bible study at the Casa in the morning, because services at Nuevo Refugio will be at night. Pastor Carlos has several parishes that he serves during the day, so his mountainside church is the smallest and last that he reaches.

Dave and Anne join our mission group for dinner. Tonight we have tamales with plantains for dinner. With our first days behind us, everyone is in a festive mood. No one knows what to expect.

Pastor Carlos has gently suggested that our women wear skirts or dresses to church. It will be cold in the clear night air, so everyone puts on extra clothing. We look like hens in a barnyard skit with plump arms and legs like sausages. Anne rolls up her slacks under her elastic band skirt.

"You look like you've gained on a few pounds," I say.

"Dave will understand," she replies with great confidence. "He's such a terrific guy."

We arrive at Nuevo Refugio as natives drift in to services. In the dim light, I think of the catacombs where early Christians secretly worshipped. Ben is there and takes Cal's hand. We sit together on a worn bench. Ben turns around and smiles at a woman who stands along the wall with a young girl beside her. I realize that this is his mother and sister. Maybe his father is dead.

I don't understand Spanish too well and not any Mayan dialect. Pastor Carlos uses both as he translates the greetings that Clyde bring to our bronze brothers and sisters in Christ. Someone begins to sing spontaneously and the small building fills with a soft lilting melody of praise, accompanied by Pastor Carlos son-in-law, who will become a pastor in a few months.

"Cantad al Senor un cantico" is repeated many times. Anne whispers that it means *Oh, sing God a new song.* There are four more stanzas of simple repetitive lines—

"Porque el Senor ha hecho prodigios"

By his holy power, our God has done wonders
For Jesus is Lord! Amen! Allelulia!

Pastor Carlos leads them as they murmur something together—perhaps it is the Creed. Then after another song, the Pastor places a small bowl of water on the table. I recognize this is the time for baptisms.

Only teen-agers and older people come forward. Then Ben rises and leans on his makeshift cane. He turns and pulls at Cal's hand. Obviously, he wants Cal with him. They wait quietly, and when it is Ben's turn, he looks up at Cal and motions, "You, first."

Cal hesitates only a moment and bows his head. Pastor Carlos dips his hand in the water, three times as he touches Cal's forehead with the incantation in Spanish, *"En al Nombre, del Padre, del Hijo, j del Espiritu Santo. Amen."* Instinctively, I understand—"In the name of the Father, and of the Son, and of the Holy Spirit".

Ben looks up at him with an angelic smile after he, too, is baptized through this holy sacrament. They return to the hard bench hand-in-hand, but Cal keeps his head bowed, touched with an emotion he can't identify, bonded to a child whose language he can't fully understand. Cal sits beside me and reaches for my hand as tears slide down his face.Ben looks up and gently wipes them away.

"Ser padrino de," he smiles.

Anne whispers, "That means Dad is now Ben's godfather."

I see Cal's trembling hand as he hugs Ben closer. An Isaiah verse flashes into my mind, *And a little child will lead them...*

It is time for a final prayer. Pastor Carlos starts out in almost a whisper. The congregation responds with soft petitions, and as time passes they grow in intensity and fervor. Moaning and pleading come from these smaller sun-tanned Christians, their hands uplifted, reaching up for the Eternal God to hear them. It is unlike anything I have known—akin to a Pentecost where people speak in different languages, yet understand each other.

They lose themselves, trancelike, as they come to the Eternal God who daily sustains their simple lives. They pour out their love for Him and each other. Their thunderous petitions shake me. I hear Clyde's and Jeanette's voices among the rising and falling chorus of anguish and gratitude. I close my eyes and cry out, too, "Lord, bless us. Bless us all!" I am transfixed, emptied of anger. Time stands still. I feel cleansed, free, touched by grace, flooded with love. I want to stay in this Holy moment—on this mountain—forever. I know before I open my eyes that my life is completely changed. Praise God—things will never be the same again! My pride is shattered. My anger is gone. My broken and contrite heart is smashed into many pieces and made whole again.

I know that I am the one who needed healing.

Gradually, the petitions cease in a cascade of fading *Amens*, until everyone is silent, thankful that God has leaned His ear toward His penitent people. The service ends and our group is subdued. We're not sure what happened to us as these native people led us to worship in their dialect and Spanish with an intensity that embraces us. We speak in low tones as we head down the mountain..

Our trip back to Panajachel is hushed. We have experienced a spiritual depth of God's people—our brothers and sisters in Christ—that we didn't expect. Our own religious expression seems colorless and shallow in some ways. We're blessed in the States by so much and we think we deserve it. These Mayan brothers and sisters are grateful just to be alive. Do our possessions interfere with our relationships? They seem to have a total trust in God, an innocent faith without the intellectual questions that plague educated people. We are learning much more from them than they are from us. The few gifts of clothing and medicine that we brought can't match the faith that they share with us.

As we enter the iron gates, Brother Bill waits there. He stops Cal. "Clyde Thorson told me that you worked for Mirron/Molten before it was sold to Colton. I was an accountant for the old Molten Brothers company. I was fired just before Mirron bought it."

Cal starts to sympathize. "I'm sorry it happened to you, too. I know about that. I got the ax several weeks ago. "

Brother Bill beams, "Getting fired was the best day of my life. I was free to do something worthwhile. I've never looked back."

Cal is puzzled. "Really? That's great—if you found something else." He pauses. "I'd settle for just a job right now."

Brother Bill gives both of us a sharp look and says, "I'll pray for you. Have a good night."

We lie in our twin beds in the dark. Cal is restless and goes to the bathroom several times. Although he is quiet, I know he's awake. He doesn't snore, as he sometimes did when we shared a bed.

Finally, I ask, "Are you okay?"

"I'm thinking about today—about my baptism. I'm shaken up by everything—the tears, the prayers, the trust that Ben wants me to be his godfather. What happened? I don't understand it."

"You don't have to understand anything. You just accept with assurance that you are a child of God. You are a part of God's family now. You will never be entirely alone again." I'll remind him of that when he leaves for San Francisco. For now, I say, "Just thank God tonight for His goodness and grace which surrounds all of us on this trip." I feel in my heart that, soon, Cal will learn the joy of helping others in a new way.

"I don't know how to pray."

I want to say that I'll teach him, but he needs other people, too. "Come to church and you'll learn from your brothers and sisters in Christ." There will be Christians, even in San Francisco (although TV news doesn't imply that!) who can help him. I didn't believe that anything could change Cal's attitude. I, too, am filled with wonder.

"Everything is so strange to me. You say the prayer tonight for me—please."

So I pray aloud in the dark, *Dear God, we thank you for today and what Cal's baptism means to him—to everyone. Keep us in your care as long as we live. And give us strength to help others in need. In Jesus' name. Amen.*

Everything is quiet. I think I hear Cal murmur, "I love you", but I'm not sure. So I lie quietly and watch the light from a huge moon dimly filter through our window. I'm at peace, too. I sleep.

Cal barely slept last night because the *tourista* malady caught him. Clyde gives him a quick exam and advises rest and lots of water with the standard pills. As I leave, Cal's eyes are closed, drifting off to sleep. Anne and I will have a workday together.

When our bus arrives, Ben waits there—a frown on his face as Anne explains Cal's absence. I walk along with Anne and Ben to school. We play a math game with third graders. Anne teaches them an action song about God's wonderful world. They hold their arms in a circle, then fold their hands in prayer and sing-song along, wiggling their hands and giggling as they illustrate falling rain.

Their teacher asks the children to tell us about their own Mayan creation story, the Popol Vuh. The sacred Ceiba tree connects heaven and earth. Hunob-hu, the god of creation, sits in the tree's crown. I think of the Biblical story of Adam and Eve in the garden and the tree of good and evil. I wonder if there is a relationship between the two accounts. Perhaps, I could pursue more of Mayan folklore if I lived here, but that is impossible. I'll return home, work in the library, and find a condo when Cal leaves for California. I'll build a new life and remember these days in Guatemala with gratefulness. I am at peace with myself and Cal.

Yesterday, the children were taught "London Bridge is Falling Down" and they beg to play it today. Anne and I are the bridge and hold hands above their heads. It's awkward to let the gate fall, especially when the victim wiggles and giggles. My arms ache and I'm punched by a wily head that tries to escape the gate. However, the children are giddy with this simple game. What significance will a sociologist find when he studies Mayan life and finds the children playing a very old English game? He may write his Ph.D. thesis on that very subject.

After lunch, Anne and I lie down on lumpy ground in the shade of tall corn stalks. We hear only buzzing flies or laughing children in the distance. It is a quiet time to look at a very blue sky and realize how far away the States and our old life seem to be.

I sigh, "A penny for your thoughts—."

Anne hesitates. "I've thought—and prayed, too—about my future. The Pastor said this trip might change us." She rolls over to face me. "I've loved this week and the children. I want to teach. I can get my degree in June, and perhaps get a master's in education next year. Maybe I can teach in a bi-lingual classroom in the States, or come back here. What do you think?"

"I think you have to pursue whatever you wish. Certainly, there must be satisfaction in working with students." I take a deep breath, afraid to ask. "What about Dave? You go off to dinner with him every night. Our group has missed you."

Anne looks off toward the mountains. "I really like Dave—maybe too much. I invited him to my graduation in June, but he'll be filming in Japan after he finishes here. He's on the road a lot. He has film contracts lined up for the next two years."

I think of Cal and his career with so much travel. Does Anne realize that Dave's career is a lot like her Dad's? She vowed she would put down roots in one place.

She continues, "I may not hear from him after I leave. Maybe, he's a guy who gives a girl a big rush and then drops her flat when she's gone."

"He doesn't appear like that to me or he wouldn't dine with you every night."

"That's very kind, Mom. You never say anything negative about anyone."

"I really believe that he's interested in you or I wouldn't say it. His eyes light up when you cross the patio."

"We'll see." She repeats with more emotion, "I like him—maybe too much"

When we get back to the Casa in the late afternoon, Cal is on the patio in deep conversation with Brother Bill. I assume he's telling him about his baptism in the native church. I see Brother Bill grasp his hand and offer a prayer. I pass by quietly to rest and dress for dinner. However, I decline to eat with the others. Instead, I suggest that Cal and I dine at the hotel next door. Soup and flan will be better for Cal's queasiness.

We sit on a covered porch near the hotel pool. The tropical plants and torches lend a romantic air that makes me feel as if I'm at a fine resort. Momentarily, I forget about our reason to be in Guatemala. Our days together will be over when we leave.

"All our frantic pace seems far away. My watch has stayed in the suitcase. I may leave it in a drawer when I get back home. I doubt if I rush anywhere again. Patience is my middle name. I could get used to living like this," I say, waving my hand at the fountain and broad-leaf foliage.

Cal gives me a strange look. "Do you realize what you just said?"

I think hard and wave my hand again. "I guess I said I could get used to living like this—."

Cal laughs, "—Funny you should say that. I have something very important to ask you."

I stiffen, unsure what he might say. "So—?"

"Brother Bill and I had a very long talk this morning—and another this afternoon. He says the retreat association will open two more hostel centers this year with plans for another next year. The board believes that Guatemala will become a prime tourist destination in the future. That means that more students and groups like ours will come down here. His group wants to provide modest accommodations for them."

"—And what does that have to do with us? With me?"

"Brother Bill wants me to be the business manager for this Casa, so he can be free to develop other sites."

I am stunned. "You—mean—live—here?"

Cal beams, "That's right. Me—run a mission center! I'm stunned myself. He studied me and thinks I'm right for the job. What do you think?"

I can't absorb what he's saying. "It's not about me. What do YOU think?"

"It's like an answer—" he grins somewhat sheepishly, "—to—to prayer. When I was fired by Colton Industries, I thought my business days were over. What good was I? A dozen others could easily replace me I realized no one cared about me or my experience. Then I came here. Everyone is so warm, so welcoming. They don't notice my leg, or snap at me to hurry. Time seems to stand still. Ben grins at me like I'm his best friend." Cal lowers his voice, "That kid has really touched my heart. I hate to leave him up there on the mountain. If WE came, we could bring Ben here to go to high school—maybe even the university." Cal's voice trails off as he mentally plans Ben's future. Cal's always been big on plans. "What do you think?"

What do I think? I hear him say "you" which must mean he wants me to come with him. "Well, I don't know what to think. First, there's Anne's graduation in June. This is your decision. I'm really not a part of it."

"—But you are! I want you with me."

I take a deep breath. Months ago I wanted to hear that from him. I'm not sure about myself anymore. I've grown too free from any responsibility connected with his life. My care during his convalescence was to be temporary.

"I—I don't know. It would be a tremendous change for me—for both of us." I smile to myself. Also, it would mean I would be rid of those Victorian drapes and Cal's hideous chair. If I lived here, I'd hang my Guatemalan tapestry on the wall and buy Cal a wicker chair with floral pillows and an ottoman to support his leg. I hesitate. Didn't I say that I'd never move again? Leave Trinity church and Arletta and my Garden Club friends? I'd miss them. It would hard to make new friends in a strange country—learn to converse in a different language.

Cal leans a little closer, "It would be a second chance for us. Brother Bill wants me for the next three years. After that, the organization may send me to their main office in Antigua. Or I might find a business opportunity here. He tells me I'm ideal because I'm still young—he calls me *young*—and have the business background that's needed to deal with Americans, especially businessmen."

I hear the excitement in his voice. "Oh, he's right about you!"

"You've made a home in a lot of different places. You made it possible for me to succeed at Mirron and then at Mirron/Molten. Without your encouragement, I would have failed in both of them." Cal continues with an enthusiasm that softens his brow's deep lines. "I need you if I attempt this. A retreat center will be a strange and new experience. I'm afraid to be alone. Come with me."

I evade his invitation with a little laugh. "What if I went native—wore a woven skirt, an embroidered blouse and thong sandals?"

Cal speaks deliberately, slowly, pleading with loving eyes. He repeats, "Please—come with me?" He leans over and kisses my cheek.

"—Give me time to consider everything." I tremble and turn away so I won't cry. Cal has made an odd proposal, but I can't say *Yes* so easily this time.

The final morning is short. We return for a communion and farewell service in Nuevo Refugio. Ben stands there, his hand tightly held by Cal. We confess our sins and receive absolution. A year ago my Pastor told me that he would pray that Cal and I would one day experience the forgiveness of God together. I didn't believe him. Now, I tremble with this miracle. We are here hand-in-hand.

Pastor Carlos blesses the tortilla and wine for the holy meal. He breaks off a tortilla piece for each to dip in the wine cup that Clyde holds. Once again, the body and blood of Christ assures us of the grace of God and the forgiveness of our sins. All is quiet and reverent in this small place with a dirt floor and a few natives communing in a circle with us.

The mothers are friendlier now than when we arrived. Maybe they're a little relieved, too, to see us go, leaving behind our strange printed material that warms their children on cool mountain nights. We are such tall people beside our short sisters. We hug and whisper affectionate farewells.

The two paid carpenters mutter many *gracias* to our men who have helped construct their new cement block foundation. Hands are clasped and shaken with grins and nods in recognition of all the progress. Clyde, Wil, and the others take more pictures. Each one proudly stands by the foundation block he set in place.

Then we form another circle, hold hands, and sing, "God Be With You Till We Meet Again" in harmony, our voices floating over the mountain like a chorus of angels. It is a Holy moment for everyone—special, and never to be repeated—a time to remember forever—when God's peace touched our hearts in a way we never expected. We wipe away tears of love and farewell, embracing our Mayan family that some may never see again.

As we climb into the bus, Ben clings to Cal's good leg, begging him to stay. Cal gives him his collapsible cane and reaches for Ben's stick. He kisses Ben's forehead and promises to come back with a *Nos vemos*—"See you later". Ben waves and calls with the other children *Dios legarde* which Anne translates and cries out, "God keep you, too." The bus pulls away.

Cal's eyes are moist. "Ben really tugs at my heart." Maybe Cal's return to Guatemala will be as much for Ben as for himself.

We spend our afternoon packing while the others go souvenir hunting. Some return with small Guatemalan flags of blue, white and yellow triangles. Many have purchased unusual and classical jade jewelry. Cal has another long talk with Brother Bill who also quizzes me for my reaction.

"I hope you will come, but it won't work for Cal if you're unhappy here."

"If I move, I won't look back. This will become my home." I take a deep breath. "Cal finds a great fulfillment in his work." I, too, must find something here and not expect him to provide a life for me. If I come—that is a decision that I must soon make.

Brother Bill gives me a long look. "I'm concerned because you must find a purpose, also, or you will be miserable."

I've always believed that I lived for Cal and Anne. I can't hide behind that sin of sacrificial pride any longer. I need a greater purpose than my own selfish desire. With God's help, I will put the past resentment and anger behind me and find a new life.

I smile at Brother Bill and Cal. "I'd love to record some Mayan folk tales and songs." I take a deep breath. "That intrigues me."

Brother Bill nods, "The preservation of an old culture is very important. We would help you."

I can't wait to tell Arletta everything. If I do come with Cal, she'll organize this major move for me with a promise that she and Boyce will visit us when the snow flies—and bring along pictures of Tummikins.

Cal and I wait on the patio for the others and our final dinner together. In a corner by ourselves, he talks enthusiastically about his new opportunity. A strange culture could bind us together more tightly or cause a final separation. Surely, we would work harder this time to make our marriage last. As we discuss possibilities, Dave strides across the patio and waves a "Hi!"

"I'm so glad to find you alone," he grins.

I start to rise, "I'll tell Anne you're here."

"No, don't go. I need to talk to both of you," he says in a serious voice.

Cal and I look at each other

Dave continues, "Anne and I have seen each other daily for nine days. I'm filled with the wonder that I discovered her down here. With all my travel, I never thought I'd find anyone. I'm very fond of her and I really don't want her to leave."

Cal clears his throat. "We want her to graduate in June. That's only a couple of months away."

"I know," Dave replies. "I want to be there when she graduates, but I want to surprise her. I told her I'd be filming in Japan. I didn't tell her I'd be finished by May. I hope she'll forgive me."

I murmur, "Of course, she will." I know a lot about forgiveness and being forgiven.

"I want to make sure that I won't interfere with any family celebration."

"—Not at all." I add. "You're more than welcome. In fact, you can stay with us. We have a guest room—." I stop and realize what I've said. Cal gives me a quizzical look and smiles. If Dave has the guest room, that means I'll be back in our bedroom with him and our king-size bed plus those awful rose-patterned drapes.

Dave takes a deep breath. "I bought her this jade and silver bracelet as a farewell gift." He holds out a heavy linked chain set with pale jade carved stones.

"It's lovely." I know that Guatemalan jade is a very precious stone. The gem is mined only here and in Burma. Traditionally, Mayan babies are given a jade bead at birth.

Anne comes through the doorway. She looks smashing tonight with her hair coiled into a top knot. She wears white slacks and a peasant blouse that shows off her tan shoulders. When Dave steps over to give Anne a welcome hug, she smiles that dazzling smile that helped an orthodontist in Hartford cruise to Bermuda one spring. Now, it's worth every penny to see her smile with radiant happiness.

They leave with promises to get back early so Anne can rest before we leave to fly home to the States tonight. This

Guatemala experience has been—ah, more than unique. It's been a fantastic and transforming time for each of us.

Cal chuckles and shakes his head. "This trip has changed all our lives. I hope you anticipate that we'll be together again in the years ahead—."

I'm still unsure. If we return together, he will grow bald and my hair will turn silver. I relax and look at the full white moon which seems so large on this balmy tropical night. I'm so surprised by what has happened to us. Surprise is among the blessings of a good marriage which begins with hope, but is really an act of faith with a commitment to the unknown. So, possibly, it will be for us again.

He asks, "What are you thinking about?"

"Oh, I'm looking at the moon. It seems so close—like I could reach out and touch it in that velvet sky."

"Oddly, I remember that same tropic moon when we went to St. Croix years ago—."

"—When old F.A. gave us a week there because you solved that Houston problem—."

"—And when you walked into the hotel dining room in that ice blue dress, every man wanted to join us at dinner."

I don't remember the dress, but I remember the moon just beyond our balcony. It lit our room with a mystical light. The stars were like thousands of diamonds. We held each other and heard a steel band softly play "Stardust" with a trembling beat. I will never forget because Anne came to us that night. Nine months later she was born and Cal cuddled and called her *Miss Moonbeam.*

Cal's voice grows deeper. "I know I hurt you terribly when I walked out. Can you forgive me? I don't know why I went off the deep end. I began to—."

I reach over and put my finger on his lips. "Don't say anything more. I made mistakes, too."

After my parents died, I expected Cal to be my anchor. I wanted to belong somewhere, but he was transferred so often, we grew apart. I resented that. Maybe we were both lost. We can't go back to our old ways. We can only move ahead, each stronger with hope—each one finding new purpose, new meaning.

There were two third parties in our marriage, but they were the wrong ones. Cal doesn't understand his involvement with Diedre. As for me, my flirtation—maybe lust that I had for Gunner—seems so terribly foolish now. Already, that experience is fading. Maybe I even imagined it for more than it really was.

However, if God is a third party in our marriage, perhaps He can prevent the ever-present danger of a power struggle between us. If I come to Guatemala with Cal, perhaps we'll find a deeper purpose than our own selfish desires.

I know that a future with Cal can offer so much. We've each gone up a rocky trail and almost fallen down a cliff. Will we see greater splendor beyond these mountains? And together, maybe more?

"—I have always loved you," Cal says

I reply, "I love you, too."

It is the truth.

The End

ABOUT THE AUTHOR

Marion H. Youngquist — Born and educated in Salem. Oregon. She's written for newspapers, magazines, and served as a church editor. She's also won prizes for her poems and plays. Her three books *Procula, Maple Tree Tales,* and *Christmas Presence* were released by Drury's Publishing. Her advice: *Write in spite of a good excuse.*

She and her husband Ted have four children, six grand-children (another deceased) and four great-grand-daughters.

www.ingramcontent.com/pod-product-compliance
Lightning Source LLC
Chambersburg PA
CBHW050342030726
47503CB00008B/2576